Praise for Bianca D'Arc's *Hara's Legacy*

5 Angels & Recommended Read   "Wow. Really and truly wow. Not only has a new world been born, but a relationship that I have never seen before has unfolded – successfully...In Hara's Legacy there's not only a unique relationship to enjoy, but a fascinating plot as well. Aliens. Come on, what's not cool about that?"

   ~ *Serena Fallen, Angel Reviews*

5 Klovers "Bianca D'Arc has hit another one out of the ball park... If you love a great futuristic science fiction tale with plenty of sensual romance and steamy ménage scenes, you will not want to miss Hara's Legacy!"

   ~ *Jennifer Ray, CK2S Kwips and Kritiques*

5 Kisses   "...a brilliant journey...Ms. D'Arc wrote every scene with sensitivity and beauty...This is a book you won't be able to put down!"

   ~ *Tara Renee, Two Lips Reviews*

5 Hearts "Fascinating!...incredibly well described...arousing and explicit...Ms. D'Arc has an amazing ability to tell her stories and I am extremely eager to read the next book."

   ~ *Marcy Arbitman, The Romance Studio*

Hara's Legacy

Bianca D'Arc

A SAMhAIN PUBLIShINC, LTD. publication.

Samhain Publishing, Ltd.
577 Mulberry Street, Suite 1520
Warner Robins, GA 31201
www.samhainpublishing.com

Hara's Legacy
Copyright © 2007 by Bianca D'Arc
Print ISBN: 1-59998-742-2
Digital ISBN: 1-59998-482-2

Editing by Jessica Bimberg
Cover by Anne Cain

First Samhain Publishing, Ltd. electronic publication: May 2007
First Samhain Publishing, Ltd. print publication: March 2008

Dedication

To my family, for believing in me when I wanted to change careers. I couldn't have done any of this without your support.

And special thanks to my editor, Jess, for being a cheerleader when I had doubts.

Chapter One

Caleb O'Hara had the gift of precognition. Even so, he wasn't able to do much of anything when the cataclysm came, except move his wife and family to higher ground well before the planet-altering event. He couldn't help the rest of humanity as the Earth was bombarded by huge crystal shards. It was a disaster that would forever change the Earth's resonances and doom most of the human population. The attack had come from space a little more than four and a half years ago. Although Earth's best observatories had seen it coming, there was nothing they could do to stop it either.

But the aliens didn't see it as an attack. They saw it as cleansing the planet of its rodent population. That some of those rodents happened to be descended from the aliens' early exploration team was a conundrum. They hadn't known humans would be fertile with their own kind and many generations had passed between exploration and the bombardment, with their alien DNA mixing with the native human population in surprising ways.

Once they discovered humans with traces of their own DNA, the aliens looked on the half-breeds as an interesting experiment. Unsure how to proceed at first, they left the survivors of the cataclysm alone for the most part. The aliens built new cities in the prime coastal areas once the tsunamis subsided. They set up colonies on every continent of the newly claimed planet, and monitored what went on up in the mountainous regions where the few survivors of humanity lived, testing subjects according to their whims.

Those left in the desolate places were sturdy, resourceful, cunning and powerful. The mix of human and alien DNA had caused unexpected changes in their brain patterns and some of those half-breeds were more than a match for the aliens.

Half-breeds, or just Breeds, as the aliens called them, were the only potential danger on this new colony world, and the colonial governors wanted them kept under control. Some wanted them killed outright, but they were hard to catch, and there were advantages to studying them. They held clues to the aliens' distant past in their very DNA and the Council decided such information was worth looking into.

Caleb hadn't known any of this when he packed up his wife, brothers and possessions, and moved to the high wilderness of what used to be the Canadian Rockies a little more than five years ago. It was called the Waste now, and small enclaves of survivors dotted the area. Most were hermits, trappers and native peoples, mostly men, and pretty much all of them shared one common trait—they were all psychically gifted in some way.

It was freaky, really, how many telepaths, precogs, empaths, telekinetics, and others had survived the cataclysm by hiding in the mountains of the Waste. A few banded together to form small villages. From time to time, the humans saw evidence of the aliens, but they never made contact, only flew or hovered above in their shiny, impervious machines.

Caleb and his brothers shared a small ranch. Caleb's gift allowed them a precious few months to set up their home and gather all kinds of supplies and books on everything from medicine to mechanics. They spent every last dime they had to set up underground tanks and apparatus to brew the biodiesel on which they ran their generators and made their home as self-sufficient as possible.

They were well hidden in a secure valley, and their livestock and crops provided plentiful food. They had enough to barter with the nearby village for equipment and things they couldn't grow. The villagers, in turn, had made a deal with the O'Haras. The village militia, such as it was, would protect them from raiders, as long as they supplied food to the village. Since the village was made up of men who knew machines, warfare and technical things, not farmers or ranchers, it was a good trade. There were few women, and all were claimed.

It had gotten so bad that most women were now partnered with two or more men. Although before the cataclysm, many women had psychic gifts, they either hadn't moved fast enough or hadn't been able to survive the harsh conditions in the mountainous regions. As a result, men outnumbered women in the Waste by about three to one. It was a difficult situation, to say the least.

The O'Hara brothers kept Caleb's pretty young wife, Jane, under their protection. She stayed hidden in the house when men from the village came to trade. It was the safest thing for all concerned. Men had been killed for their women. Caleb swore he would keep Jane safe, no matter what.

He'd known Jane all her life. All the O'Hara boys had protected and loved Jane as a child. As youngsters, the boys hadn't quite realized the power of Jane's empathic gift, but she always knew when one of them was hurting or unhappy, or just needed a friend. She was a part of their lives from the time she was just toddling around and they loved her, each in their own way. She loved them too, but it was Caleb she'd married. He

9

was the eldest, the protector. And it was his precognitive gift that had saved them all.

She would do anything for him and he knew it. If a stray desire crossed his mind, moments later she would be fulfilling it. She was that open and receptive to him, and he loved every minute of it, and every inch of her.

He loved her sassy mouth and the way she would take all of him down her throat. He loved it when she purred, the vibration of her vocal chords causing chaos in his body. And he loved the way she would stroke him, not just his cock, but his chest and arms and face, when she wanted to comfort him. She could read him so easily, as if they were perfectly attuned to each other.

But he knew she could read his brothers just as easily, and it had bothered him at first. She told him what they were feeling in an effort to help settle family disputes. He knew the other two men were feeling a level of sexual frustration that was almost unbearable and that they envied him for having Jane. They had perhaps always been jealous, but the shortage of women was making it doubly hard.

Jane didn't come right out and say these things to him when he asked her to read his brothers, but her blushes and vague replies said all he needed to hear.

℘∞℘

"Justin is mad as a hornet about something." Caleb slapped his work gloves together to rid them of the perpetual dust. He laid his hat aside and took off his jacket as he stomped inside the big kitchen, greeting his wife with a smacking kiss.

Jane put her coat on and picked up a wire basket. "I have to get the eggs anyway, maybe I'll try to see what's up with him."

Caleb stayed her with a hand on her arm. "He's in a foul temper, Janie. Don't let him upset you."

She patted his hand, then reached for the doorknob. "I won't. But, Caleb, he needs a friend."

Caleb muttered as he watched her traipse down the path toward the chicken coop and nearby barn where Justin kept his Harley.

"What he needs is a woman," Caleb growled, knowing Jane couldn't hear him, trying hard not to let guilt flood his mind. Jane would be back like a shot then, and he would have to explain why he felt guilty about being the only brother with a wife.

He'd tried desperately to hide the guilt caused by his belief that he'd stolen Jane out from under his brothers' noses. He'd always known his youngest brother, Mick, was sweet on her, but he'd been away in grad school. Of course, Caleb also suspected the middle brother, Justin, would have courted her too, had he been home at the time her daddy died. Caleb felt like a heel. He was supposed to protect his younger brothers, not cheat them out of the best woman in the world.

At the time, he'd figured they would find other great women, eventually. Now though, with the shortage of women, the prospects were grim, and Caleb felt worse each day and each night he spent in Jane's loving arms.

Caleb watched her through the kitchen window, but staggered as he was hit by a vision. It clouded his senses in a way he hadn't felt in years. At least not this strongly. Not since the dire revelation of the alien invasion had he been gripped so tightly by his gift. He slumped into one of the hard wooden chairs, letting the vision take him where it would. Surrendering to it, he feared what he might see, but resolved to use his gift to protect his family—the most important thing in his life.

Jane collected eggs and set the basket down on a shelf where it would be safe while she went to find Justin. He was really touchy lately and always refused her offers of a friendly ear. Still, if she got close enough to him, she could read his emotions and at least give Caleb some clue as to what might be wrong. Caleb was the problem solver of the family, but he needed something to go on before he could put his quick mind to work to find a solution. Jane's empathic powers had provided those much needed clues in the past and she didn't mind helping him in this small way if it meant she could help the other men as well. She loved them all and wanted them to be happy.

Justin was the rebel son. Two years younger than Caleb, he'd been a hell raiser back in the old days. He had luscious, chocolate brown hair he kept military short, wicked tattoos and a sleek, black Harley Davidson motorcycle he worked on in his spare time. That beauty purred like a mountain cat and seemed to be the love of his life. Justin was quiet now, quieter than he'd been before the cataclysm. His dark eyes watched everything, and he seldom smiled. Jane could feel the turmoil he kept hidden from everyone but her, but lately he rejected every overture of friendship she made, preferring to deal with his dark feelings on his own.

Justin was a telekinetic of amazing strength. He had once used his power to save his brother's life when a piece of farm equipment threatened to crush him. From across the field they were working back in Montana, Justin saw the axle break and tons of metal list, collapsing on Caleb. Justin's hand shot out to direct his power as he ran across the field, keeping the heavy object from descending fully while Mick and some of the workers pulled Caleb to safety. It had been a magnificent rescue, but it had let the cat out of the bag as far as Justin's gift was concerned. He'd taken his bike and hit the road a week later, not to be seen for the next five years.

He'd kept in touch, calling his brothers each week to check in, and when Caleb told him to come home, he'd done so without question. He'd come home only to help pack up and move to the Waste. If he'd been taciturn before, now he was downright solemn. He never talked about his five years away, but he had picked up a huge two-headed dragon tattoo across his chest as a memento.

Jane saw it once in a while when the temperature grew warm enough for the men to strip off their shirts as they worked. And once, she'd practically crashed into Justin as he walked out of the bathroom after a shower. She couldn't help but stare at the masterful image etched into his skin and fought the odd desire to touch his chest and trace the powerful lines.

Justin was telepathic as well as telekinetic. All the brothers had some telepathic ability, and he'd probably picked up on her half-formed desires. Since that day, he'd been careful to be fully clothed whenever he had a chance of running into her.

Jane knew Justin usually hid in the big stall he'd arranged to house his Harley and the various tools he needed to keep it in prime condition. It was about the size of one of the large birthing stalls in the barn, but unlike the rest of the building, it was spotless, with nary a sliver of hay in sight. The concrete was oil stained, but there were good lights in there so Justin could easily see into the engine of his beloved machine. There was also a huge stack of spare parts and fluids he'd managed to stockpile that would ensure the machine functioned well for the next twenty years at least. Caleb's precognition had allowed them time to stock up on all sorts of things that were unavailable or hard to get now.

Jane approached slowly, seeing light through the partially closed door. Justin had made this small room his personal retreat. There was a space heater, a comfy chair, and a small cooler with the bottled beer she'd learned how to brew for her men. They'd loved that little surprise, and a smile dawned as she thought of their reaction when she'd served up the first batch a few months ago.

The door was ajar just a few inches and she approached cautiously. Justin's temper was unpredictable, though she knew he would never hurt her. Still, she didn't want to alienate him. She hated when he turned away from her. Only Caleb could console her when Justin shut her out and of course, then Caleb would have words with Justin for hurting her tender feelings and only make the situation worse. If at all possible, she wanted to come out of this encounter with nothing more than the information Caleb needed, and no overwhelming emotions that would cause further strife between the brothers.

She edged forward into the small patch of light that spilled into the dark barn. "Justin?" she asked tentatively, not wanting to startle him. His reactions were lightning-quick and she'd learned not to sneak up on him unless she wanted to risk bodily injury.

"Go away, Jane."

The words held anger and she heard a frantic sort of rustling as she pushed the door wider to peer inside. It was obvious what she had interrupted and she felt her cheeks flame. Justin's magnificent tattooed chest was bare, his fly was open, and one hand was barely covering his thick erection.

She was caught, like a deer in headlights, her mouth forming a perfect "O" of surprise that only made things worse.

"I'm sorry," she said quickly, feeling waves of his anger, desire and turmoil that literally took her knees out from under her.

Justin saw her begin to crumple and moved to catch her.

"Dammit, Jane," he growled, catching her in his arms. He brought her into the room and placed her on the overstuffed chair. He left her there while he tucked himself in and forced the zipper up. It hurt like hell and when she gasped, he looked up to see her wide eyes watching him. He nearly came right then and there.

"Fuck!"

"Justin." She sounded almost afraid of him. "I'm sorry. I just...got overwhelmed by your anger." Her sympathetic eyes made him squirm. "I'm so sorry."

He knew he had to get himself under control or risk hurting her more. Her damned empathic senses were too closely attuned to the O'Hara boys. She'd always been able to read him like a book and he knew his anger and turmoil could hurt her.

"No, I'm the one who's sorry." He turned his back while shrugging into his shirt, hoping the tails would hide his hard-on, though there was no way to ease it while she was there. He was gathering calm, trying to smooth out the jagged emotions riding him while she recovered from the shock, but his deep breaths just brought home her warm, feminine scent and it was hard. And he remained hard.

"Jane, are you okay to go back to the house yet? I need a few minutes here."

He heard her stand. He thought he felt a disturbance in the air, as if she reached out to touch his back, but stopped before she made contact. He was relieved she didn't. If she touched him, she would feel everything he was feeling multiplied ten-fold and he didn't want to subject her to that.

"We need to talk about this, Jus. I want to help you." Her soft voice almost unmanned him.

"Janie, for God's sake, please just go."

"No."

He was so startled, he turned to face her, the muscles in his jaw jumping with tension.

"But I'm going to wait outside while you...do what you have to do. After, we will talk. I care too much about you to let you continue as you've been. Something's eating you and I'm half afraid it's me. I don't want to cause you pain, Justin. I'll leave if I have to. I want you to be happy. I don't want you to hate me."

"Sweetheart, I don't hate you. Far from it." The sight of tears in her beautiful brown eyes brought him under control and he was able to offer compassion. Now that was an emotion only she had ever been able to spark in his warrior's soul.

"But I'm making you unhappy. I can feel it."

He reached out tentatively, hesitating before he made contact. He knew the only way to convince her was to let her feel what he was feeling at this moment. He couldn't let her leave. Not only would Caleb kill him, he would kill himself if any harm befell her. She needed his reassurance now, not his anger or his lust, though God knew he wanted her and had for most of his adult life. He squashed that thought as he prepared to touch her, concentrating on his care, his compassion and his love. Pure thoughts and emotions that would comfort her, if he could just keep them under control.

She pressed her cheek into his palm, her eyes flooding again as she absorbed the waves of pure emotion he sent. The tears helped him like nothing else to keep his libido under control as he curved his hand to cradle her head, tunneling his fingers into her soft auburn hair.

"I care about you, Janie. I don't want you to leave. I want you to stay here, continue to make Caleb the happiest of men, and drive me and Mick crazy, okay?" As a joke, it wasn't much, but she smiled anyway. "Besides, who would brew my beer? Mick's too busy being Doctor Dolittle and I don't know one end of that contraption you use from another."

She smiled at him and broke the contact, reassured. "I know you're unhappy, Justin. If it's not me, then what? Caleb and I want to help you in whatever way we can."

He stalked to the other side of the Harley, watching as she perched on the arm of his overstuffed easy chair. "So Caleb sent you down here to see what I was feeling, only you got more than you bargained for, eh?" He could almost laugh at the situation, if he wasn't feeling so raw at the moment.

"We love you, Justin. We want to help you. Come on, tell me what's really wrong. I don't like to see you men fighting with each other."

He let the silence stretch until she shocked him with her next bold question.

"Is it sex?"

"Jane, you don't want to talk to me about that. Believe me." His tone was hard, unrelenting, and he hoped she'd get the message and drop the subject.

"Come on, Jus. I've been married to your brother for almost seven years now. I know all about sex. And I know you weren't a priest in the old days. You had your share of women swooning at your feet, beguiled by your mysterious eyes and bad boy rep. And now there are no women for miles around."

"Except you," he whispered low, challenge in his gaze.

"Except me." She nodded slowly, swallowing hard.

He cursed and shook his head with renewed anger. "You can't possibly mean to take me on, Janie. You're Caleb's wife and that's that. It's best for all concerned if I just stay away from you for a while."

Jane didn't know what she'd meant by her challenge, but she hated seeing Justin so full of turmoil. She loved him, as much as she loved Caleb and Mick. They were her family, her saviors, her life, and she would do anything for them. She turned to go, shocked to find Caleb there in the doorway, a look of concern and compassion on his face.

Justin spun around when she gasped, his eyes hardening as he saw his brother standing there.

"Perfect." He swore. "Just perfect." He shook his head. "I suppose you heard."

Caleb faced his brother with a frown. "Not all of it, but enough. Justin, I—"

"Save it." He grabbed his helmet off a peg and rolled the Harley out of the barn. He had a duffle already attached to the back. Jane realized he'd planned to leave long before she'd come out to the barn.

"Justin, please don't go," Jane pleaded with him. She was afraid if he left now, he'd never return. Those five years he'd been away had hurt her terribly. She didn't want to live through that again. She needed all the brothers, together, with her. "Please."

Justin turned to her, his eyes pained but resigned. "Just for a little while, Jane. I need to think some things through. I promise you, I won't go for good without saying goodbye."

She sobbed, turning to Caleb. His arms came around her while his eyes flashed fire at his brother.

"Go. But you damned well better be back in three days. That's the limit of my patience." Caleb guided Jane aside while Justin rolled the bike out the door. He led her to the chair, settling her there before he left to join Justin on the dirt driveway that led from the barn.

Chapter Two

"It hurts her when you're gone." Caleb stepped into his brother's path. "She pined for you those five years you were away."

Justin looked as if he'd been sucker punched and Caleb knew his brother hadn't quite realized that little fact.

"She was nearly as bad when Mick was in school, but at least she knew he'd be back on holidays and she knew where he was." Caleb kicked a pebble out of the drive. "She needs all of us, Jus. Her emotional bond to us is strong and her own feelings very fragile. I'm afraid if you leave us for good, she'll never be truly happy again."

"God, Caleb! Don't lay this on me." Justin looked up to the sky as if for strength. "If I stay, I'll make her miserable too. I can't control what I feel anymore and I don't want to hurt either of you."

Caleb sighed. "You love her, don't you?" Justin's eyes hardened, but he refused to speak. "I don't mean like a brother. I mean, you want her, right? Like Mick's always wanted her too."

"Jesus!"

"It's okay," Caleb said resignedly. "I knew Mick loved her from the start, but back then... Well, it was easy to find women, and he was in school. You were gone and she needed one of us to bring her into our family. She belongs with us. I figured Mick would get over it. But now—"

"It's impossible," Justin said with resignation. "It's just frustration. Any woman would do."

Caleb looked up at him with a raised eyebrow. "You think so?"

Justin refused to answer, just put on his helmet and straddled the bike.

"You go find a woman then," Caleb advised. "Fuck her good and hard and then tell me if it satisfies you like just the thought of fucking Jane."

"God, Caleb! Have a little mercy. This is your wife you're talking about!"

Caleb nodded. "And I love her more than life. But I'm not the one she should have married. I stole her from Mick, or maybe even from you, if you'd been home. She always followed you around when she was a kid. More than either me or Mick. She was fascinated by you, and I think she still is. I've seen the way she looks at you."

"All the more reason for me to go." He kicked back the stand and balanced the bike as he prepared to start the powerful engine.

Caleb reached out to put a hand on his brother's shoulder. "Things have changed in our world, Justin. I know it's hard to accept, but the world we knew is over. We have to adjust to this new way of living and find a way to all be happy. One life is all we get and we were luckier than most. Don't ruin it by running."

Justin looked up into Caleb's eyes, questions circling visibly in his own. "You've seen something, haven't you?"

Caleb nodded once and shook his head to halt further questions. "Go to the village. You'll find a woman there. Give her this." He handed over a gold chain and crystal pendant that had been in their family for generations. Justin's eyes widened. "Do reconnaissance. See what's going on and bring back news. The future isn't clear to me yet and I need more information if I'm going to be of any use to this family."

"Caleb," Justin grasped his brother's hand firmly and with purpose, "you've already saved us many times over. You're our leader." He let go, but his dark eyes sparkled with new purpose. "I'll get the information you need and I'll be back."

"Three days, Jus. No longer. And fuck that woman long and hard. Bring her some pleasure to remember you by. If she likes you, I think it could help us in the end."

Justin knew better than to question Caleb's cryptic words, having lived with them all his life, but Caleb knew this was by far the oddest set of instructions he'd ever given anyone.

"I'll be back in three days."

With a roar, the big machine started and Justin took off down the dirt road. Caleb turned with a sigh to see Jane waiting in the open doorway, her dark auburn hair glinting in the sun. He wasn't sure how much of the conversation she'd heard, but probably quite a bit judging from her stormy expression.

"Do you really think you stole me from your brothers?" she asked, making his breath catch. It was his deepest, darkest secret, and now she knew. He wanted to collapse right there on the spot and cry like a child, but he had to be strong. For her.

"Didn't I?"

His tone was desolate, and her eyes filled again. She stepped forward, into his embrace, loving him. "Never, Caleb. I love you with all my heart."

She reached up and kissed him then, not objecting at all when he took the kiss deeper and backed her into the barn with an urgency they hadn't felt in a long time. She didn't object when he pushed her into Justin's hideaway, kicking the door shut behind them. And she didn't object when he peeled off her jeans and panties in one move, dropping them to the side of the big easy chair. He plopped her down into the chair and knelt before her.

He spread her legs wide, dangling them in the air above his shoulders as he smiled. She was wet for him already.

"I love you, Jane. I love everything about you." He bent over her to lick her, pausing at the hard nubbin at the apex of her thighs. Sucking her into his mouth, he felt the contractions in her tummy, signaling her excitement. He moved lower to stab his tongue into her in sharp bursts, making her come with little effort. He knew she loved it when he went down on her, probably as much as he loved her going down on him.

But he was a desperate man with no time for finesse. Lowering his jeans just enough, he knelt in front of her, his cock at just the right height with the chair to do the job. With a bold thrust, he impaled her, his hands sliding up her legs to hold them high above as he shafted her.

He loved the small cries she made as she neared climax, spurring him on. He drove into her over and over, his cock a tight fit even after years of loving her. It never got old with Jane, she matched him so well, was open to every one of his desires.

"Faster!" she whispered.

He liked being open to her desires too. When she sent what she wanted directly into his mind, in her rare bursts of telepathy, the sex had been unbelievably good. But Jane wasn't a strong telepath and only deep emotion got her thoughts through to him—or maybe it was his own gift of telepathy joining them at such times.

He sped up, swirling his cock inside her to bring that little extra pressure she needed. Within moments, she was shivering and contracting around him, milking his spurting cock for all it was worth.

"God, I love you," he whispered, licking a drop of sweat from the side of her neck as he collapsed over her. He released her legs and they came to rest on his back, crossed daintily as she held him tight within her.

"Never doubt my love for you, Caleb." She kissed his neck, making him want to fuck her all over again, but while the spirit was willing, the flesh was weak. He needed time to recover.

Caleb straightened, meeting her sultry eyes as he rested against her. "I do love you, Jane. But I still feel like I got away with something when you agreed to marry me. I caught you at a low point in your life. Your father had just died and neither Mick nor Justin were around to fight me for you."

"Would you have fought for me?"

The idea seemed to titillate her and he was amused. He was forever learning new facets of this wonderful, magical woman who was his wife.

He growled, bending down to nip at her shoulder. "You bet your sweet ass I would have fought for you. Back then, I would have died to keep you all to myself." She stilled and he straightened once more, his gaze holding hers.

"And now?"

He considered for a moment, all levity gone. "What I told Justin is true. The world as we knew it is over." He lifted off her and was oddly pleased by her short whimper of protest as he withdrew. He pulled up his jeans and handed her the panties and jeans he'd turned nearly inside out in his earlier haste. He had to smile at that. They hadn't been so hot for each other in months, though their sex life was never dull. Still, the added edge made it even better, though he hadn't thought it possible. That she was adventurous sexually was a good thing which might just make what had to come next palatable.

She dressed quickly, trying to keep him in her line of sight. No doubt she was feeling his every emotion, so tuned was she to him, but he had no solid answers. Still, he owed her some explanation of his conflicted feelings.

"What have you seen?" She stood, fully dressed now, and took his hand. They walked out of the room and back through the barn toward the house, picking up the eggs along the way as he tried to put his chaotic thoughts in order. She waited patiently, having been through this with him before.

"Change is coming. Big change." Only his hand in hers kept her calm, he knew. She could feel everything he felt and he had to work to channel his emotions, to reassure her. "The aliens are curious about us, but they don't see us as people. They see us sort of like we see the cattle, or maybe more accurately, as we see insects. Interesting, but not useful for any real purpose and quite disposable."

"Did I just hear Justin roar away?" Mick's deep voice intruded on the moment as he joined them.

Mick was the youngest O'Hara brother, who'd grown steadily quieter and more serious since the cataclysm. He'd almost finished veterinary school when Caleb called him home. He doctored the animals and the family when they got sick, and ran their small herds. He also took in strays and doctored them back to health. Birds with broken wings, baby animals who'd lost their mamas, they all came to Mick. Somehow, he could communicate with them—not like he used his very strong telepathy to speak with his brothers, but it was communication, nonetheless. He could calm them and reassure them and let them know he would help. It was a useful gift on a ranch full of animals surrounded by wild forest.

Mick had brought small gifts to Jane, even as a child. Her first kitten had been a gift from Mick, and the puppy that followed a few years later. He'd helped her with school science projects, incubating duck eggs until she had her own small flock living on her daddy's pond back in Montana. He'd been a scamp and a good playmate to her while she was growing up. He was the closest in age to her, but he'd been away in veterinary school when her father died and Caleb had stolen her heart.

He had golden hair and flashing blue eyes—the only one of the O'Hara boys to inherit their sainted mother's laser blue gaze—while Justin had deep brown pools that seemed to see into the darkest parts of a person's soul, and Caleb's eyes were a warm, grassy green. Both older brothers had dark brown hair, though Caleb's was so dark as to be almost black.

"Yeah, Justin just took off for the village." Caleb sighed and looked at Jane. "And there's something you need to hear. I was just telling Jane what's coming. Or what I think is coming."

Mick whistled between his teeth, taking off his work gloves as he started toward the house with them. "That bad huh?"

Caleb nodded grimly. "Could be, if we're not ready for it."

₧CC₩

They gathered at the big kitchen table and Jane poured cups of strong coffee all around while Caleb once again marshaled his thoughts. He was a very deliberate man, a thinker as well as a doer, and he had thoughtful ways that had always comforted her in times of trouble.

26

"So what is it?" Mick prompted, impatient as always.

"The aliens are coming," Jane supplied, wanting to give Caleb a bit more time to prepare his words as he saw fit.

Mick sat back, both hands on the table, clearly shocked. "What can we do?"

"I've already asked Justin to do some reconnaissance while he's in the village. There's a woman." Caleb's eyes squinted as if he was looking into the distance, and Mick leaned forward in interest at the mention of a woman. Women were so scarce nowadays, it was a bit of a shock to hear one was involved somehow with Caleb's vision of the future. "She's different. I think she's one of the aliens."

"And you sent Justin off to find her?" Mick was quite obviously upset, though he tried to make his complaint sound like a joke. Still, his words were clipped and his face flushed ever so slightly.

Caleb smiled ruefully. "Actually, I sent him off to fuck her."

"What?" Mick was incredulous now.

"I don't quite understand it myself, but it's important that someone from this family form a bond with her. She's powerful, and cold, but I think she's the key to our survival."

Jane stood from the table, trying to hide the sharp emotions that shot through her at the idea of what Caleb had sent Justin off to do. If she didn't know herself better, she'd think she was jealous of the idea of Justin having sex with the woman. An alien at that!

Caleb continued talking with Mick, oblivious to Jane's shock. "They're coming. And it's not going to be pretty, but there's not much we can do to stop them. At least not this time. But in a few years..." Again his eyes squinted. "There's hope, that's all I can see right now. But not if we don't get this alien woman sympathetic to us. That's Justin's job."

27

"Damn," Mick grinned boyishly, "how'd he get so lucky? I haven't had a woman in just as long as him, but I guess I don't rate in your visions, eh, big brother?" Jane's gasp had Mick looking sheepish. "Sorry, Janie. I didn't mean to be crude."

Jane could feel the heat of a blush in her cheeks but moved back toward the table. Her family needed her.

"It's okay, Mick. I think I understand." She moved her hand to cover his on the table and was nearly overwhelmed by the flash of desire he unwittingly broadcast to her before drawing away.

Caleb's gaze flowed between his wife and his brother with a sad sort of understanding. "There's more, but I don't think you'll want to hear this."

Mick turned back to them. "After that revelation, what could be worse?"

Caleb shifted uncomfortably in his chair. "This is of a more personal nature, and has to do with the frustration I know you and Justin are both feeling."

Jane flushed, remembering how she'd walked in on Justin earlier that day. He'd had his hand fisted around the longest cock she'd ever seen, his eyes closed as he sat in that damned chair, jerking off. Undoubtedly Mick was just as sexually frustrated. If Caleb was right in thinking Mick had wanted to marry her years ago, the whole situation had just gotten even more complicated.

Couple that with the flash of desire that still had her reeling from when she touched Mick's hand, and her thoughts turned downright shocking. But the serious expression in Caleb's turbulent green eyes and the emotions she could feel rolling off him in waves warned that he too was facing some rather odd and unsettling thoughts. Mick must have sensed the changed mood in the air. He stood, palms held outward.

"You're right. I don't want to hear this."

Caleb carried on though, planting a scandalous seed in the youngest O'Hara brother's mind. And in Jane's as well.

"The world as we knew it is gone, Mick. There are no women for you to make a life with. There's only Jane and she's been in love with all of us since she was old enough to know what love was."

"That's enough, Caleb." Mick's voice growled low in warning. Jane couldn't handle fighting between the brothers. She went to Mick, daring to touch his arm, preparing herself as best she could for the onslaught of his emotions, but he was under tight control this time.

"It's all right." Her low voice caught his attention, making him face her, making his sparking blue eyes meet hers. "Just hear him out."

"God, Janie!" The passion in his gaze and the feelings she sensed gave her hope she could hold the family together even through the trial to come.

Caleb stood, facing his brother, remorse clear in his expression.

"I owe you an apology, Mick. Probably Justin too, but you especially. When Jane's dad died, you were in school and Justin was gone. I thought there'd be plenty of girls who could make you forget Jane. With her empathic gift and her understanding of our own special abilities, I knew she belonged with us. I always figured it'd be you, or maybe Justin, if he ever came home. I didn't expect to have her, but by God, I love her." Caleb seemed to run out of steam as he sat back down, practically collapsing in his chair.

Jane released Mick, feeling the compassion in his heart as he realized his strong older brother was human after all. Things would be okay now. The air between them all was beginning to clear.

"You think I should have married Jane?" Mick sounded as if the idea wasn't all that foreign to him. That surprised her. Jane was learning a great deal today. Things she'd never suspected.

Caleb nodded in answer to Mick's question, his expression miserable.

"Well, I didn't," Jane said forcefully, reminding them both that she was there. "I married you, Caleb, so you're stuck with me."

He smiled as she'd intended, but Mick's eyes were still troubled.

"He's probably right, though, Jane." Mick's serious tone surprised her. "If I'd been finished with school, I would have been after you like a shot. But I had nothing to offer you at the time. I thought it was for the best that you married Caleb. He'd inherited the ranch and he could support you."

Jane's eyes widened as she stared at Mick. Only now did she feel the emotions he'd been so adept at hiding from her for so long. He'd wanted her all this time and she hadn't known.

"Dammit, Mick, how'd you learn to hide your emotions from me?" That, more than anything, had her head spinning. The rest she couldn't quite assimilate yet. She needed to think.

Mick smiled, a sparkle in his blue, blue eyes. "Fooled you, huh? Well good. It's not healthy for a woman to know every thought in a man's head."

His teasing made her smile even though she was still in shock about the revelations of the past hour. "I'm not a mind reader, Mick."

"And thank God you're not!" Mick joked, but there was an edge to his words that didn't escape any of them.

"With the way things turned out, well, Mick, I'm sorry." Caleb's quiet voice was full of remorse. Mick shrugged, but Jane could tell he was deeply moved by his brother's words.

"It was fate. That's all."

"We can't change the past, that's for certain, but the future..." Caleb squinted again and both Jane and Mick caught their breath at what he might reveal. "The future is foggy. Like it hasn't been since before the cataclysm."

"Is there anything we can do?" Mick was serious, but he was never serious for long. A devil entered his eyes as he teased his brother once more. "Other than having Justin seduce an alien woman, that is? And dammit, why didn't you pick me for the job?"

Jane chuckled and Caleb smiled despite the grim vision of the future in his head. "There's one thing more we can do, and I'll need your help, Mick. You're the closest thing we have to a doctor and I need to know..."

Jane felt the difficulty Caleb had with whatever he was going to say and moved closer to him, supporting him. The regret in his eyes spoke to her.

"Whatever it is, we'll work through it together." She held his big hand to her lips and kissed it gently, offering comfort.

He grasped her hand so tight it hurt, but she said nothing. He needed her to be strong now. It was rare that he leaned on her. More often it was the other way around. But this time, she sensed the despair in his soul and knew she would do anything to remove such desolate feelings from the man she loved more than life.

"Jane, I know you've wanted a child and I have to wonder if there's something wrong. I want Mick to find out why we haven't conceived, if he can."

She gasped at the sudden overload of emotions—her own and Caleb's mixed with Mick's shock and sympathy. Tears ran down her face. Caleb had managed to stun her.

"Okay." She took deep, calming breaths. "If Mick can help us, I'll do whatever he asks for the tests."

"I think the problem might be with me, sweetheart, and I'm so damned sorry."

She hugged him close. Mick shuffled a bit, his own emotions tightly under control once more, his face grim.

"How will this help when the aliens come?"

Jane knew Mick's businesslike tone was for Caleb's benefit. He needed something to focus on that would remove him from his own sense of failure and loss.

Silently, she thanked Mick, throwing her thoughts at him the way he'd taught her as a child. She hadn't attempted to use the very modest telepathic skills he'd taught her in over a decade, but was gratified to see him hold her gaze and nod. He'd heard her, though he was probably the only one strong enough telepathically to pick up on her weak signal. Caleb straightened, releasing her.

"If Jane is pregnant when the aliens come, they'll spare her. That I can see for sure. If Justin is successful with the alien woman, there's a good chance they'll leave us all in peace, but the odds tip in our favor if Janie is pregnant." The anguish entered his eyes again. "But whose child? If I'm sterile, it's got to be either you or Justin, Mick."

Jane collapsed into her chair as she realized what he was saying.

"You mean you want me to artificially inseminate her? Like she was a cow or something? Jeez, Caleb!" Mick looked both alarmed and disgusted.

"No."

That single word from Caleb hung in the air, with all its implications. The three of them stared at each other.

"First things first." Caleb finally broke the silence. His shocking words had given them food for thought, "Can you run tests to see what the problem is?"

Mick nodded shortly. "I can try."

"Test me first, then if I'm okay, we'll see about Jane, but I don't think we'll have to go that far." Caleb's eyes hardened and she could feel grim resolution wash through him. "We have a very short window of opportunity. If Justin is following my directions, he's making a baby as we speak."

Jane was shocked yet again. It was a day of revelations that had her reeling. Caleb laid one of his hands over hers.

"Giving the alien woman a child will make her more sympathetic to you. It's coming clearer now. I saw you both together in my vision, both round with pregnancy. She doesn't understand us. She doesn't have the same emotions we do. She's so cold, it's scary, but I think you'll have pregnancy in common if my visions hold true, and it could be the key to saving us all."

"So that means we have between three and nine months before the aliens come in earnest," Mick said, reminding them all of the bigger picture. The brothers wore grim expressions.

"That's about the size of it." Caleb nodded. "Both Jane and the alien woman were showing. There was no doubt they were both heavily pregnant in my vision."

"Dear Lord." One thought became instantly clear in Jane's turbulent mind. "I'm really going to have a baby?"

Caleb grasped her hand. "You're going to be a wonderful mother, Jane. I've wanted that for you for a long time."

Bittersweet tears of joy gathered in her eyes as she clasped Caleb's hand to her heart. "I love you so much, Caleb. You're going to be the best father."

"Uncle, at least." He shrugged, trying to hide his feelings unsuccessfully.

Mick went to the door and opened it, reminding them of his presence. "We don't know about that yet, Caleb. If it's within my power, I'll make it happen for you both. You deserve a child together."

Jane kissed Caleb on the cheek and rushed over to Mick before he could leave, needing to share the love and joy in her heart.

"Thank you, Mick." She threw her arms around him and kissed his cheek much like she'd just kissed Caleb.

Mick met Caleb's eyes over Jane's head and Caleb nodded his understanding as Mick's arms tightened uncontrollably, just for a moment, around the girl he'd loved since childhood.

Chapter Three

Damned if Caleb's visions were ever wrong, Justin thought as he rode up to the village's only rooming house on his Harley. He'd stayed there several times when negotiating trade deals with the villagers or when he just needed to get away from the ranch for a while. Jane's disturbing presence chipped away at his control until he thought he'd go mad if he couldn't have her.

But she was his brother's wife. It didn't matter that Justin had known and loved her most of his life. He knew she cared for him deeply and he even knew she found him attractive. Her admiring looks and the unconscious way she followed him with her eyes were proof enough of that, but it made him uncomfortable, to say the least. He'd had to stop in the woods to stroke his cock and give himself some blessed relief from the hard-on she'd witnessed. That little encounter would be good for a few hundred fantasies and though he could have wished she'd never found him jerking off in his garage, in a perverse way he was glad she had.

He'd suffered in silence so long. He wanted her so badly. Only his love for her and the love and respect he had for his brother kept him under control. But perhaps most disturbing of all were the veiled hints he'd gotten from Caleb that somehow he just might be able to have Jane after all. He hoped to God that didn't mean Caleb had foreseen his own death, because he feared that most of all. The thought of losing Caleb, like nothing else, had helped him get his head screwed on straight. Caleb was their leader and Justin vowed to do whatever his brother asked to help the family survive his dire visions of the future. Caleb had never been wrong before.

So there he was, parking his beloved Harley in the middle of the ground floor room, right next to his rented bed. He didn't trust leaving the bike outside where anyone might steal it, and it didn't take up much space. He hadn't seen the woman Caleb mentioned yet, but knew enough to trust his older brother's vision. If Caleb said he'd find a woman and screw her brains out, then he definitely would.

And just in time too. Justin didn't think he could survive much longer without sticking his dick in a warm and willing pussy. Jerking off was fine to relieve the pressure, but it had been so long since he'd fucked a woman, he could barely see straight. Masturbating to visions of his sister-in-law was some kind of sin, he knew, but he couldn't seem to help himself. He loved her and he always would. No matter what.

Justin settled his pack and bike in the small room, then left, locking the door securely behind him. He needed to do the reconnaissance his brother had requested, and he needed to find the woman.

Justin licked his lips and headed for the saloon. A couple of guys had set up a distilling operation and made some decent brews using different plant sources, including some of the grains he and his brothers grew and harvested. He could check in with the guys at the bar and get the latest news while discussing what they needed in the way of supplies from the ranch. Plus, he could get something stronger than the beer his sister-in-law brewed for him. He needed a little extra kick tonight after the disturbing revelations of the morning.

Justin pushed open the door and headed for the long bar, answering a few friendly greetings from the other men. The owners of the place kept order by virtue of the fact they were the only ones in town with booze. They could refuse service if a man got too unruly. Being refused service in the saloon was a fate worse than death for most men these days when liquor was the only easy form of relaxation available.

He spent time in the saloon, learning the news and negotiating an order for more grain from the owners, but aside from the stiff shot of some kind of new bark brew early on in the conversation, he kept his wits about him. He didn't know exactly what Caleb wanted him to learn here, but he would watch carefully in order to make a full report to his big brother. He'd learned in the old U.S. Army how to do a proper job of recon, and he knew from long experience Caleb could use even what seemed to be insignificant information to verify his visions.

After a few hours, Justin headed back to his room to get some sleep. It had been a long day, and it only seemed to get longer when he noticed the door to his room was ajar. A light shone from within, so whoever was in there didn't seem to fear discovery. Still, Justin was instantly on alert. He moved quietly toward the door, hoping for the element of surprise as he pushed it open with a crash.

What he found inside gave him pause. It was a woman. But was she the woman Caleb had foretold? With the scarcity of women, it was hard to believe she could be any other.

She had tightly coiled, icy blonde hair and slightly pointed ears. She was tall and statuesque, with a fey quality that enchanted him on sight. She had small breasts and a willowy body, which was not his favorite body type in a woman, but he was so hard and desperate, he would fuck almost anything with a cunt.

She looked up in surprise as he entered, but no fear. She was an odd one, he thought, and she dressed in clothing like he'd never seen before. The fabric seemed to change color as she moved, fitting like a second skin against her tall form. She was thin and tall like the old fashion models, but she had a coldness in her sky blue eyes that chilled him.

"Who are you and what are you doing in my room?" Justin asked calmly, his eyes cataloging everything. He sensed no immediate threat from the woman or anything else in the room. Stepping inside, he closed the door behind him with a stray thought, a show of his telekinetic power to let the woman know who and what she was dealing with. He was gratified to see her eyes widen and a somewhat pleased expression settle on her lips.

"I am Mara."

Her voice was like music, though it held no warmth. Justin realized this woman must be an alien. There could be no other explanation for her otherworldly appearance, total lack of fear of him, and the fact that she was running around apparently alone in the settlement made up mostly of single, hungry, horny men. And there was the voice. Tales abounded about the soothing, musical nature of the aliens' voices, though Justin had never heard it for himself. Until now.

"Well, Mara," he moved boldly forward, "what brings you to my bedroom in the middle of the night?"

She straightened to her full height, which was close to his own six foot three, and stared him down. "I go where I wish, Breed."

"Is that so?" Justin unbuttoned his shirt. He watched her eyes flare with heat that she couldn't hide. Oh yeah, he thought with satisfaction, she would be under him in no time, her tight little pussy dripping with his come.

"I saw you ride in on this," her hand gestured gracefully toward the motorcycle, "and became intrigued. I have never seen such a machine."

"It's called a motorcycle and there were many of them before your people came."

Her eyes shot to his. "You know what I am?"

Justin shrugged. "It's easy enough to guess. You look like an elf."

"A what?" He was glad to see he'd gotten her attention.

He shrugged as he threw the shirt aside and unbuttoned the top button of his jeans. She seemed fascinated by the huge double dragon tattoo that covered most of his chest. Chicks really did dig that tattoo. Lord knows he'd gotten some fantasy mileage out of Jane's fascinated eyes on his dragon. He didn't know if he was really looking forward to fucking this alien woman, but if he kept thoughts of Jane firmly in mind, maybe he could keep his dick up all night for her. Hell, a desperate man couldn't afford to be picky.

Caleb had said to fuck her long and hard. Fucking her once or twice wouldn't be a problem for a man who hadn't had warm pussy in years, but keeping it up after the first few times would be another story. Justin hadn't ever liked to have sex with just anyone. He'd always enjoyed it more when there was some affection in the joining to make it special. Casual sex just hadn't had much appeal for him, though like any guy, he'd indulged in it more often than not.

Justin crowded her, relieved when she stood her ground, even sending out one of her pale fingers to trace the swirling lines of his tattoo the way he'd known Jane had wanted to when she caught him coming out from a shower. He stifled a groan as his cock hardened and expanded.

"We have legends of fey folk who look like you. Tall, pointy ears, and fair-skin. We called them elves in the old country where my ancestors are from. It was called Ireland or Eire. I can only guess now that Ireland was populated by descendants of your people, though they spread out and immigrated across the globe."

"I had not heard of such before, but it does make sense. We sent an advance party, of course, but they were lost to us centuries ago, after surveying the planet and finding it suitable for our colony."

"My guess is they liked it so much here, they stayed." He smiled and stepped close enough so his chest touched the tips of her small breasts, gratified to hear her breath catch. "And they fucked like bunnies, spreading their DNA all over the planet, which I would assume the mothership hadn't intended."

She shrugged, dragging her tight nipples up and down his chest. "If such is the case, it is an unforeseen complication. We had no idea until just recently that we could breed with humans. But the idea is intriguing."

Justin moved away. "Intriguing, hmm?" He lowered the zipper over his straining erection. "Are you intrigued enough to want to try a human on for size?"

"You are not human," she said quietly, her eyes almost covetous on his rigid shaft. "You are a Breed. I have encountered several like you in my research."

He nodded, sliding one hand around her waist, surprised to find the shiny material of her jumpsuit warm beneath his fingers.

"A telekinetic Breed." He nuzzled her neck. "What gifts do you have?" Her breath came quickly now, and she was getting hotter for him, if he were any judge.

"None," she said on a soft moan. "We do not have the same abilities as Breeds do."

He tucked that knowledge away for Caleb's perusal. They'd always assumed the aliens had similar, or perhaps stronger psychic gifts than them. It was surprising to hear they didn't, but Justin was careful not to let his astonishment show. If she were lying, she was a damn good liar, but he'd bring all his information to Caleb and see what he could make of it.

"So that's what brought you here, hmm? You want to experience a Breed's gifts up close and personal?"

She nodded as he kissed her neck, then moved to her lips, smothering her gasp of surprise as he thrust his tongue into her hot mouth. Her hands moved between them and suddenly, she was naked. Justin liked that. He liked it a lot.

Her features might be cold, but her body burned hotter than normal human skin, warming him immediately. He growled low in his throat in appreciation as he cupped her small breasts, trailing kisses down her neck to pert nipples that beaded for him as he licked and blew, teasing them.

"Have you ever been fucked by a Breed before, Mara?" His growled question overwhelmed her senses. Truly, Mara had been unprepared for the reality of the male Breed. He was so sure of himself and so strong physically. What little she'd seen of his telekinetic power intrigued her and his cock looked hard and long.

"No." She answered his question, her scientist's mind always on the matter at hand. "But I've been intrigued by your people for some time. I'm studying your DNA."

"How about I give you a semen sample right up your pussy?"

She nodded, surprised at how easy her mission here was being accomplished. "I may require several of your samples," she warned him.

She felt it was only fair to tell him that having been chosen as her test subject, she would expect certain things from him, but he showed no signs of stopping. If anything, his attentions to her nipples grew stronger and his caresses bolder. She'd never known nipples could be so sensitive, but his sucking and gentle bites made her very excited. She studied the effect until her knees unexpectedly buckled, but he was there to catch her, his heavily muscled arms easily carrying her to the wide bed.

He stood above her, looking down, his dark, intent gaze sending sparks into her bloodstream as he focused his telekinetic power on her. It was truly a wonderful experiment. He parted her legs using just the powers of his mind. Her arms were held in place above her with his thoughts. This telekinetic power was very interesting, and stronger than she would have credited. His cock seemed to get thicker as he examined her body and she offered a small smile she'd seen her human subjects use to convey invitation to their mates. It must have worked because he settled between her legs and fingered her pussy.

"It's good to see that you're made the same as a human woman. Everything's in its usual place, except," he tilted his head as his fingers disappeared up her pussy and she squirmed, "your passage is a bit longer than most women I've fucked before."

Her scientific mind thought about his observation, pleased that he would share his discoveries and experiences with her. She'd been lucky to find this articulate Breed on her first foray into the small village.

"Probably because I am taller than most of your women. Everything is in proportion, you see."

He grinned, showing even, white teeth as he positioned his cock at her wet entrance. "Yeah, same with me. My dick is longer than most men's, but you'll take me easily. I've always had to be careful not to hurt smaller women, though I like the way a small cunt feels around me." His eyes were clouded as he pushed easily into her. "But you don't want to know any of this, do you?"

She tested the strength of his hold by trying to move her hands. She noted his eyes tracking her movements and a moment later, the hold on her arms released. She rested her hands on his shoulders, meeting his gaze.

"On the contrary, I want to hear anything you wish to share. In return I will share with you, as is only fair." Her body trembled in pleasure as he began to thrust. "What are you called?"

"Justin," he panted, his dick twitching in eagerness as her warmth surrounded him. "I'm sorry, I can't last long this first time, but I'll make it up to you."

"It's all right. Come inside me now, Justin." She caressed his muscular shoulders. They were pleasing in a very masculine sort of way. This Breed was quite a specimen. He thrust hard a few more times and came in a flood, filling her womb. She purred with satisfaction as she felt the wet release within her channel. She thought he would leave her then, but he surprised her by staying, propping himself up on his hands as he loomed over her.

"I haven't had a woman in years." He kissed her once, gently. "Please forgive my bad manners." He continued the kiss and nibbled on her skin, exciting her in ways she'd never experienced.

Truthfully, she was astounded by the Breed's good manners. He was considerate of her comfort, releasing his power over her limbs at the first sign she wanted to be free. He was also well spoken and more intelligent than she'd been led to believe of the wild-living Breeds. His articulate descriptions of his past experiences would be helpful in her research and he appeared to have a quick mind, able to gather evidence and come to fast conclusions. It was all more than she'd hoped to find among the Breeds she'd selected for her experiments. He also had a great deal of stamina. She was surprised and pleased to feel him grow hard within her once more.

"When was the last time you had sex with a female?"

He pushed himself up, rocking slowly within her as he met her eyes. "Since before your people's attack on the Earth."

"It was a retuning, not an attack," she felt compelled to say as he pulsed harder into her body. She was close to some peak she'd never climbed and didn't want him to stop. He became ruthless in his thrusts as she urged him on. She was slave to her own body in those moments, the physical reaction from her pleasure centers making it hard to focus on the conversation. That had certainly never happened before. But the Breed seemed not to experience the same difficulty. Curious.

"Maybe it was innocent from your perspective, but my great-grandfather was a Shaman. What your people did to the Earth changed it forever." The Breed kept thrusting as she struggled to follow his words. "Your people killed many millions of sentient beings. It was wrong." He seemed angry, but it only made her hotter as he thrust into her hard and fast now. She barely heard his words any longer, though somewhere in the back of her mind they were stored for later examination. She could only concentrate on the incredible sensations he was producing in her body.

With a pulse of telekinetic thought, Justin repositioned her legs around his waist, allowing him to push even more deeply into her. Still, he couldn't quite reach the end of her gripping warmth. She was built extra long for a woman, with a long torso and long limbs. She had a long channel as well, her passage held him completely, but he missed feeling the ridge of a woman's body up against the tip of his cock. He imagined what it would be like to fuck Janie this way, with her petite build, and it was enough to renew the fire in his veins.

But he'd be damned if he came again without bringing Mara off as well. He reached between them with one hand and teased her clit, watching in satisfaction as she jerked. A few moments of pinching her clit and she came with a squeal that nearly left him deaf. He powered through the discomfort in his ears and finished her with a thick load of cum she seemed to milk from him with her own powerful orgasm.

Her pussy was now so hot, it nearly scalded. Relief flooded him when he pulled out, releasing his mental hold on her legs. Justin flopped down at her side and shut his eyes, willing the strength back into his body. He had to find reserves of energy to make her come again and again, all night long. For one thing, Caleb expected no less. For another, she was the only willing female he'd encountered in years and he didn't know when he might be so fortunate again. His cock needed as much as he could get from her to hold against the future when he would again be in the impossible situation of loving and desiring a woman he couldn't have, but had to share the ranch with.

Plus, he knew he needed to somehow gain this woman's sympathy. She was so analytical he could easily see her ordering all their deaths without a single shred of remorse. His family was at stake here. His beloved brothers as well as the woman he loved more than his own life. He would do anything—fuck anyone—to help keep them alive and safe. There was no question of leaving now. He would stay with Caleb, Mick and Jane, and see the family through the coming crisis.

With that thought firmly in mind, he turned back to the alien woman, noticing for the first time her pale blonde locks had come loose from the intricate hairstyle, to drape enticingly around her head. She had beautiful features, if he could just overcome the cold, alien light in her pale blue eyes.

"Are you ready for more?" he asked bluntly, watching with satisfaction as her breath caught.

"Give me a moment more, then I will be ready for you again." Her tone was clinical, almost detached, but her skin was hot when he reached out one hand to caress her nipples.

"What was that noise you made?"

"Did I hurt you?" she asked, a bit of calculation entering her expression.

Justin shrugged, palming one small breast now as he bent to lick the other one.

"No, I was just surprised. I've never heard a woman make such a racket before, and I thought your people were noted for their beautiful voices."

"Powerful, if not always beautiful," she agreed. "It is one of our many strengths, but also some would say, a weakness."

"How so?" He nipped at her body, sliding two fingers into her wet pussy.

She shuddered at his slightly rough treatment, but answered his question. She was a regular font of information and he had to believe she was either so confident in her people's strength she could discount any possible threat from his fellow survivors, or she intended to kill him when this was over. He could believe either one from this alien woman. He'd be on his guard, but would get as much information as he possibly could to bring back to Caleb. It was his mission and he hadn't failed his family yet.

As a sort of insurance, he used his lesser talent of telepathy to send out a silent call to Mick. Mick was the only one who might be able to hear him over this distance. And Mick could be trusted to pass on whatever information Justin could send him telepathically if this bitch really did plan to kill him after he had served his purpose.

"We vibrate on a higher energy level than your human ancestors." He could barely believe she was answering his question so calmly while writhing in pleasure from the fingers he was stroking in her pussy. "Our explorers were treated to survive it, but we had to retune this planet's energies before the majority of our people could be comfortable here."

Justin settled himself between her legs. This time he didn't have to use his telekinetic powers to keep her legs spread wide. No, this time, she did it eagerly.

"So that's what the crystal bombardment was all about?"

She nodded and moaned, the sound having an otherworldly quality to it as he slid into her. She was even hotter than before and he pushed her hard and fast toward orgasm. Each of his powerful thrusts drew a cry from her lips, lifting her off the bed, but he couldn't come, even though she found her pleasure twice at least, ringing his ears with her loud cries each time.

He withdrew. When she would have reached for him, he used his gift to immobilize her. With just his thoughts, he turned her over on her stomach, raising her slim ass in the air. He rubbed his cock over the line of her spread buttocks and down into her as she began to tremble again.

"Don't worry. You're going to love this. Trust me."

"What are you going to do?" That damned clinical tone was in her voice again and it grated on his nerves.

"Have you ever been fucked in the ass?"

Her pussy clenched around him and he could tell the idea excited her.

"I need your sperm in my womb," she reminded him and he was taken aback at how adamant she sounded. The last thing he wanted to do was antagonize her.

"Maybe later then." He nipped gently where her shoulder joined her long neck as he drove in deeper. Several hard thrusts later, he came hard within her as she shuddered with release. He let go then, allowing her to roll away. She lay on her back, watching him with those calculating eyes in a way he didn't like.

"What is that symbol on your chest? Were you born with it?"

Justin laughed at her assumption. "No, ma'am. It's a tattoo. An artist drew it on me over several days using a needle to inject ink into my skin."

She trailed her hand over the design, particularly the dragon's tail that wound around and around down past his navel to the base of his cock.

"Why? What does it mean?"

"It's a dragon—a mythological creature that breathes fire and symbolizes strength. I liked the design and I was young and somewhat foolish. It hurt like hell when the artist was doing the work and for a few days later, but she made it up to me."

"A woman did this?" Mara seemed fascinated.

Justin nodded with a smile of remembrance. "Jolea was very talented in many ways. I let her talk me into this as a way to keep my mind off other things."

"But she is not your mate?"

Justin shrugged. "As far as I know, she died in the cataclysm. She didn't have any psychic gifts that I saw and she lived on the West Coast. Chances are she died in the tsunamis."

"You said you hadn't had a woman in a long time. So then you are unmated?"

"I don't have a wife." Justin found it disconcertingly easy to talk to this woman, whom he didn't know from Adam. Probably because she was a stranger and would never be part of his life, he felt free to tell her things that he normally would keep inside. "But I am in love. I've loved one woman for just about as long as I can remember, but she's not mine."

"You've never had sex with her and still you claim to love her?" Mara sounded genuinely interested.

Justin faced her. "I don't know much about your people, but humans form very strong emotional attachments to each other and to places and things. We love freely and most of us love very deeply. I grew up with Jane and I've loved her for many, many years."

"Then why can't you have her? Is she dead?"

Justin shook his head, his eyes dropping. "She belongs to my brother."

"So why can't you share her?"

Justin looked up at the puzzled alien woman asking the question that had plagued him ever since Caleb began to hint that maybe Jane would be willing.

"In the old days," he tried to explain, "when there were about equal numbers of men and women, most civilized people believed that one man and one woman formed the family unit with their children. A man and woman would get married and their union would be legally recognized by the state and everyone else. Before your people came, Jane married my brother. They are together and faithful to each other according to the old traditions."

"But I've noted in my research that many Breed men will share the same woman." She looked simultaneously confused and fascinated, as if the survivors of humanity were lab subjects to be studied.

"Only out of desperation. Most women in the old days would have only one man after they married him. They might have sex with others before marriage, as did men, but after marriage, they were supposed to be faithful to each other."

"This is fascinating. I had no idea. But why do you cling to the old ways? Surely you realize your world has changed?"

"Out of respect for Jane and for my brother, Caleb. Though Caleb said something very similar to what you just said the last time I saw him. I'm beginning to think that maybe my frustration and anger at not being able to have a woman of my own is affecting Jane. She's a strong empath, you see. She can feel what I feel, even from afar. I think my presence is hurting her."

"And you don't want to hurt her?" Mara was savoring the idea as if it were a foreign concept. Justin thought perhaps it was a good thing to give this alien woman a true idea of the emotions humans—or Breeds, as she called them—dealt with. Maybe he could win her sympathy, or maybe a little understanding if she was truly as cold as she seemed.

"It hurts me to hurt her. I would give everything I am to keep her safe and happy."

"I never knew how devoted Breeds could be to their mates. It explains a great deal."

"Your people don't feel as strongly as we do?" Justin wasn't sure if she would answer his question, but thought it was worth a try to ask. Caleb had sent him here to gather information and he'd do his best to learn as much as possible while he had the chance.

"Generally speaking, we don't have strong emotions of any kind. Once in a while there's a throwback, but they usually become reclusive and go mad after reaching full maturity."

"Throwback?" Justin echoed her word. "Then your people did have strong emotions at some time in your past?"

She nodded. "So the historians tell us. In generations past, our males would go on matequests, looking for their resonance mates."

"Resonance mates?"

"The one who could join with them for life, balancing their energies and keeping them sane." Her voice was dreamy, filled with something like wonder, if she truly could feel such an emotion. "Without their resonance mate, our males would usually go mad, which is why our military was full of single men. They killed at alarming rates until our geneticists stepped in to alter our breeding and remove aggressive tendencies. I surmise that over the centuries, not only was aggression removed from our DNA, but also any other kind of strong emotion. That's why humans seem such insignificant savages to us."

"Then why are you here with me?" He realized that his dick was ready for another round as he watched her nipples harden in his hands.

She sighed as he squeezed her breast. "I'm conducting an experiment."

"What? You want to feel how Breeds fuck?" He raised her to her feet and brought her to the bathroom, stopping only to turn on the water and adjust the temperature.

"Yes, that, and I want to study your DNA and how it meshes with my own."

He smiled devilishly at her. "So that's why you want all those 'samples' of my sperm, huh?"

She nodded perfunctorily. "Yes, I want you to impregnate me."

Justin rocked back on his heels as he realized the implications of what she'd said. For all he knew, she could already be carrying his child. And she wanted it. To study it. Oh God!

"You want my child as some sort of lab experiment?" His voice rose as his anger increased.

She seemed to realize he was upset and placed her hot hands on his shoulder. "I would not hurt the child. I would try to love it, if I am capable of that emotion. Many of our females develop love feelings if they choose to give birth, but I have never had a child, so I don't know. You have my word I have no wish to harm the child."

"Yet you would study it and subject it to clinical tests. And you're not even sure you could love it! And I would never see it or hold it or even know its name. I can't believe this!"

"You realize I may already be pregnant?"

He groaned. "That just makes it worse."

"I could grant you special privileges, I suppose. In return for your continued cooperation." Her head tilted in the way he'd come to realize meant she was thinking.

"What kind of privileges do you think you can give me? I live in the Waste and I won't abandon my family."

"Or the woman you say you love, yes. I understand. But my people are coming. We will be studying this area in some detail, taking subjects to study. I could promise to leave you and your family as they are if you willingly come inside me a few more times. That should do it."

He was torn. "But what of the child?"

She stepped under the spray of water, adjusting it hotter. "I don't know if I will be capable of loving it. If so, I will keep it. If not, I may be willing to give it to you for safekeeping. I know little about raising young and as long as you will grant me access to visit and study it, I may let you keep it."

"I feel like I'm making a deal with the devil."

She smiled as she rinsed her skin under the steamy shower. "I am just a scientist and not any sort of deity. But I will make that deal with you, if you live up to your part."

What could he say? His dick was already hard and she was female—and more than willing—if not of his species. He wanted in her pussy as many times as she would let him. But most of all, he wanted his family safe. Caleb had sent him here, probably knowing he would be offered such a bargain. Caleb had sent him to keep the family safe. And he would do it.

It pained him to think of this cold woman giving birth to his child, not even knowing if she could love it. But he had her word she would not harm the babe and if by chance some miracle happened and she could love the child, it might just help her have some compassion for the test subjects her people were going to capture and study when they invaded the Waste. Justin sighed heavily, all his options boiling down to only one.

"All right, you win." He caressed her slick shoulders. "Now turn around and let me in. I want a shower and I want your pussy. Preferably both at the same time."

She made that throaty noise he was beginning to recognize as her sound of arousal and turned to the wall, bracing her hands on the cool tile. "That can be arranged, Justin."

He enjoyed the tone of her melodic voice and wasted no time joining his straining cock to her hot body. He pumped her from behind, enjoying the hot spill of water on his chest and across her back as she leaned against the side wall of the tub. The warm water dripped down to pool between them and it was almost enough just seeing his cock pumping into a warm, wet pussy to make him come right then.

But she needed a little more stimulation and he vowed to make this night one she would remember always as the best sex of her life. So he brought his hands up to squeeze her nipples. Hard. She squealed in the way he now knew signaled impending climax, so he did it again. And again.

She climaxed around him, her warm tunnel milking him as he allowed himself to watch the red lips of her pussy caressing his shaft. It was a sight he hadn't seen in a long time and probably wouldn't see again any time soon after this night was over. So he promised himself he'd enjoy it while he could and live with the consequences of this night's decisions when they arrived. If things worked out like he expected, that would give him about nine months to figure out a way to get his child away from this heartless bitch.

After their shower, Mara collapsed on the bed for a short nap. But Justin's mind was reeling and only the tentative touch of his brother's telepathy cheered him. Mick was as good as his word and had come down the mountain to the village at his silent request. Justin couldn't go out to talk to his brother and risk Mara waking, but he could and did use their telepathic gift to fill Mick in on everything that had so far transpired.

Mick promised to stay in town in case his brother needed some backup, and agreed to follow Justin home from a distance, watching his back trail. With plans made, Justin allowed himself to close his eyes for a short respite. He had a woman to fuck when he woke, for the first time in too many damned long years, and he needed his strength if he was going to do it right.

Chapter Four

It was two days before Mara was ready to leave Justin's room. They'd fucked on every surface in the room, the dresser, the shower, the bed, the chair, and even his Harley. She'd been hot and insatiable, and Justin was downright dirty dog tired after the marathon session. He had a grimly satisfied smile on his face as he packed up his belongings, Mara watching him as if she was trying to figure him out.

Reaching into his saddlebag, he found the pendant Caleb had given him and remembered what his older brother had said before he'd left. He stood, fingering the gold chain that had been in their family for many generations, trusting in Caleb's precognition that he was doing the right thing.

"Mara," he took her hand in his. "I think I understand your people a little better now." He watched carefully, hoping she would show some kind of emotion, but all he got was the cold analytical stare he'd come to expect from her. "This pendant has been in my family for many generations and I want you to have it now. For the child. Just in case. I want you to give it to him or her so they'll have a piece of their father's heritage and know that I cared." He took her hand and folded the chain within, shocked when the pendant glowed at her touch.

"What is this?" She seemed almost as shocked as he was.

"I told you. It's a family heirloom. I want you to keep it safe for our child."

"By the First Shard!" she exclaimed, holding the pendant to the meager light. "I think this is a piece of the Home Crystal from my people's ancient homeworld." She turned wide eyes to him. "How did you come by it?" She sank onto the bed, holding tightly to the precious pendant.

"It's from my ancestors. It's been passed down from one generation of O'Haras to the next."

"O Hara? What did you say?" Her shock seemed only to increase.

"O'Hara. It's my family name."

"I thought you said your name was Justin?"

He nodded, not quite understanding. "It is. Justin is my first name. O'Hara is my last name. It is the name my family shares. Caleb O'Hara is my oldest brother. Mick O'Hara is my youngest brother. And Jane O'Hara is my sister-in-law, which means she's married to my brother." He wanted her to know all their names so she could keep them off her list of test subjects. He wanted her to keep her bargain and keep his family safe. "Why does this surprise you so much?"

"I did not know you have more than one name. My people do not."

"Then how do you keep everybody straight?"

"I was designated Mara 547,326 at birth. On this planet, I am known as Mara 12, since I am the twelfth in order of rank presently living here. The numbers keep us separate. They keep the line of Mara straight, as you put it."

"God! You number your children?"

"It is efficient."

"And cold," Justin said shortly, unable to keep the horror from his voice, but she didn't seem to comprehend it. "So your family name is Mara then?"

"I suppose you could say that. There are many Maras. Are there many O Haras?"

Justin nodded sadly. "In the old days there were many. Ireland is the origin of my family name, which is where I believe your advanced exploration folk probably settled. Many thousands of O'Haras lived there before the cataclysm. But a lot of O'Haras emigrated to other countries, as my ancestors did when they came to the North American continent in the late twentieth century. I don't know how the other O'Haras might have fared, but my family all shared psychic gifts that allowed us to adapt to the new vibration of the Earth that your people caused. I assume if we did, other O'Haras might've survived as well. But why are you so interested?"

"Hara was one of the Founders. He was one of our greatest explorers and leaders. It was he who led us away from the homeworld when our sun exploded. It was he who found this planet and several others for us to tame and settle. He was lost to us on a long ago expedition, but if what you say is true, he settled here on Earth and you are of his line." She again fingered the pendant. "I cannot believe otherwise. If you are not descended from Hara, there is no way you could have claimed a piece of the Home Crystal. Only the Founders were allowed shards of the Home Crystal and many of them disappeared with the Founders. Justin, do you really want to give this to me? It is a sacred relic of my people and worth more than I can tell you."

She held it out to him but he closed her hand over the pendant once more. "Take it for the child. Promise me you will give it to him or her from me in case something should happen to me. That's all I ask."

"But, Justin—"

He held a finger to her lips, staying her objections. "It was foreseen that you should have this. I never argue with my brother's powers."

"He can foresee the future?" Her clinical tone was back, but she was still stroking the crystal in her palm with her thumb.

Justin nodded. "His precognition saved us from the cataclysm. He knew what was coming months in advance and we came up here and set up our ranch. He also sent me to you. He told me there would be a woman waiting for me in the village, and that I should love her as well as I knew how and give her this crystal. As the eldest, it was his to guard and pass on, and he foresaw that it must go to you. I don't know why, but I don't question his vision. He's saved my life too often for me to question him now."

"I don't quite understand, but I will keep this safe. For the child, as you request. And when the child is born, I will seek you out so you may see it and learn if I have developed love feelings for it."

"As long as you come in peace, you're welcome on our ranch." He quirked his head up at her as he secured his saddlebags. "I think I'd enjoy seeing you while you were still pregnant." She looked at him with that darned clinical curiosity, but he still felt a need to tell her how he felt. "I've never made a woman pregnant before. I'd like to see it, feel the roundness of your stomach and feel the baby kick. The drive to procreate is very strong in most human males. I guess I'm no different. If you can manage it, I'd love to see you while you're still big with my child. It'll probably be the only chance I'll ever have to have offspring."

She nodded calmly. "I will try to accommodate your request but I can make no guarantees. I will have much work to complete in the coming months."

He strode up to her, pulling her close for one final kiss. "Just promise me you'll try to remember that we humans have deep feelings. What seems inconsequential to you is devastating to us. Remember that when you perform your tests, and be kind, Mara. I sense you have a kind heart buried somewhere deep down inside. Look for it, Mara. Let it guide you in your dealings with humanity." He knew it was asking a lot, but she looked as if his words were at least making her think.

"I will leave now," she announced, putting on her shoes.

Justin stepped up behind her, taking the necklace from her hand and securing it around her neck, tucking the glowing crystal into her form-fitting jumpsuit so it wouldn't be seen. It was up to her whether or not she'd tell her people about this "Home Crystal" thing. He kissed her cheek and she returned the gesture with an odd light in her eyes.

"Thank you for keeping your end of our bargain, Justin O Hara. I will keep mine. On this you have my word." She bowed her head once to him and left the room without a backward glance.

"I hope like hell I can trust you, Mara," Justin mumbled as he surveyed the wreck of the bed and double-checked to make sure he had all his belongings. With a mental nudge to Mick, who was next door, he rolled the Harley out of the room and started her up. He knew Mick would watch his back to be sure he wasn't followed, then make his own way home to the ranch.

It felt good to have his brother watching his back. They'd always been close, but in the years since the cataclysm, they'd worked together as a team, struggling to keep the family safe and to survive in the Waste. It hadn't been easy. At first, they'd had to struggle to set up the herds and crops. They'd had bad years, but they'd worked together and overcome not only the elements, but also the criminals who'd tried to harm them every now and again.

The Waste was not a safe place. At first, the challenges had come every few weeks, but after a year or two, as the Earth settled, so did the people who were left. Plus, the O'Hara brothers had learned to work together to defend their home. They'd all taken pointers from him on how to work as a military unit. Justin counted himself doubly blessed to have received the best military training the old world had to offer, and to be able to use it to defend his family in this brave new world.

Only recently, the strain had become too great. The brothers hadn't been in any life or death situations lately and they'd grown lax. That would be remedied now the aliens were coming. Justin only prayed they were equal to the task. He also knew they'd been sidetracked by the mounting frustration that came from having Jane around all the time and no ready sexual outlet available to work off their own steam. It was all fine for Caleb. He had Jane. But Mick and Justin had been getting desperate and that made them irritable. Irritable, sexually frustrated men didn't make the most reliable or reasonable defense force.

They'd have to fix that somehow. The time was coming when they'd probably have to defend their home and family again if Caleb's visions were accurate—and they always were.

Justin set off for the ranch, thoughts of the future heavy in his mind.

₧яј₨

"I'm glad you're back safe." Caleb greeted him as he pulled the Harley into his small garage. Justin was bone tired, but the frustration he'd been feeling for months was mercifully dulled. He'd enjoyed the hot pussy he was presented with, but it was just sex as far as he was concerned. It hadn't meant much to him or to the emotionally cold woman who'd chosen him to impregnate her.

But he had to believe it had been worth it. He'd gotten his rocks off, and he'd bartered his sperm for the security of his family.

"Three days. As ordered, sir." Justin eased his harsh words with a slow grin of the sexually satisfied.

"Now I know just how obnoxious I look every morning," Caleb muttered, slapping his brother on the back. "I want to hear everything you learned, but I think first you need a nap."

Justin laughed as they headed back to the big house. "The short of it is, we're safe from the aliens for now. Mara's most likely pregnant with my child and in exchange for my sperm, she leaves all of us in peace when her people invade the area."

"Good God! I'd hoped it wasn't true." Caleb was grim.

Justin turned on him quietly, his eyes growing somber. "You knew about this? You knew and you didn't warn me?"

Caleb sighed with regret. "It didn't come clear until after you'd left. The visions have been increasing steadily instead of easing off. I'm sorry I couldn't tell you more before you took off."

Justin grabbed his saddlebags and headed toward the house with Caleb. "I understand, I guess, but it doesn't sit well with me, Caleb. Giving life to a child who might never know me. Doesn't sit well at all."

They walked in silence for a time before Caleb answered.

"I can't guarantee anything, Jus, but we might have a chance to get the child back. We might be able to raise him."

Justin stopped dead in his tracks, hope lighting his dark eyes.

"A son?" Caleb nodded and Justin felt the sting of tears he refused to let fall. He was going to have a son—one he might never know. Fate couldn't be so cruel. Not if he had anything to say about it. "How can we help him?"

Caleb looked off into the distance, shaking his head. "I'm not sure yet, but I know there's a chance. I feel it in my bones. And I feel like it's something we have to do. We have to make it our goal, Justin, to raise that child as our own."

Caleb started as Justin clapped him on the back, bringing him back to the present.

"Then that will be our goal," he said shortly. "That and keeping all of us alive through what's to come."

Justin began walking again, stopping at the back door to turn back to his eldest brother.

"Thanks, Caleb." His eyes shifted down. "Thanks for giving me hope."

Silently, he went into the house and sought his own room. He needed to think, but right now he needed sleep more. Thought would come later.

ഇരുഃരു

Two days later, Caleb sat quietly while Jane and Justin cleared away the dishes from lunch. It had been a strained and silent meal, the tension running high between the two brothers. Mick was still off in his laboratory, running tests, and the uncertainty was killing all of them slowly.

"When I was just a child, before Mick was born," Caleb reflected, garnering all their attention, "I caught the mumps. There were vaccines for that, of course, but some of my friends—the immigrant workers' kids—were outside the system and hadn't had their shots. Even some of us who'd had the shots got sick. My face blew up like a balloon and it hurt real bad." He turned to Jane, taking her hand and holding tight. "It's probably the reason we've never been able to conceive, Jane, and I'm so sorry."

She went to him, cuddling close. "It's okay, Caleb. There's nothing for you to be sorry for. Mick will come through for us. You know he will."

Caleb allowed her to comfort him for a few short moments, but then guided her gently away, back to her seat. She went, her expression sad.

"Yes, I'm sure Mick will be able to help us—eventually."

"That'll have to be good enough," Justin said, breaking into the conversation. He didn't like the direction this was taking and he wanted it stopped before it tore them asunder.

But Caleb sighed, not rising to the anger Justin expected. "No, it won't be good enough. Not for me and Jane, not for you and especially not for Mick."

"Don't go there, brother." Justin growled.

The back door opened and Mick sailed into the kitchen, oblivious to the tension. "I've got all our results. Jeez, I don't know how to say this, so I'll just come right out." The silence thickened. "I'm sorry, Caleb, your suspicions were correct. Your sperm count is low, but it is still possible you can father a child, given the proper preparation and timing. I'll get started on that right away, if you like."

Caleb waved his brother to a chair, no emotion showing on his stoic features. "Don't bother just yet, Mick. How are you and Justin?"

Jane gasped, but didn't say a word.

Mick eyed him steadily. "You know we never caught the mumps like you did. We're both normal."

Caleb sighed. "It's got to be one of you then."

Justin stood from the table, knocking his chair to the floor behind him with a clatter. "And what about Jane? I want no part of this, Caleb. It's bad enough you sent me to the village into the arms of that cold bitch so she could do God knows what to my son." His voice broke on that thought and he turned to flee from the room, but a soft hand stayed him. It was Jane of course, feeling everything he felt, sympathizing with him and trying to make it all better. But this was something even she couldn't fix.

"I've already agreed, Justin. I can't stand to see you two suffer anymore. I suffer with you, you know."

"God, Jane," Mick stood too, shock clear on his face. "Think about this!"

She turned to him, not releasing her hold on Justin. "I have. I love you all, don't you get it?" Her voice rose as her frustration grew. "I can't bear to see you in pain. Any of you. I know times have changed. If we were back in the old world, I would have been happy to live out my life monogamously with any one of you. But we're not in the old world. We can never go back to the old ways. Caleb helped me realize that. His visions have helped him accept it too. We've both talked this over and we've agreed that since I love you all equally, I should be allowed to express that love equally. As should you."

"Caleb, talk some sense into her!" Justin ground out, desperate both to have her let go of his arm and to pull her tighter against him. He was confined to do neither as both would hurt someone he loved. To push her away would hurt her. To pull her in would hurt Caleb. It was a no-win situation.

Caleb sighed and Justin squirmed inwardly. He knew that sigh.

"I've lived with this gift all my life and haven't always liked what it's shown me, but I've learned to make peace with what came. As have you all." Caleb looked at each of them in turn. "Mick, there is no other woman in your future. I'm sorry. I haven't wanted to tell you that. Especially since Jane probably should have been yours from the beginning. But that's my sin."

"Come on, Caleb. Even I know you can't see the past, only the future. There's no way you could know that Jane and I should have been married any more than Justin and Jane should have been. The past is past. We have to live in the now and the future. That's where your gift comes in handy. It's saved us in the past and it will save us now. If I live my life alone, well then, so be it."

"But you won't live your life alone. You'll share it with us. With Jane and me and Justin."

Mick nodded. "Just like we do now."

"No, not exactly. We all have to change and grow and accept that we are all each other will have for some years to come. At least until the children get older."

"Children?" Justin asked. "Whose children?"

Caleb looked around the room. "Yours, mine and Mick's."

"But if there's no woman for me—" Mick was thinking out loud when his eyes grew angry once more. "Oh no. I am not forcing myself on Jane because you had a warped vision."

"Who was the mother of my child?" Justin asked quietly into the angry silence.

"Children," Caleb corrected him. "You'll have more than one. You'll have several with Jane too. Starting with the one that will be born about nine months from now. I'm sorry, Mick. This first time, it has to be Justin because of Mara."

"I think I'm going to be sick." Mick said, clearly not censoring his words.

"That's nice. The idea of giving me a child makes you sick, Mick? Well hell, don't wait around for your turn. You're not getting one!"

Mick looked astounded, then hurt. "Janie, I didn't mean that the way it sounded. It's just—"

"All so different than what we expected our lives to be in the old world." Caleb finished his brother's sentence, effectively drawing all attention back to him. "I know. But it's an adjustment we have to make if we want to survive. If we want to give humanity a chance."

"Humanity? Since when did we become the saviors of the entire race?" Mick wanted to know.

Caleb rounded on him. "Since Justin impregnated an alien woman with the power to say whether we live or die. Everything hinges on her and her child. Justin's child will have powers we can only dream of, and he will be able to change the world."

Everybody looked at Justin with varying degrees of suspicion and respect.

"Wow. Damn, Jus, sounds like you fathered the second coming."

Caleb snorted at Mick's hushed words. "Think more along the lines of Merlin instead of Jesus and you might be right." Now that he had their full attention again, he continued, "Regardless, we have to do everything in our power to change Mara's mind, to give her some inkling of understanding of human emotions. For our own sakes and for the sake of our people. If we do this right, Justin's baby will change the world and make it safe for humans again. Maybe even within our lifetimes."

"But, Caleb, that woman is made of ice. Her DNA has been altered so that no emotion remains. How do we show her what it means to feel?" Justin sighed wearily as he ran one hand through his dark hair.

Caleb's gaze zeroed in on Jane. "We have our sweet empath to show us the way. And if she's pregnant at the same time as Mara, they can compare notes on their conditions. Mara is a scientist. She will want to study Jane to see what a human gestation is like compared to her own. If the test includes a fetus that's from your DNA, Jus, it will be more appealing to her scientific mind. Sorry, Mick."

"Jeez!" The youngest brother winced. "Don't apologize for not wanting me to cuckold you!"

"You're still thinking of the old days, Mick," Jane turned to him. "And even then, some people had open marriages. Many cultures allowed multiple wives. Just think of this as female revenge. I get to have three husbands." Her teasing tone tried to lighten the mood, but the subject was too serious for laughs.

"Is that what we'd be? Second and third husbands?" Justin wanted to know.

"There's no second or third about it," Caleb said firmly. "We would all be her husband. And she's our wife. Not just mine alone any longer. I've been selfish."

"And I've been insensitive." Jane chuckled. "Imagine that, with all my empathy, I couldn't bring myself to release the old ideas long enough to realize I could ease your pain. I know what you two have been feeling around me for months now. Justin's better since his trip into town, but Mick, you're so on edge, it hurts just to be around you."

"Then don't be around me," Mick said angrily. "I'll clear off so you won't be subjected to my anger and my unnatural desires."

But Caleb raised his hand calmly. "That's not the answer. And your desire for Jane isn't unnatural. You've wanted her since she was sixteen and you saw her come down the stairs in her prom gown. You told me that back then, remember? You told me that when she was old enough, you'd marry her come hell or high water. You just didn't count on me swooping in and claiming her before you got your chance." Caleb shook his head in guilt and regret. "But we're going to fix that now. We're all going to put aside the old ways and make this family work. I know it's not going to be easy, but it's the only way for us all to survive. If even one of us leaves, we all die, and humanity doesn't stand a chance."

Mick shook his head angrily. "You don't cut us much slack with your visions, do you, Caleb? Jeez! Our little family, responsible for the fate of humanity? As if keeping just ourselves alive wasn't hard enough."

"I hear you, brother. But we don't deal the cards, we just play the hand we're dealt. And I've never had a clearer vision of what has to be done. So much is riding on us, we have to do whatever we can to help that half-alien child." He looked at Jane with loving eyes. "And that includes giving up my selfish desire to keep Jane only for myself. I know you both love her and I know she loves you. You'll be good to her and frankly—though it shocks the hell out of me—just the thought of you two with her is damn arousing." Caleb pushed back from the table and smiled to ease the rising tension in the room. "There's no one else on Earth I would share her with."

"And no one else on Earth I would welcome into my heart and into my body," Jane echoed, looking at Justin and Mick with affection in her teary eyes. "Only you three. I've loved you

69

all as long as I can remember. I want a bunch of children with you. And I want to know each of you like I've gotten to know Caleb over the years we've been married." She turned and stepped into Justin's arms, giving him no choice but to embrace her.

Justin met his brothers' eyes over Jane's head as she snuggled into him. He was already aroused and the fire in his eyes told the other two all they needed to know. But Jane turned in his arms to look at Caleb and Mick, focusing on the youngest brother.

"I know how badly you need me, Mick. I feel your hunger. It has to be Justin first, to give me a child, but if he has no objections, I'd like to share the experience with you too. I could take you in my mouth," she offered shyly, pleased to feel Justin's arms tighten around her middle and his cock swell against her butt.

"Jeez!" Mick sucked in breath as if he'd been sucker punched. He was aroused, she could see, as she held out one trembling hand to him. Her empathic senses were feeding off their arousal and it made her feel quite daring. Mick held out, but when Caleb stood to push his shoulder, sending him toward her, Mick's resistance crumbled and he took her hand, allowing himself to be pulled into the embrace.

Sandwiched between the two brothers, Jane smiled as she rose up on her tiptoes to place a kiss on Mick's shocked mouth. She ran her hands through his blond hair as she'd often longed to do and caressed his stubbly cheek, smiling into his eyes.

"It's going to be okay, Mick."

She kissed him with more pressure then, willing him to let loose with the passion she could feel him holding back. He gave in with a tidal wave of emotion, flooding her empathic senses with a rage of need and caring that almost overwhelmed her. She caught the motion out of the corner of her eye as Caleb moved the chairs out of the way and placed himself off to the side of the sturdy kitchen table. She saw the wisdom in the scene he was setting. If they broke apart to go to the bedroom, second thoughts might interfere with the joining that simply must take place in order to save them all. Better they let passion overwhelm them right here in the kitchen this first time, with all of them present, so they could break the ice, so to speak.

Jane reached around Mick as Justin ground against her bottom. He was as lost in sensation as Mick was, though Mick had always been more stubborn. She knew she had to focus on him until all his inhibitions were crumbled to dust. She kissed him for all she was worth, savoring the feel of his tongue, the similar but different taste of him as he let go with her for the first time. It had been so very long for him, he was almost immediately out of control, and she smiled as she caressed his wide, muscled shoulders and washboard belly.

She unbuttoned his shirt as his breathing increased and then her hands were against his hard chest, tangling in the light dusting of hair she found there. He was more compact than either Justin or Caleb, standing just under six feet, but he was all muscle and had those All-American blond good looks that had always made the girls swoon back in the old days. He was powerfully built, his chest and abdomen bulging with rippling muscle as she stroked him. But he trembled with need of her and she hurried her mission to free the pulsing cock that pushed against her belly through their clothes. She was sidetracked only momentarily when Mick scooped her sweater off over her head, leaving her only in a lacy white bra as he kissed the swells of her breasts over the cups of the thin material.

She felt Justin's hands at her back, undoing the hooks and pushing the bra straps down her arms as Mick groaned in appreciation, kissing her nipples and sucking them into his hot mouth while Justin kissed her neck. She opened her eyes to meet Caleb's green gaze over the blond head of his brother. She reached out empathically and felt her husband's arousal and satisfaction. She blew him a kiss as he stroked his own arousal, then yelped as Justin reached his hands right into the stretchy waistband of her pants and cupped between her legs. God, his hands were hot! And his fingers were definitely longer than Caleb's, and a bit rougher as he swept them through the curls covering her mound and delved into her folds.

Justin's aroused chuckle made her squirm. She could feel the emotions coming off him—a sense of surrender to the inevitable and arousal at the idea that he would finally have her and father her first child. There was that driving will to procreate she had sensed in Caleb as they'd tried so hard to have a child, and that same satisfaction that meant he knew he would be coming inside her in short order. For that reason, his strokes were slow and unhurried, in sharp contrast with Mick's frenzy. The poor man hadn't had a woman in years and he was as desperate as she'd ever seen a man.

"Mick," she spoke gently as she moved back slightly. "Let me sit on the table."

Mick moved away as Justin let go, but he didn't go far. Justin positioned himself between her legs as if staking claim to her pussy. Mick stood at her side, seeming unable to let go of her breasts, even as she unbuttoned his jeans and worked the zipper down over an amazing arousal. He was hard and ready, and when she clasped him in her hands, he trembled.

Looking up at Justin, she sought his understanding. Justin nodded once. Mick was in a bad way and he needed her attention.

72

Justin could wait a bit, though not long. He'd waited a lifetime to have a woman he loved this much come to him and he would not be denied now that he'd finally given in to the crazy world they now inhabited. Jane felt all of his emotions, sitting up to kiss him as she began to stroke Mick's cock with her hand.

The first taste of Justin was shocking. His mouth was spicy and hot, his kiss demanding in a way that neither Caleb's nor Mick's had been. He was a bad boy through and through, his kiss cutting her no slack, his hands digging into her waist and thigh with erotic urgency. She smiled into his kiss, licking his lips with a final caress as she lay back on the table. She then turned to take care of Mick.

Chapter Five

But Justin had other plans. Instead of waiting for her to suck Mick off, then come back to him, he continued to tease her even as she tongued Mick's cock and finally took him into her mouth.

Mick groaned in pleasure, and so did Jane as Justin lifted her a few inches up from the table. He pulled down her pants and underwear in one smooth motion and repositioned her at the edge of the table, kneeling down to spread her muscular legs around him. He unbuttoned his own shirt and pants, all the while enjoying his first view of Jane's creamy pussy. He'd dreamed of her like this—wet, for him. He'd jerked off countless times to this fantasy, but the reality was a hundred times better than any fantasy he'd ever come up with. He could see the little nubbin of her clitoris throbbing as his fingers spread her inner lips wide.

He had to taste her. He had to know what she felt like against his lips and tongue. And he ached to know just how far inside she could take his long cock before he felt the delicious ridge of her cervix. She was a small woman, but she had long, sleek, muscular legs and he wanted to kiss every inch of them, in due time. He dropped his shirt on the floor, rubbing his bare chest along her inner thighs while she moaned around his brother's cock. Justin had been in wilder situations in the past, but never with his brothers, and never with a woman he loved down deep in his soul. The combination made him hotter than he'd ever been before. He made short work of his jeans and boots and then was back between her legs, worshiping her with his tongue, swirling it around her clit, relishing each of her sighs as he memorized the feel of her luscious body.

She tasted divine. Better than anything he could have imagined, and she was so responsive and warm, he could barely keep from coming as he stroked two fingers into her, testing her. He groaned when he realized she could take almost all of him in her petite body. It was as if she'd been made to his own specifications. Her pussy felt perfect and he couldn't wait to really get inside her.

Mick was nearing his release, if Justin was any judge, though he hadn't witnessed his brother's release since they'd both been boys sharing girlie magazines. Still, Mick hadn't changed much from the carefree youth he'd been back then. Justin recognized the signs as Mick's eyes practically rolled back in his head at the pleasure Jane was giving him. Who knew their little Janie enjoyed sucking cock so much? Justin never would have guessed it, but his gaze shot to Caleb, realizing his older brother knew damn well what Jane liked and what she could do. Hell, he'd probably taught her how.

Justin decided there and then that if he was going to continue in this haywire relationship, Jane would learn a thing or two about how to please him before he was through. That thought firmly in mind, Justin couldn't wait any longer. He stood, knowing from his glance at Caleb that all three brothers were getting off on this, and took his place between Jane's spread legs. With a shudder he watched every inch of his cock sink into Jane's sweet pussy, groaning as he felt the welcome of her tight body.

She practically screamed around Mick's cock as she came right away, bathing Justin with her cum, lubing the way for her to take nearly all of him. But her petite body still allowed him that much-needed abrasion that told him he'd filled her as much as she could take. It nearly undid him, but he gritted his teeth, enjoying every moment of his first time with Jane. How he'd dreamed of this moment!

But never in his dreams had he imagined he'd be sharing this experience with his brothers. Oh, he'd enjoyed the occasional ménage a trois when he'd been on his own those five years, but never would he have imagined sweet Janie agreeing to such a thing. And he couldn't imagine any man he would want to share her with. But seeing Mick's cock in her luscious mouth made Justin realize the only men who made any sense sharing Jane's delicious body were his brothers. They'd all grown up together. They all loved each other. It was almost natural that if she was willing to share, it would be with the three of them. And at the moment, he thanked God she was willing to share. He knew now he'd finally been inside her, he could never go back. Jane was a fire in his blood that would never be quenched.

He rocked her toward another orgasm, watching with pure male gratification as his brown pubic hair meshed with her lighter colored curls as his hard cock slid into her rosy pussy. She moved eagerly under him, still sucking Mick as she moaned her pleasure.

Mick came with a shout and Justin realized he shouldn't have been surprised when Jane swallowed it all down like an old pro. He knew from their youth that Caleb loved it when a woman swallowed his cum. Apparently he still did. He'd taught her well, but she didn't know everything, Justin thought with satisfaction. He imagined Caleb was fairly pedestrian in his sexual tastes and aside from the fact he was stroking his dick with a smile on his face as he watched his brothers fuck his wife, he'd never been kinky as far as Justin knew. But Justin had learned a thing or two about kink while he'd been on his own, and he would show them all with great pleasure, if they were agreeable.

From the sounds Jane made as she sucked the last of Mick's cum, she would be more than agreeable. That was their Jane. Always the adventuress. She'd take all he had to give and return it tenfold. He couldn't believe he was finally inside her. He couldn't believe her response to him. But he believed it when she turned her face up to him with a satisfied smile, Mick having collapsed on a chair over by the wall.

"I love you, Justin," she said simply, feeling everything he was feeling in that moment. "Make me come again, and give me a baby, please."

"Well, since you ask so politely," Justin teased her, increasing his pace. He was careful though, knowing he was too long for most women. But he hadn't counted on her appetite or her empathy. She knew his every emotion, and when he was holding back, she countered with her gentle understanding. With a devious smile, she hooked her legs around his waist, laying herself open and pulling him hard and deep within her.

"Easy, Janie. I don't want to hurt you." It was all he could do to gasp while she tormented him with her luscious body.

"You won't hurt me, Justin. You would never hurt me," a glint entered her eyes as she lay there, looking up at him, "unless you thought I'd enjoy it." Her shy smile had him thinking of all the ways he could have her, if she was as agreeable as she seemed in that moment.

"God, Janie! Have you developed the ability to read minds as well?"

"Not yet, but I will admit," she said between pants for air, "Caleb warned me he thought you were probably a little kinky."

She smiled like an angel and he groaned. "And having two men at one time isn't kinky enough for you?"

His words whispered into her skin as he bent to kiss her breasts. He'd wanted to suck her nipples ever since she'd hit puberty. She was well-endowed without being top heavy, just perfect in his opinion, and he'd waited a lifetime to see her pretty tits and worship at them.

He sucked one big juicy nipple into his mouth and bit down gently, just enough to make her gasp. She seemed to like it, so he moved to the other one, pausing only to admire how rosy her slightly abused tit had become. He licked it in apology before biting down on the other one and this time, she screamed as she came in a tumultuous flurry of clenching muscles and gripping thighs which spurred his own release.

He shouted as he sank into her, jetting his sperm deep into her body, hoping like hell for the second time that week he'd planted a child in a female's womb. He would think of the irony of that later, since he'd been very careful to not impregnate any of his former lovers in the old days. Nowadays he was just like Johnny Appleseed, planting his kiddies whenever he got the chance.

The thought made him smile as he regained enough strength to lift up and look down into Jane's beloved face. She was smiling too, mirroring his emotion as she so often did. "I love you, Jane. I always have."

She reached up to stroke his face and pulled him down for a tender kiss. "I know, Justin."

"I guess you do at that."

She stroked his chest, her fingers tracing over his dragon tattoo. He was uncomfortable with his emotions laid bare, but

Jane always knew how to soothe him. Justin pulled away from her when he heard a chair creak, yanking him back to reality. He'd lost track of when Caleb came in his own fist, but all three brothers wore the satisfied looks of men who had recently achieved sexual release. Guilt crowded in on him when Caleb came forward and he tried to flee, but Jane clamped her legs around his hips and wouldn't let go.

"It's done now, Justin," she said calmly, rising up on her elbows. "The four of us are truly one. And you can't back away now. We still have to make sure I'm pregnant."

Justin groaned in dismay, but Caleb put his hand on Justin's shoulder, even as he stood trapped between Janie's legs, her pussy open to him, and his dick getting hard at the sight.

"Don't panic, Jus. This is as it must be. I've accepted it. So has Jane. You and Mick have got to come to terms with it too. But the first order of business is getting her pregnant. This time, that's your job, so she's sleeping in your bed for the foreseeable future until we're damn good and sure she's pregnant. Mick," Caleb shot a look over to their younger brother who still appeared shell-shocked, "you'll have to monitor her and let us know when the deed is done for certain."

"And then you can have my pussy too, Mick. I promise."

All three of them groaned at her coquettish tone, just imagining sliding into her wet hole. But Justin was still at the gates of paradise and his cock was getting harder by the moment. He tried to turn so Caleb wouldn't see, but it was no use. His cock was just too damned long.

Caleb chuckled, noticing his brother's predicament. "You need her again, Justin. Just as she needs you. Don't feel guilty about it. I've lived with my guilt for years and only now do I realize it was all for nothing. Take her, Justin. She wants you. Give her what she wants. Give her your love."

"Damn, Caleb." Justin growled as his brother pushed him toward the place he most wanted to be. His dick was already aligned, ready to sweep into her pussy, but Caleb's powerful push sent him deep within her. Jane gasped though she smiled up at him, reveling in his inability to stay away from her, no matter what his head told him. His heart was leading him now and well she knew it with her strong empathic link to all three O'Hara brothers.

"Fuck her for me, Justin. Truth to tell, she's always been just a little too hungry for me to satisfy alone. Maybe with all three of us doing her, she can get all she wants and needs."

"Is that true?" Justin demanded as he began to move within her. "Do you really want more?"

Caleb laughed and slapped his brother on the back. "She always wants more. She's damned insatiable!" Justin saw her gaze shoot lovingly to Caleb's just over his shoulder. Caleb knew her best of all the brothers, at least this way, and she didn't deny his words. In fact, she blushed and nodded, sending Justin's tension level up another notch.

"Insatiable, hmm? That sounds like a challenge." Her gaze was drawn back to him with a wary kind of excitement. He couldn't help himself as he was swept up yet again into the sweet sexual fulfillment of being inside Jane. He began to thrust harder, pulling her long legs up, holding them there with a thought as she squealed. He mentally glued her hands to the table as he pistoned into her. He was only dimly aware of Caleb setting himself on one side of the table while he motioned Mick to the other.

"Let her hands go, Jus," Caleb ordered and he did, watching with an odd kind of fascination as she reached out to either side and grasped his brothers' cocks, stroking them up and down with an expert touch. Oh yeah, the O'Hara brothers were going to come in buckets tonight.

Jane smiled up at him as he pounded into her. He was rougher this time, but she seemed to like it and he couldn't control himself. He loved her and he was having her. Having her while she willingly stroked his brothers' cocks. Who would have ever believed it? Sweet little Janie was hungry for O'Hara cock and it didn't matter to her which brother got her off. She wanted them all.

But more importantly, he could read the love in her eyes. That had always been the magic thing for him, seeing the love only a sweet woman could give to a man. Janie had always looked at him with love, but now, while he was inside her, it was a whole new ballgame. He was finally free to return the love, the desire and the affection. He was finally free to love her as he'd always wanted to do.

Little by little he was coming to terms with this odd new relationship. If it meant he could have Jane openly, then so be it. He would do anything to have her. He would do anything for her. He loved her that much.

For her part, Jane felt Justin's acceptance and it reassured her. She let go, coming hard with the triple-stacked emotions of desire, passion and love coming at her from all three men. It was like no aphrodisiac in the world. It was manna from heaven for her empathic senses. She cried out as she came around Justin's obscenely long cock. She never would have guessed what he'd been hiding in his pants. It was only slightly thinner around than Caleb's but it was by far the longest one she'd ever seen.

She absolutely loved the feel of it bumping up against the end of her channel, sliding as deep as he could go. It made her come in a way that Caleb's thickness never had, but then Caleb had an attraction all his own. He was so thick around, he somehow managed to rub her clitoris just right with every stroke, so she wasn't complaining. She wondered what Mick's curvy cock would feel like. It was definitely intriguing, and his salty cum had tasted divine. She could tell he'd liked her sucking him off almost as much as Caleb enjoyed it. And that was saying something.

She cried out as Justin increased the pressure, stroking her harder than Caleb ever had, and deeper. She looked up at Justin with love, seeing the strain on his chiseled features, feeling the hot desire coming from him and his two brothers as they watched. It was mind-blowing and almost more than her sensitive empathic senses could take, but she realized in that moment it was something she could easily become addicted to.

"Harder, Justin. Please!" she cried, knowing he needed to hear her acceptance of his violent loving.

"Shit!" Justin swore as he lost control. Feeling Jane taking him in and seeing the acceptance on her face as she begged him for more was like nothing he'd ever experienced. He felt her pulsing around him, felt the nearly desperate milking of her inner muscles and he couldn't hold back any longer.

He slammed into her with more force than he wanted to subject her to, but she liked it. Hell, he realized, she loved it! Jane came in a rush, jerking his cock and coaxing him into a blinding release as he collapsed over her. He was so wrung out, his knees wouldn't support him at first. But he could feel her kissing his neck with small pecks of adoration that had his cock twitching in the aftermath, still cradled within her warm body.

"Give us a minute, will you, boys?" He heard her say, and then dimly heard Mick and Caleb walk away.

He dragged the remnants of his strength together and lifted up as much as he could to look down at her. He didn't know what he would have said in that moment, looking into her eyes of love, but it didn't matter in the end when she reached up and kissed him so sweetly he could have cried.

"You needed that, Justin. And so did I. I don't ever want you to hold back with me," she whispered just to him, his brothers out of range to hear what they were saying. "I'll always know." Her eyes twinkled up at him and he groaned as he reached down to kiss her sweetly.

"Damn," he said after a moment, looking up to see where Caleb had got to. He and Mick were leaning against the counter on the other side of the big kitchen. "How do you deal with her always knowing what you're feeling, man?"

Caleb smiled and his green eyes went hot. "It took some getting used to, but if I know her, she'll ride you hard until you wouldn't even dream of holding out on her. And she'll make you want to tell her every damn last thing on your mind too."

Justin pushed up, his strength returning, and traced her breasts because he just had to. He loved the shape and feel of her and he could tell from the smile in her eyes, she damn well knew it. And liked it.

He pulled out, knowing his brothers were waiting, but he also knew she would be in his bed all night long and probably for several nights to come until they were sure she was pregnant with his baby. He stroked her smooth belly, a joyful light entering his eyes. This was very different than the stud service he'd performed for Mara. This time, he knew he would see his child be born and grow, receiving all the love this generous woman had to give. He knew his brothers would be good to the child, love it as he would and teach it how to survive in this world gone wild.

"I think Justin's liking the idea of fatherhood," Caleb teased as he moved back to the table.

Jane hummed and nodded as Justin stroked her skin. "I'm liking it too. I like the idea of giving you all children and raising them here on our ranch, safe from the rest of the world. We'll start our own colony of little O'Haras."

"Starting with Justin's," Caleb agreed, looking down into Jane's eyes as he put one hand beneath her back and helped her sit up.

Justin stayed close, his hand moving to her hip because he couldn't quite bear to let her go just yet.

Chapter Six

Jane looked for Mick and found him sitting in a kitchen chair, watching them all, his hand barely covering a thick erection, and realized she'd left two of her men hanging—quite literally. A devilish light entered her eyes as she looked from Mick to Caleb to Justin. Justin winked and she knew he understood. He let go of her and watched as she took Caleb by the hand, then turned to Mick and led them down the hall to her bedroom. She liked the emotions coming from Justin as he watched her rounded ass stroll down the hall between his two brothers. She liked the passion she felt from him, as well as the heated need Mick was generating and the hot admiration coming from Caleb. All together, the feelings they were broadcasting made her hot and damn near as insatiable as Caleb had claimed she was.

Pleasing these men pleased her, as it always had. Just now, it was sexual pleasure they all sought and she was more than willing to accommodate them. Caleb had been right to tell them about her hunger. Caleb could please her, she knew well, but he'd needed to find a way to let his brothers know she could take all they could give. He'd needed to make this easier on all of them and he knew they wouldn't accept her word for it. They knew she would do anything for them, including lie about her own desires. But Caleb wouldn't lead them astray. He never had and she knew they trusted he would always have her best interests at heart. She knew all that, but she still felt bad Caleb had to downplay his own sexuality even the tiniest bit to help his brothers along.

She would make it up to him, though. They both knew it. But for the moment, she was learning the feel of Justin and Mick in a whole new way. And the emotions coming from Mick were turning desperate. He needed her so badly and was very reticent about claiming her. Turning to Caleb as they entered their bedroom, she gave him a pleading look. He let her hand go as he sat on the bed. She held on to Mick's hand tightly as she led him near the single window, taking a seat on the old wooden chair and positioning him in front of her.

With gentle caresses, she lowered the zipper on the jeans he'd hastily pulled up. He trembled as he watched her pull the pants down, freeing him from his briefs as well, never leaving off touching him for a single moment. She leaned forward to kiss the tip of him and he groaned. She smiled and moved to caress his balls. They tightened.

She took him in her mouth then, knowing he was near the edge. He'd waited so long with little or no relief and he could wait no more. The earlier release in the kitchen had only dulled his need. He was a desperate man. She needed him to find his pleasure and she didn't care how quickly it came, just that it came for him now. He needed it as the other brothers hadn't. He was the youngest and the one who'd had the fewest women in his time before the cataclysm. But she had him now, and over time she would make sure he experienced everything he'd missed. She drew him deep and sucked, gently fingering his balls, thinking about how he might feel when he finally took her pussy. It was enough to draw the moisture from her hot folds and make her squirm. A groan from the other side of the room made her eyes open.

She caught her breath when she looked up to see Justin watching from the doorway. He had one long arm braced on the doorframe, the top button of his jeans undone, and she could see the zipper straining over his rigid length. The look in his eyes as he watched her go down on Mick was amazingly hot. Amazingly tender too, in a mix that confounded her and tightened her nipples. He didn't miss that either as his gaze caressed her breasts, jiggling and bouncing as she moved up and down on Mick's cock.

She tore her gaze from Justin to find Caleb stroking his dick with a profound smile on his face. He rose and came near the window, placing one large hand on her back, as if urging her to increase her pace on Mick's quivering dick. She did so, looking up at Caleb, drowning in the feelings of admiration and incredibly hot passion coming off him in waves. She then set her gaze on Mick, letting him know she was there for him in that moment. For him alone.

His blue eyes shone down into hers with a wetness that could have been tears of relief. Caleb took Mick's hands and placed them on her hair, showing him silently how to massage her scalp in the way he knew she liked. She groaned around Mick's hard length and felt him begin to come. Staying with him, she took him as far down as she could, sucking hard to encourage his release. At the same time, she squeezed his balls gently, in the way Caleb had taught her and was gratified when she felt the first jets of Mick's seed spill down her throat.

She swallowed over him and continued to suck, knowing the convulsive action of her throat added to his pleasure. Or maybe it was just the idea of her swallowing his cum that turned him into a rampant fireball in her mouth. Either way, she was well satisfied with the results as he released his load in her mouth for the second time that day. He shouted and trembled and would probably have collapsed had Caleb not been there to catch him around the shoulders and usher him to the bed.

"You did good," she heard him say to Mick, patting him on the shoulder. "I know you never had many women, before. Don't worry."

Only then could she identify the uncertainty that had emanated ever so slightly from Mick all night long. She'd come to realize that of the three brothers, he was the only one who had found some way to successfully mask his feelings from her, but she would break down his walls. She knew she would.

She went to him now, sitting at his side as he recovered on the bed. "Did you ever have a girl suck you back in the old days?"

"Jeez, Janie. Give me a little credit!"

She smiled as she stroked his thigh. "I'll take that as a yes. But I'm betting it wasn't often. And maybe you never had any girl swallow before, huh?"

Mick continued to look uncomfortable, but she could tell Caleb was loving the dirty—and necessary—talk. She stroked Mick's abdomen with her gentle fingers, soothing him. "It's okay, Mick. You missed so much. But I promise you won't miss anything from now on. I promise you, okay?" She kissed his cheek to seal her words, but he took her by surprise as he wrapped his arms around her waist and pulled her into a drugging kiss.

His tongue swept into her mouth with a magic all its own and a kind of desperation she'd felt in him before. She soothed him as best she could, pressing her breasts to his chest and returning his kiss until he seemed satisfied. He let go of her mouth only to hold her tightly against his chest, kissing her temple and down to her ear as he whispered to her.

"I love the taste of me in your mouth, Jane." She squirmed as his hot words drove her higher. "Thank you, sweetheart. I've never felt anything half as good as your mouth on me." He let her go with a final caress and stood, leaving the room.

"Will he be all right?" Justin asked when he was out of earshot.

Caleb shrugged and looked at her.

Jane nodded slowly. "It's been hardest for him, I think. Somehow he's learned to hide his emotions from me, and I didn't quite realize. But he'll be okay, I think."

She returned to the chair, crooking her finger to Caleb who was still clearly eager to feel her wet mouth. She began to caress him with her hands in the ways he'd taught her and was pleased to hear his breath catch.

"Mick never had the same rampant sex life as you two before the cataclysm. He had fewer experiences to back up his imagination and help him find relief."

"But you're going to change all that, right?" Caleb said with a pleased smile as he cupped the back of her head, coaxing her to his cock.

She smiled up at him. "You better believe it." She allowed Caleb to guide her then, in the subservient way he sometimes liked. She gave over control of her head to him and made the purring noises in her throat she knew made him tremble. It wasn't long before she felt him take up a smooth rhythm to fuck her mouth and she held on for the ride, sucking and purring as she'd been taught.

"Jesus, Caleb," she heard Justin swear as he came right up beside them. "You trained her to do this?"

Caleb's affirmative answer was a long and heartfelt groan as he tightened further still. She knew he wasn't far away from orgasm now. She sucked harder and then gasped in delight as

Justin's hard hands came around her from behind to pinch her nipples and play with her breasts. Her pleasure increased as did her suction on Caleb's cock. With a shout, he came in her mouth, forcing her to swallow his cum.

She enjoyed every minute of it, but the old activity had a new twist to it now with Justin stroking her breasts, adding to her pleasure. Caleb removed himself from her mouth, allowing her to suck the final drops from him, then Justin grabbed her around the waist and lifted her to her feet. He held her from behind, stroking her breasts as Caleb leaned down and kissed her deeply.

"I'm taking her to my room," Justin said, almost as if he were daring Caleb to argue, but the older brother nodded in acceptance.

"Take care of her, Jus," Caleb instructed as Justin swung her up into his arms and carried her down the short hall to his own room.

She'd never really spent any time in his private domain, only entering to drop off laundry or bring him something he'd requested. She giggled as he threw her down on his oversized bed. He'd had to build it special for himself since he was taller than average and he'd wanted a comfortable bed. She'd always wondered how it would feel to sleep on such a grand platform and now it looked like she was going to find out.

Justin looked down on her for a moment, naked before him and then she felt the first stirrings of his telekinetic power again as he looked at her arms and spread them above her, then did the same with her long legs, spreading her pussy wide before him with only a thought. He smiled and licked his lips.

"I've come inside you twice already tonight, sweetheart," he reminded her. "I can see my sperm mixed in with your juices." Her stomach muscles rolled as his words excited her. "You have a beautiful body, Jane, and I never knew what a dirty girl you really were under that innocent exterior. Caleb's been a lucky man."

She felt what he felt as he teased her, his aim only to push her to her limits and see how far she might go with him. Little did he know she was prepared to go wherever he led. But she'd make a believer out of him eventually and she relished the thought of convincing him.

"Tell me what you like, Jane," Justin watched her soft skin shiver as he rasped his hands over her delicate ribs. He sat at the side of the bed, caressing her with his hands, his eyes, while she looked up at him, almost dazed with resurging pleasure. And just from the touch of his hands! Damn, but she was responsive to him. It amazed and humbled him.

"Anything you want, Justin." She swallowed visibly as he continued to tease her skin, his fingers roaming the undersides of her sensitive breasts.

"Anything, Jane? Really?" He quickly tweaked a nipple and she gasped in shock. He looked carefully for any trace of fear in her eyes, but there was none, amazing him yet again. But he wouldn't push her. This was Jane, after all. She was delicate and sheltered. She'd only ever had one man before tonight. He knew damn well that she'd come to Caleb a virgin.

She nodded up at him. "Anything," she repeated, breathless now as his fingers played with her nipples, pulling at them, squeezing them, then caressing them after a hard tug.

He was so tempted, but this was Jane. She was to be protected at all costs—even, perhaps especially—from him and his own selfish desires. He didn't want to hurt her or scare her. He wanted to cherish her and let her know how special she was to him.

"I don't think you're ready for some of the things I want to do with you, sweetheart." He bent down to lick one of her straining nipples, sucking the peak into his mouth. She popped free a moment later and he blew air across the wet tip, making her shiver in delight. "Let's stick with the things you know for now, just until we get used to each other a bit, okay?"

Slowly, she nodded. Her eyes were half-closed in her pleasure, but he could read excitement there. He didn't really know how far Caleb had gone with her. Aside from a penchant for being sucked, Justin didn't know all the particulars of what his older brother liked or expected from a woman. But that all had to change now, if they were to survive this unorthodox arrangement.

"Do you like it doggy-style?" he asked in between licks of her other peak. She started at the blunt question and he smiled as he applied his teeth ever-so-lightly to her nipple, adding to the pleasure she was feeling.

She moaned her agreement. "Caleb doesn't do that too often," she said on a gasp. "But I like it." Justin sat back then, watching as she strained to follow him, arching her back, eager for his touch.

"All right then," he said with relish as his eyes sparkled over her. "Get on your knees and spread your legs wide, sweetheart. I want to cover you."

She laughed then, knowing the ranch term. "Like a stallion covers a mare?"

He nodded slowly, holding her eyes. "I might even bite your neck, if you get frisky."

"Is that a promise?" she asked flirtatiously, reassuring him and driving him wild at the same time.

He was amazed to learn that shy little Jane was a wildcat in bed. He felt the same protectiveness toward her he always had, but it was spiked now with a sharp stab of lust. He'd always wanted to protect her from his darker desires. Hell, he still did. She was just not ready for some of the things his twisted mind could come up with, but damn if she wasn't hot for him, eager to please. And please her he would, stretching her boundaries, but never dragging her sweet innocence into the dark desires that burned in his soul.

The time for those games was over, lost with the rest of humanity, and the few women who liked it. Justin would have to be satisfied with what Jane would allow him, and the glimpses of heaven he'd had so far in her tender arms more than made up for it, he thought with a smile of purely male satisfaction. He watched her take the position he'd ordered. She was a submissive little thing and he'd have to watch himself not to push her too far, but he liked her eager puppy look as she shyly turned her head to watch him over her shoulder. She licked her lips unconsciously and it made his cock stand stiffer, just seeing her eagerness for his possession.

"Rest on your forearms and stretch wide, sweetheart," he ordered her in a gravelly voice that he barely recognized as his own. He hadn't been this hot for a woman in his entire life. "That's it," he said, kneeling on the mattress between her spread cheeks, using his hands to spread her even farther, looking possessively down at the tight holes he uncovered. Her pussy was dripping with need, the tempting, tight bud of her anus contracting in shock as he placed one long finger over it, pressing gently.

"Ssh, darling, don't worry." He dropped down then to cover her back with his warm chest, rubbing her all over as he leaned to nibble on her neck. She moaned, driving him higher. "You're so beautiful, Jane. You've always been the most beautiful woman in the world to me."

His whispered words made her shiver and he heard her cry out with satisfaction as he bit down on her earlobe. His long cock poised at the edge of her entrance, dipping in just slightly to tease her. She was panting now in anticipation and he smiled against her neck as he felt her juices flowing over the head of his dick, making him slippery.

He eased inside her, using one of his hands to position himself and one to grasp her around the waist, controlling her movements as he brought her back against him, possessing her fully.

"You fit me like a glove, Janie. I love how you feel around me."

"Justin," she whimpered, her legs trembling in pleasure. "You feel so good."

She cried out as he began to move, his long dick and the angle of penetration bringing her a little extra nudge inside as his balls slapped against her clit in a rhythmic motion. She came and came, riding waves of orgasm as he took her higher, not letting her rest between. She was crying as she rode higher than she'd ever been before, as he stroked her inside and out, moving her body on him and controlling the ride utterly.

He jerked her upright against him when he felt his own release near, not wanting to let her come down, but knowing he couldn't sustain this level for both of them much longer. She was the wildest woman he'd ever known, her hands reaching back to claw at his shoulders as she squirmed and shivered in release, riding him as he pushed her up and over the edge of passion, the edge of reason. When he started to spasm inside her, she screamed, but it was a sound full of pleasure, full of fulfillment and it made him come harder than he ever had.

He sat behind her, within her, holding her tight against his chest. He held her generous breasts, loving the sensations of her writhing on his cock as her orgasm went on and on. Her contractions dragged cum from his body in long, lengthy spurts that seemed to last and last.

Finally, his dick slowed its eruptions within her body, but aftershocks abounded, small twitching movements of her hips bringing bursts of pleasure to him even after the storm he hadn't thought he would survive.

"I wish I could stay like this forever," he whispered in her ear, using his hot tongue to lick the salt from her skin, to plunge gently into the whorls of her ear and caress. "I've never come like that before, sweetheart. With anyone."

Jane sighed and the delicious tension eased from her body at last as he held her. "Me neither." Her eyelids drooped as she leaned back against him, her petite hands stroking his arms as they held her tight. "I'm completely wrung out."

Justin smiled in male satisfaction. "Me too," he said on a sigh, lowering them both to the bed, but he didn't leave her body. "Let's sleep for a bit."

He nipped her neck as he snuggled her into the curve of his body, using one big hand to bring a blanket up from the foot of the bed to cover them. It was more for her sake than his, since she might get cold, but he liked the idea of cocooning them together, enjoying the thought of being free to sleep with her, and within her.

"Go to sleep," he said, but it was a wasted effort. She was already breathing lightly, her mind deep in sleep in his arms.

Jane woke to motion and heat. She felt the long thickness stroking into her from behind, already inside her, and she realized with shock that the length belonged not to her husband, who often liked to wake her this way, but to his brother Justin. He, she had learned well the night before, had the longest cock in the family, and one that was guaranteed to go as far inside her as she could possibly take him.

In that moment of confusion before memory returned she was scandalized, but then she remembered the way he had taken her in the kitchen and Caleb's amazing arousal and acceptance of what they'd all done. And she remembered the way she'd fallen asleep with Justin still inside her after that last explosive orgasm. Maybe he'd never left? She had no idea how much time had passed since she'd come apart at the seams. She only knew they were covered now by a light blanket, snuggled in reassuring warmth and he was moving within her, making her crazy for him once more.

"Justin," she gasped.

As if that was the signal he was waiting for, he sped up his strokes, and she moaned.

"It's about time you woke up," he whispered, planting teasing kisses on her shoulder. "I've been dying back here."

"Apparently you're not dead yet," she said as she strained against him. "Oh, that feels so good!"

"That's it, baby. Come for me now." One heavy arm at her waist pulled her back against him, while he reached around with the other and toyed with her clit, making her jump. Justin had such a tender touch when he wanted, and he was learning just where to use those long fingers of his to make her tremble with need as he rocked them together.

His loving was different this time, less urgent than that shattering release before she'd slept, but no less exciting. His hands were different than Caleb's, but just as filled with love and approval of whatever she did. A woman could get used to this sort of thing, she decided happily as she moved the way he asked with his big hand on her middle. She reveled in his groan of pleasure as she rocked back against him, deepening the curve of her back to take him as far as he could go within her.

He came with a groan she felt against her skin as she spasmed only a moment later.

After long minutes, he let her go and turned her so she was on her back. He leaned over her, bracing himself on his elbow as he traced the delicate features of her face.

"You know I love you, don't you?" He smiled as she reached up to run her fingers through his hair. "Do you realize how much?"

"I'm beginning to get an idea. Justin, you've been holding out for so long. I'm sorry we didn't come to this a lot sooner."

He shrugged as he lay back, his thoughts faraway. "It's as it was meant to be. Caleb wouldn't have seen this in his visions if the time wasn't right. And I, for one, never would have agreed to this if his vision hadn't said it was necessary. I respect you too much for that, Jane. You were never meant to be three men's plaything."

She leaned up to see his eyes and the pain hidden in their depths. "You're right. I'm not a plaything, and I would never agree to that. But to be loved by the three of you?" She stroked his face, then down his neck and to the swirling patterns of the dragons covering his chest. "I've belonged to the three O'Hara brothers since I was six years old. Probably even before that, but I remember I was six when I first wished for one of you to marry me."

"Wished?" he asked, intrigued.

She nodded sagely. "On the candles of my birthday cake. From age six on, that was the wish I made every year."

"You're kidding." He reached up to tuck one of her curls behind her ear.

"Cross my heart," she said with mock seriousness, taking his hand and making his finger trace an X across her left breast as they both smiled.

"Okay, maybe I believe you. But even so," his hand cupped her breast, squeezing gently, "I bet you never wished for me."

She traced a circle around his nipple as he reciprocated. "There you'd be quite wrong." She leaned over to lick the dragon's nose, right above his heart. "You were the first one I wished for. You don't remember, I'm sure, but the week before my sixth birthday you killed a snake that would have bitten me. You were my hero ever after, and I thought it only fitting that you should marry me when I got old enough. I knew even then that you would put yourself in danger to protect me."

Justin's emotions were in turmoil, she could tell, and something fragile was blossoming inside his heart. She gave him a moment to come to terms with the idea she had loved him so long, tracing the swirls of the double-headed dragon that decorated his muscular chest with seeming attention, all the while paying a deeper sort of attention to the emotions he was feeling.

Even she was amazed by the depth of emotion her revelation brought out and she felt his discomfort. Justin was a man of controlled passions. He didn't like getting worked up over anything, and when he exploded, look out. She didn't want to make him uncomfortable, though she did think it was good to stretch his emotional boundaries especially now that she could tell he was feeling residual guilt after their explosive lovemaking. Still she didn't want to push him too far.

She nibbled on one of the dragons gracing his muscular chest, arriving at the flat male nipple caught between the dragon's teeth. Taking a hint from the dragon, she did the same with her own teeth, smiling with daring satisfaction when he gasped. She licked him then, letting him go for now as she lay her head on his chest, enjoying the warm feel of him, the steady rise and fall of his muscles beneath her cheek.

"The next year, I wished for Mick. He'd given me a kitten for my birthday and I thought he was the sweetest, gentlest boy I'd ever known. He was so serious when he taught me how to take care of my kitty, I thought maybe I could teach him to lighten up."

"So that's why he became the nasty little prankster that put epoxy in my shoes. It was all your fault." He stroked her hair as they lay quietly, smiling at past memories.

She nodded against his chest. "I'm afraid so. After that I kept daring him to new bits of deviltry and he was amazingly devious in the things he came up with."

"It's that scientific mind of his. Give him a problem and he'll come up with the most creative solution, every time."

She felt the pride Justin felt in his brother's accomplishments and the total lack of jealousy. She even felt his delight as he thought of Mick's practical jokes through the years and how he'd made them all laugh—and keep on their toes around him.

"You've been working behind the scenes all this time, haven't you, sweetheart?" he asked as realization dawned. "You've been challenging us and nurturing us your whole life."

"Mmm," she agreed sleepily, rubbing against his chest. "I decided early on that you all belonged to me, no matter what. You three were like me, with your special gifts, and you understood me and protected me."

"When did you start wishing for Caleb?" he asked, as if unable to prevent himself from voicing his curiosity.

She yawned. "Oh, not until much later. He was so much older, I had to grow up a bit before I came to truly appreciate him. But I'm afraid for a good few solid years there, he was the one I wished for, once I understood he was the one who kept you all together. I later realized my reasons for wishing for him were a bit selfish. I knew if I had him, then I'd have all of you because there was no way he would let either you or Mick stray far from us for long."

He sighed, his rumbling laugh reassuring her as well as the flood of emotions she felt from him. "Well, you got all of us, but in a way I bet you never expected."

She reached up to place her finger over his lips, silencing his words and his residual guilt.

"In a way I never dared dream. In a way that will fulfill my deepest needs and desires. I never would have asked for this, but now that it's within my grasp, I'm going to enjoy every single minute."

He pulled her face up for a long, heated kiss, exploring her lips with a gentle need that overwhelmed her senses.

Chapter Seven

Justin sighed heavily as he sat on his large bed the next morning, watching her, echoes of guilt consuming him as he heard the unmistakable tread of Caleb's boots down the hall past his door. Jane was awake and looking at him with those beautiful brown eyes that seemed to see everything. He knew she was probably reading his emotions, but he couldn't help it.

It nearly tore him apart, waking to find her nestled so trustingly in his arms. It was a dream come true. A troubling dream at that. He thought of what they'd done the night before and the essential reason why they had done it and practically growled.

"Do you really want this, Jane? Do you really want to have my baby? It's Caleb's baby you should be having, not mine." He could barely look at her, sprawled naked and enticing before him, on his bed, in his domain at long last. He'd thought this day would never come. Oh, he'd fantasized about her, but that wasn't real. He never would have acted on any of those fantasies. Not until Caleb had told him he must, and that he approved, of all things. Justin still could hardly believe it.

Jane's touch startled him, her hand coming to rest on his chest as she moved closer. She knelt at his side.

"I feel your guilt, but Justin, there's no use for it." She shrugged, unable to hide her feelings from him for a change. "I wanted Caleb's baby. I still want Caleb's baby." She sat back from him a bit, his eyes following her unhappy face. "But we've been trying for years. Caleb assures me that Mick will come through for us eventually. His visions have shown him that at least, and it gives us some hope, but Caleb's scared, Jus. His visions haven't been this bad since before the attack and in a way, they're worse, he tells me. He doesn't sleep much anymore. He wakes from dreams of the future in a cold sweat, trying to sort through the images, but they're confusing to him. When I ask, he tells me the worst ones are of the alien city and their culture. Things he has no way to really interpret since no human has ever lived to tell about their cities once they've seen them."

Justin ran a hand through his hair, expelling a harsh breath. "Damn, I had no idea it was that bad."

Jane faced him, clutching one of his pillows as if for comfort as she nodded gravely. "It's bad. And it's been getting worse since it started that day you left the ranch. The visions are coming hard and fast now and he's having a hard time sorting through it all. Last night was the first time I've seen a smile on his face in days."

Justin shook his head in irony. "I still can't believe letting Mick and I take you on the kitchen table brought a smile to his face."

"He wants a baby." She shrugged again. "It really doesn't matter to him if you're the father. He wants me to have a baby. He knows I want it too and he wants to make me happy. Any baby in this family will be his baby too. It will come under his protection, as we all do."

"And what about all that saving the world stuff, Jane?" Justin was having a hard time with the reality of the past few hours, but Jane seemed calmer than he was.

She nodded gravely. "Saving our family first, Justin. We have always come first in his heart. The rest of humanity, well, that's just a bonus—and only one possible interpretation of his visions. He's not entirely sure of all that yet. A lot of that stuff, he tells me, is from his visions of the aliens and he has no frame of reference to interpret from. He's started writing it all down so that maybe we can figure it out later, if we learn more about them."

"My brother Nostradamus," Justin marveled, only half-joking. He had never taken Caleb's gift for granted. It still amazed him how his big brother could and did protect them all—often at the sacrifice of his own happiness. In this case, at the sacrifice of his marriage. "I love him, Jane. I never tell him, but he's more than just a brother. He's so damned good to all of us and all I do is take." He turned to her with tears in his eyes, shocking her, he could see. "As I take and take from you, sweetheart. You deserve so much better." His hand came out to stroke over her hair with a gentleness welling up from his heart like he had never known before.

She shoved aside the pillow and sank into his arms, surprising him with the ferocity of her response. "I'd give you anything, Justin. Anything."

He hugged her close. "I know that, sweetheart, and I'll take it all."

"But you still feel guilty."

"Don't you?" he asked her in a moment of necessary candor. "You're Caleb's wife, Jane. Not mine or Mick's." He saw her eyes darken as he looked down at her, letting her know with a gentle squeeze what he needed. "Tell me the truth now."

She looked down. "I admit it's still strange to me," she said at last. "Caleb convinced me to try last night but I didn't make him any promises when I went into the kitchen. I'm kind of shocked at myself now—at how easy it was for me to go to you and Mick. I never thought I could do that."

Justin's blood started to rise yet again at her hesitant words. "You took all three of us and it made you horny as hell."

She smacked his arm, but not hard, a blush rising from her chest to her cheeks. "I thought I was the empath in the family."

He kissed her cheek with a swooping buss that made her giggle. "It made me horny as hell too, Jane. Mick and Caleb too, if their groans of pleasure were any clue." He squeezed her again, his dick stirring as he thought back over the hours past. "Hell, I never thought Caleb would get off on watching his woman get fucked by two other men. I never thought he was that adventurous."

"Not just other men. His brothers," she reminded him. "He wouldn't let any other man near me, and neither would I."

His eyes cleared as he bent down to kiss her deeply. "I know that, sweetheart, and it makes it even more special." He bared another small portion of his soul to her. "I've done threesomes before, Janie." He watched her eyes widen with a sort of delicious shock. "It's never been like it was with you, and Mick and Caleb. It was better than I ever thought it could be. And I want to do it again."

"Me too." She hid her face in his chest as her whispered words made him hard as hell once more.

"Dammit, Jane!" he growled, pushing her down on the bed and rising over her warm body. "I can't believe I finally have you in my bed." He tensed as the reality of her gorgeous body under him shook his senses once more.

"I can't quite believe it myself." She touched his cheek, nearly unmanning him with her gentleness. No one had ever been so gentle with him, big and burly as he was, and he

104

realized only now what he'd been missing. "But I'm glad, Justin." She reached up and kissed him. "I'm glad to feel your anger drain away. I'm glad to feel your tension ease. I'm glad I can do that for you, and for Mick."

He kissed her then, settling his hips into the groove of her legs, just pressing his hardness into her folds, making no move yet to take his place inside. He stroked her with his body, raised up on his forearms to look down into her face as he rubbed every inch of him he could over her petite frame. It was a delicious sensation and he was pleased to feel her shiver of delight as her eyes sparkled up at him intimately.

"I'm sorry I was so hard to live with these past few months. I never meant for you to know how much I—" Damn, it was still hard to admit to wanting his brother's wife, even after having been pushed—quite literally—into her arms.

"How much you wanted to fuck me?"

She surprised him again with her blunt talk, as well as the devilish, daring light in her eyes.

"And what would you know about that? I thought I was hiding it pretty well."

"Yeah, growling like a bear every time I walked into a room was really subtle. Following me with your eyes." She kissed his chin as she laughed up at him, stilling his heart for a moment with her beauty. "And jacking off in your garage was no clue at all to your level of sexual frustration. Justin," her eyes teased him with mock severity, "lust has been pouring off you in waves since just after we moved here."

"If you think I was bad before," he warned her with a nip to her tender neck, "just wait and see how bad I get, now that I know what it's like to come inside you." He thought about that a moment as he slid his cock through the wet folds of her pussy, teasing them both. "Think what it's going to be like when

I see your tummy round with my baby. Damn, sweetheart, I didn't think I could get any harder, but just the thought of you carrying my child—"

He couldn't finish the thought as she squirmed beneath him, undoubtedly feeling the wave of his emotions, his wonder and his lust with her deep empathy.

"Come inside me now, Justin," she said on a whisper, and he could do no other than comply, sliding down and into her, filling her, stretching and pushing right up against the depths of her, the way he liked. He growled in her ear in momentary satisfaction.

"Damn, sweetheart, you're so tight." He ground his teeth, trying for control, but her delicate whimpers were going to take him straight over the edge. "You're like a dream come true. My dream come true."

"You say the sweetest things when you're inside me."

He grinned. "I always aim to please, ma'am."

She whimpered as he rubbed just right inside her, up and tight. "I'd say your aim is damn near perfect."

Justin laughed, then grunted as he bore down on her. The woman was electric, like holding a lit firework in his hand.

"Jane!" he groaned as he felt her go off like a Roman candle around him, her inner muscles shivering, clenching and quaking, massaging his cock in a way that only she could. He came in a burst only seconds later, joining her in ecstasy, lost in the wonder of claiming her and loving her out in the open as he'd always secretly dreamed.

ഗൗങ

"Damn, Jus, what did you do to her last night? I almost busted down your door when she screamed." Caleb watched his blushing wife carefully as she buttered her toast. Justin's room was between the other two brothers' bedrooms so both Mick and Caleb had heard the sounds of pleasure coming through the shared walls.

Justin straightened, some of his male pride showing in a face that was still a bit uncomfortable speaking about their sexual exploits—and excesses—openly.

"I would never hurt her, Caleb. You know that." He sought his brother's gaze, the message clearly passed with his abrupt glower.

Caleb laughed at his brother's discomfort, but moved to reassure the younger man. "I know you like the back of my hand, and I know you wouldn't hurt our Jane. But damned if I didn't want to join you when I heard the noise coming from your room last night."

Justin eyed his brother speculatively. "Maybe next time, you should."

Caleb rocked back in his chair, excited by the idea, Jane could see from the fire in his eyes.

"You think that's a good idea?"

Justin nodded solemnly, looking from Caleb to Jane to Mick and back again. "I think it's the only way this is really going to work. And I think," he ruffled Jane's tousled curls with a saucy grin, "Jane would like it."

Caleb sought out Jane's eyes. "Is that what you want, honey? Are you willing to take us together like we did at first?"

It was clear to her that Caleb was hesitant about the idea and for some reason he thought she wouldn't want to have more than one man at a time. They'd done it that first time as a way to prove to his brothers it was really okay. He'd explained it

107

to her before it happened, when he was trying to convince her, but she realized now he didn't quite understand how little convincing was really involved. She'd wanted them all for a very long time. And she wanted them—together—again.

"Um, Caleb..." She was unsure of his reaction and dreaded the thought of possibly hurting him with her newfound desires. "I liked it." She looked down, embarrassed by what she'd just admitted. "A lot more than I thought I would."

"Well, hell!" Caleb was shocked, but filled with a kind of lust she hadn't felt from him since the early days of their marriage. The emotions swamped her, making her bolder. "You like having two of us at once?"

"One, two or all three of you. I liked it all, Caleb. And I want to do it again." She felt the approval and inexplicable pride coming from Caleb and Justin as her words registered with them.

"Damn." Mick swore behind them. His eyes were dazed as he watched her, keeping his distance, the wanting that never quite left him these days very palpable to her empathic senses.

Taking it as a good sign, she pushed a little further. "I think Justin's right. I think the only way we can work this is if there's complete openness between us all. I don't want any one of you to think I don't love you or want you. And I don't want to feel that way either. So, no secrets. No mine or yours. Only ours. As of last night, I belong to all of you. And you three belong to me." She looked at the eldest for confirmation of her daring words. He was their leader in all things, but especially in this. "Right, Caleb?"

Caleb surprised her, his eyes bright with a wetness she didn't expect. But it wasn't sadness, it was pride and acceptance. It was happiness that she was willing to do as they needed, to compromise her expectations of what her life would be to accommodate what must be done. To love them enough to save them all.

Caleb came around the corner of the table to kneel at her side. "You're amazing, Jane." He kissed her, hiding his tears against her skin. When he had better control of his emotions, he eased away, cupping her cheek in one big palm. "You give us everything, honey. You are our salvation."

She grew concerned, noting the dark circles under his eyes. "Were you up all night again, writing down your visions?"

He nodded and stood, pulling her head to his chest, caressing her hair as he hugged her tight.

"They're getting worse." His voice was bleak. "I don't understand half of the things I'm seeing, and it's as if because I'm not getting it, they're repeating and repeating, each time only slightly different—slightly more detailed. It's like nothing I've ever experienced before."

"You're writing down the details?" Mick asked, stepping up to the table, concern clear in his expression. He took a good look at the weariness etched into his brother's face.

Caleb nodded. "As much detail as I can capture. Then the vision repeats and I get more to write down. It's as if they're coming in small doses so I have time to write down what I don't understand."

"Like your subconscious is only giving you as much as you can handle at one time?" Mick reached for his brother's wrist and timed his pulse.

Caleb leaned against the counter, letting his brother do the family doctor thing. "I guess you could say that. I hadn't thought of it that way, but it makes sense."

Mick looked up at him. "The human mind is an amazing thing. I wouldn't be surprised if that isn't exactly what's happening."

"Wow." Jane watched them from the table. "Is he okay, Mick? Is there anything you can do to help him sleep more?"

Mick released his brother's wrist, shaking his head. "We know from past experience the visions have just got to play out. I can give you some vitamin supplements though, to help keep you healthy while this runs its course, and Justin and I will take over your work on the ranch for the time being." Mick didn't even glance over at Justin, knowing without having to ask that he would agree. "I think you should spend whatever time you can asleep. Stay in your room, let the visions just come, and sleep when you can."

"I can help you write things down," Jane volunteered. "And I'll stay with you today, while you try to sleep."

Mick nodded. "Good idea. You take care of him, Jane. Justin and I will take care of the ranch. The sooner he gets through this cycle of visions, the sooner he can rest. We should do everything in our power to help that happen."

Caleb was too tired to protest as Mick ordered him around, but he saw the sense of his plan and went along with it. Jane took Mick's orders to the next level though, making chicken soup and tucking Caleb into their big bed after she was sure he'd eaten it. He slept for at least an hour before the vision came again, and when he woke in a cold sweat, Jane was there with a warm blanket and even warmer embrace.

"I found the notes you were making and read through a bit while you slept." She held him close, her body comforting him like nothing else. "I hope that's okay."

Caleb stroked her hair as her head rested against his chest. "I'm amazed you could decipher my writing."

She chuckled and leaned back. "I'll admit it was a challenge, but I managed. Now why don't you tell me what to add to your notes while you rest? When I've written it all down, you can try to sleep again."

Caleb leaned back against the pillows she propped under him, snagging the nape of her neck in one broad palm before she could leave his side. He pulled her down for a lingering kiss.

"I missed waking up with you in my arms this morning, honey, but I was comforted by the game of thinking what Justin was doing to you that made you scream so beautifully." His eyes glinted as he watched the humor, excitement and hunger blossom in her gaze. "Maybe we should do some remodeling. Do you think we could build a bed big enough for the three of us?"

"Four of us, Caleb," she said daringly. "And I don't know if Mick would go for it, but I'm pretty sure Justin would."

"I know I would." He kissed her again, with rising passion. "I've never shared a woman in my life, but just the thought of sharing you with them gets me hot like I've never been before."

Jane tucked her head against his chest. "Justin told me he's done it before."

"I'll be damned." Caleb chuckled. "I just knew that boy was kinky." He pulled back so he could look into her eyes. "It doesn't scare you, does it? You know I'll never let him do anything you don't like."

She nodded. "More than that, I know he would never hurt me, Caleb. I feel it from his heart. Just like I feel it from yours. I know I can trust you both, and Mick too, though he's harder to read lately. I'm more than comfortable with you O'Haras directing my sex life."

"Dear God, when did we get so lucky as to deserve you?" Caleb kissed her again because he had to.

Bianca D'Arc

She made him focus briefly to write down the vision and then coaxed him back to resting, but he wouldn't let her leave. He pulled her into the bed with him, wrapping her up tight in his arms as he drifted to sleep again, only to awaken about an hour and a half later from another vision of a possible future.

Soothing him again, she helped him write down the confusing things he saw and they repeated the cycle of sleeping for a short time, waking, writing down what he'd seen, then trying to sleep again. Jane slept too, since she'd spent most of the night before experiencing Justin's way of pleasure. When she couldn't sleep any longer, she rested in Caleb's arms, thinking about the future and the fact that she might already be pregnant with Justin's child. The idea made her feel warm and fuzzy, and brought a profound love into her heart for Caleb, who was so genuinely happy at the thought of her having a baby—even if it wasn't his.

The baby *would* be his though, she knew in her heart. He would love it as his own, and protect it the way he protected all of them, with his visions, his sacrifice, and his deep and abiding love. She couldn't wait to put the baby into his big hands for the first time, watching as he learned how to deal with the tiny bundle, learning with him and his brothers, how to care for the child of their hearts. Mick would watch over the baby, doctoring its boo-boos, gauging its progress, and making it laugh. Justin would teach it things, dare his child to push its limits, nurture it with his special brand of love and discipline it when needed. She knew Justin would be the real disciplinarian of the three brothers. Just as she knew her baby would have Caleb twisted around its little finger from the moment of its birth. Caleb would be its beloved daddy.

And it would be that way for all of her children with the brothers, no matter who was the biological father. She hugged the idea of having each of their babies to her heart, knowing it

112

was the one enduring gift she could give each one of them in this world gone crazy. It was the tiny taste of immortality every one of them wanted, the chance to sire the next generation of humanity, and pass on what they were and what they'd learned. Each of them would have that chance, she vowed, knowing Caleb had seen the truth of her thoughts in his visions of the future. It was a comforting thought.

ೋ✿❀

Just before dinnertime Mick looked in on Caleb, finding Jane awake and looking at him from within Caleb's tight embrace. Mick watched them for a long moment, his emotions held tightly in check, as usual these days.

"How was he today?" Mick whispered, not wanting to disturb Caleb's sleep.

"He keeps waking up. The longest stretch of sleep was almost an hour and a half. I guess he's had about four hours total."

"Not great, but enough to keep him going for a bit." Mick crouched at the side of the bed, facing her. "You look good there, in his arms."

He could see she was surprised by his words, but he needed to say them. He'd thought of nothing else since he'd come in her mouth—twice—the day before. He still could hardly believe it. His conscience was hounding him, his sense of what was right and what was wrong turned upside down by the incredible feelings she'd unleashed within him.

"I can't betray his trust again, Jane. No matter how much you say it's right, I can't get past the idea that it's really terribly wrong."

"Don't say that, Mick."

He was about to turn away from the pain he saw in her eyes when Caleb stirred, rising from behind Jane to pin Mick with a stern gaze.

"Damn, Caleb. How long have you been awake?"

"Since you started flapping your gums. Mick, you are the most pigheaded little shit!"

"Don't get mad at me because I don't want to betray you."

"You betray us all!"

Mick rocked back, surprised by the vehemence in his brother's tone. Caleb was usually slow to burn and even slower to anger, but he was as close to rage as Mick had ever seen. Mick was more than surprised. He was shocked.

"Honey, show him what I mean. Show him the notes." Caleb nudged Jane's shoulder, releasing her from his tight embrace. He watched her with hunger and love as she crossed the room to the small desk where she'd been helping him with his notes. She gathered them up and handed the sheaves of paper to Mick silently.

"Read that," Caleb ordered. "Then tell me what'll happen if we don't continue on this course we've set. Read that and tell me if you can see any other solution to the trials that are coming."

Mick was shaking when he sat in the comfy chair by the window. He was curious and more than a little afraid of what he might read in the notes of his brother's most recent visions. Caleb had never written them down before. This was a unique chance to understand a bit of what his brother saw.

Mick read in silence. There was a lot to get through and much of it was hard to understand, since it related to the aliens. Jane left quietly, saying something about fixing dinner, while Caleb took a fresh piece of paper and began recording whatever new visions he'd received. Mick was enthralled by what he read, and the interpretations Caleb had mused on in his notes, having many years' experience with deciphering what his visions meant. But the interpretations here were wide open, many questions presented by the visions of the alien cities that were unanswerable by their limited human knowledge.

But those were questions for many years from now, if Caleb was reading them right. What was most important were the clearer visions of what would happen to them in the very near future...when the aliens came to the Waste.

"My God," Mick whispered when he read the clearest, and most disturbing, of the images Caleb had recorded. "I never realized what a burden this is for you."

Caleb looked solemnly at his brother. "More than you know," he agreed. "But it's mine to bear and I've learned how to deal with it for the most part."

"Why didn't you ever tell me?"

Caleb shrugged. "What could you have done, Mick? I know you're a miracle worker with medicine, but there's nothing anyone can do to relieve the pressure of my visions or what they portend. I just have to interpret them and deal with them as best I can."

Mick stood and walked over to his big brother, the man he had looked up to all his life.

"I don't know what to say, Caleb."

Caleb threw the pad he'd been writing on aside and stood to face his brother. "Say you'll love Jane and treat her well. Say that I can trust you with her happiness. Say you'll accept the one gift she and I can give you in this crazy mess of a world we live in."

Mick looked away, uncomfortable. "Jeez, Caleb. This doesn't feel right."

Caleb grabbed him by the shoulders and shook him hard. Just once.

"Did you read what I wrote in those pages? Did you read the part where if even one of us leaves, we all die? Do you understand that you won't be able to survive here at the ranch without her? Without the love she can give you? Without the release she can bring you?"

Mick felt like he was going to fly apart. "I read it, dammit! But Caleb—"

Caleb pulled him into a bear hug like he used to when Mick was a kid, crushing him close and slapping him on the back. His voice was gruff in Mick's ear and he sounded near tears.

"There's no other way, Mick. No other solution for any of us. Take what she offers and treat her well and she'll save us all. Reject her and kill us all—her included." Caleb let him go, pushing away to grab the pad on the bed and throw it with the other papers Mick had read. "Tell me you can kill her, Mick, knowing what I've seen. Tell me you can kill me and Justin too, by refusing her."

"I can't," Mick whispered, in pain. "I love her too." He broke down then, sinking to the side of the bed, running his hands through his hair in despair. Caleb was calmer, placing his big hand on Mick's shoulder and squeezing lightly.

"It's really a no-brainer, Mick. We all share in her love, we live. If even one of us denies what we all feel, we're all as good as dead. We have to present a solid front to the aliens when they come. If we act together, they'll keep us together. If we stay separate, they'll kill us off one by one."

"I don't want to hurt you, Caleb. She belongs to you."

Caleb shook his head as he sat at his brother's side. "She belonged to me legally, for a few years, true. But she's always belonged to all of us, Mick, since she was a little girl. Now she's a woman, and we have to treat her as such." Caleb patted his brother's back, offering comfort. "I don't see it as a betrayal. I see it as a necessary step in the evolution of our lives. She's as much mine now as she is yours or Justin's."

Chapter Eight

Jane felt the firestorm of emotion coming from the bedroom. More of it was from Caleb than from Mick, it was true, but Mick was so desperately upset, she could feel even his fierce control slipping, allowing the depth of his despair and sadness to sweep over her. She sank to her knees in the middle of the kitchen trying to withstand the storm.

Justin found her that way when he came in from the yard. He picked her up, holding her close as she shook with reaction, and she felt his worry too.

"What is it, Jane?"

She nodded toward the bedrooms. "Mick and Caleb."

"Hell, I'll kill them myself." He tried to let her go, but she clung to him.

"Leave them for now," she begged. "Mick has got to come to terms with this now. Caleb's got to make him understand."

"Understand what?"

"I read Caleb's notes about his visions. Justin, it's scary." He ran his fingers over her hair, soothing her as her eyes filled with fear for the future. "If the four of us don't face this together, we're all going to die, one by one."

"Ssh." He soothed her, wrapping her tight in his strong arms. "We'll face it together—all four of us. Nothing can separate us."

"Nothing but guilt," she whispered, afraid to the depths of her soul this would be the stumbling block that would kill them all.

"Guilt?" She nodded at his questioning look. "For sharing your love? Sharing your beautiful body?" She nodded again, his warm eyes comforting her as he let her feel the conflict that still resided in his own soul. "It's hard to take, Jane, but I'm willing to trust Caleb. If he says this is what we have to do, then I'll do it. With pleasure."

She could feel the teasing in his heart, the understanding that being her lover was anything but a chore, and the passion that swept through him whenever he thought of her body beneath his. But she felt the crescendo of emotions in the other room too, and it hurt to feel the turmoil and pain coming from two of the men she'd loved all her life.

"Read what Caleb wrote, Justin. You'll understand the necessity then." She moved out of his arms and toward the bedroom. She couldn't take any more of the pain coming from the other two men. Justin followed her, slowing her progress.

Justin captured her loosely from behind as they approached the open bedroom door. He sought out his brothers' eyes before allowing Jane to go to them, and was relieved to find some semblance of calm had returned to them both. By the way Jane had been trembling when he'd come in, he'd expected to find blood on the walls or some other horrific scene. What he found instead, was two men sitting on the side of the bed, looks of frustration, sadness and stunned acceptance over an impossible situation clear on their faces. He let Jane go, watching Mick carefully as she knelt in the small space between the two men, placing her hands on both of them as if to hold them to her.

"Is everything okay in here?" Justin looked from one to the other as he entered the room.

"As okay as it's going to get, I guess." Mick sighed heavily. It was a frustrated sound.

"Good." Justin nodded, his gaze stern. He had no sympathy for Mick just now. "Jane was trembling on the floor of the kitchen when I came in."

"Justin!" she admonished him.

"You think I wasn't going to tell them what their emotions did to you, baby? They've got to think first if they plan to fight around you."

"Oh, Jane, I'm sorry." Mick gripped her hand. She moved into his lap, cuddling into him as if to give him comfort. Mick looked thunderstruck at the warm woman on his lap and Justin saw Caleb smile.

"Now do you see what I meant when I said she belongs to all of us, Mick? She's known that since she was a little girl. She nurtures us. And she always has." Caleb stroked Jane's hair as she pressed her cheek to Mick's chest.

"Are you through being angry?" she asked Mick in a small voice.

"Can't you tell?"

"You're hard to read lately." She tugged on his collar, meeting his eyes. "And I'm telling you right here and now, I don't like it. But I felt your anger and your guilt and that's got to go, Mick. If you read what I read in Caleb's visions, you'll know it's true."

"I know it, darlin', but that doesn't make it any easier to swallow."

"Don't talk to her about swallowing unless you mean it, Mick," Justin joked darkly, enjoying the hot flush his words brought to both Jane and Mick's fair cheeks.

But he effectively broke the mood of the moment, as he'd hoped. Things would be okay eventually, as soon as he and Mick came to terms with the changes in all their lives. It was easier now that he'd spent the night in Jane's loving arms, thinking hard about it all and talking over some of it with her. But Mick hadn't had that experience yet, and his emotions were still fragile, Justin figured. He'd come around. He had to, if Caleb's visions were true. Which reminded him that he wanted to read those notes too.

Justin walked over to the small desk and picked up the wad of papers.

"Do you mind if I read these, Caleb?"

"Be my guest." Caleb stood, giving Jane and Mick time to recover from their embarrassment. He winked at Justin as he joined him by the desk. "You're the only one of us who's ever seen one of the aliens. Maybe you'll be able to understand more of what I've been seeing. Personally, I'm at a loss." He shook his head and sighed. "But, Justin, I should warn you, there's some stuff in there that could be painful to read regarding your son."

Justin felt his heart clench at his brother's warning and the sympathetic look on his strong face. He nodded tightly.

"It's better to know, Caleb. I've always believed your gift was given to our family for a reason."

"I pray you're right, Jus."

Justin reached out to grasp his older brother's shoulder, squeezing tight for a moment.

"I'm sure of it." He walked toward the door with the papers in his hand. "I'm going out to my garage to read these, just in case. Keep Jane busy in the house and keep her occupied. I don't want her to suffer needlessly."

"You're a good man, Justin."

Funny how Caleb's approval still made him feel good, just like when he'd been a kid, stomping around in his big brother's shadow.

ℰᎾᏟᏰᏬ

Jane went out to the small garage to check on Justin three hours later. She entered tentatively, afraid of what she might find, but unwilling to wait for him to return to the house any longer. Caleb was sleeping again and Mick had been placated for the moment. Now it was Justin who worried her. She'd expected him to come back long before, but he'd remained outside. She received impressions of his emotions, dimmed by the distance and his attempts to control himself, and she knew he was hurting. That was something she couldn't live with.

"I'm keeping your dinner warm." She pushed the door open to his garage. Justin sat in his easy chair, staring straight ahead, the look on his face breaking her heart.

"You read Caleb's notes?" he asked before she could say more.

She nodded and approached him. She wanted to soothe him. His emotions ran high and the closer she got to him, the deeper she felt his agony.

"It'll be okay, Jus. We'll find a way to make it okay for him."

"So much rests on those tiny shoulders, Janie." His voice was rough around the edges and she climbed into his lap as he pulled her close. She held him while he wrapped her in his powerful arms, seeking the comfort she gave freely. "And so much uncertainty."

"Caleb says we have a chance, Justin. A chance to show him we love him. A chance for him to know you. We've got to take that chance and make it reality somehow."

Justin nuzzled her neck, seeking her strength.

"It's such a slim hope, sweetheart."

"But the alternative is unacceptable," she said, conviction lacing her words. He looked up, as she'd intended, seeming surprised by the steel in her tone. "We'll make this work. I promise you. I'll do everything in my power to give your son the chance to know you."

He kissed her then, the emotion flooding him pure and true, causing her to gasp.

"You're the best thing that ever happened to me, Jane. I don't deserve you, but now that I have you, I'll make sure the four of us stay together. There's no way I'll let any one of us put your precious life in danger. For as long as you'll have me, I'm yours."

"You've always been mine. You just didn't know it."

"Now we have to work on Mick. From what I read, it'll take all four of us to stand against the aliens."

"I think after reading that," she nodded toward the stack of papers at their side, "he's beginning to understand what has to be. I don't think he's easy with it yet, but he's coming to terms with it."

"A night in your arms will remove any lingering doubts," he said with a glint in his eye that made her warm inside. "As soon as you're pregnant, you need to be with him, prove to him like you did to me that you're really okay with this."

She chuckled. "More than okay, if you'll remember correctly."

"How could I forget?" He nipped her playfully as he lifted her in his arms, rising to his feet. He really was incredibly strong, she realized yet again as he carried her from the small garage to the house.

He deposited her on her feet in the kitchen, finding Mick already seated at the table, just finishing up his dinner. Justin joined him, pulling the plate Jane had left for him from the still-warm oven. Jane sat between the brothers, drinking the cool glass of milk Justin poured for her before he sat.

"How soon will you know if Jane's pregnant?" Justin asked Mick perfunctorily, causing Jane to nearly choke on her milk.

Mick shifted in his chair. "Well, I sort of knew Caleb and Jane were trying to get pregnant before we moved up here, so I stocked up on supplies to help with that. I have some test kits that will tell us pretty accurately a few days after she conceives."

"That soon?" Justin looked over at Jane speculatively.

"I asked Jane about her, uh, cycle." Mick shot an apologetic look at Jane as he discussed the intimate details of her body. "And now is a very opportune time, so I expect the deed will be done shortly if it's not already."

Justin nodded as he ate heartily. "Good."

"What? Can't wait to get rid of me?" she joked, knowing that wasn't the reason behind Justin's questions, but wanting to lighten the mood.

"Never that, sweetheart." He took a moment to cover one of her hands with his and squeeze reassuringly. "But Mick and Caleb need you too. I don't want to appear greedy."

She laughed outright at that while Mick stewed in his lingering guilt. She touched his hand, wanting to feel what he felt, but he pulled away.

"None of that, Mick. You treat her right." Justin admonished him. "If she wants to know what you're feeling, you let her. You know she needs it."

"Dammit, Justin. Don't tell me how to behave. I may be younger than you, but I'm not stupid. I don't want to hurt her any more than you do."

"You've got a funny way of showing it." Justin turned back to his meal with a shake of his head.

"Boys! This has got to stop." Jane beseeched them both, reminding them she felt their tension and it wasn't a pleasant experience.

Justin leaned over and kissed her cheek. "Sorry, sweetheart." His eyes moved pointedly to Mick, sending a silent message.

Mick leaned over and kissed her other cheek, sighing as he followed Justin's silent order.

"Sorry, Jane," he said quickly, but she whipped around to catch his face between her palms and kissed him. She ran her tongue over his lips, making him gasp, then stood, taking Mick's hand as she tugged him to his feet.

"I believe you owe me more than just words, Mick." Her sultry grin was making him sweat, she was happy to see. She winked at Justin as she led Mick daringly from the room.

"Jane, I don't think this is a good idea," he protested weakly as she walked with him down the hall toward his bedroom.

"I think it's the best idea I've had all day, Mick." She smiled at him as she opened the door and pointed him toward the bed.

She made him sit while she reached for the hem of his T-shirt. But he stopped her.

"You don't have to do this."

"I know I don't have to, but I want to, Mick. I want to do this for you. And I want to do more than just this, but it'll have to wait until we're sure I'm pregnant." She pulled the shirt over his muscled chest. Mick was more compact than his brothers, but he was golden. Sun-colored hair and a lightly furred chest, tan from the outdoor work he loved. His blue eyes sparkled and his muscles were thickly roped, solid and oh-so-touchable. She'd always admired his All-American looks, and practically drooled now as she reached for the button on his faded, work-worn jeans.

Again his hand covered hers, stilling her motion. "Jane, really."

She met his eyes and moved her hand down over the fly of his jeans where his erection pressed so heavily, pulsing against the fabric. She squeezed gently and licked her lips as she gazed into his eyes.

"Really, Mick. I've always been attracted to you. Since I was a little girl. Growing up, you were my best friend, and my favorite fantasy. Didn't you know how I lusted after your golden boy looks when we were in high school?" He'd been three years older and way out of her league, but he always spared time for her, had always been kind to her, when others weren't so charitable to the emotionally strung-out teenager who felt things too deeply.

"Is that true?" He was breathless as she eased the zipper down.

She nodded solemnly. "You have a mirror. I'm sure you know how handsome you are." She blushed and concentrated on what she was uncovering so she wouldn't have to meet his eyes. "But it was your heart that drew me. Always your kind heart and the compassion in your soul."

He nudged her face up to his with a knuckle under her chin. "Yours is the truest heart, the purest soul, Jane. You're the center of it all and you've always been the woman of my dreams."

She gasped as she felt the rush of emotion he fed her as he bent to kiss her parted lips. He took over the love play then, bringing her slowly onto the bed with him, kissing her deeply, his tongue caressing her mouth in ways that made her whimper in need and passion. He drew her up beside him, shucking his jeans and briefs, aligning himself with her warm body, still protected by her own clothes.

"Just this, Jane. Just this," he said almost reverently, as he removed her top and the lacy bra she wore beneath it, kissing the skin as he exposed it, worshiping her with his warm mouth. He circled one nipple with his tongue, wetting the tip with due care before blowing a light puff of air across it, making it pucker in response. He pushed at the hardened tip with his tongue, playing with it, daring it to harden further. She squirmed, wanting to be closer.

"Mick, please!" She offered up her breast to him and he finally pulled the tip into his mouth for a long, hard suck that made her moan. He used his tongue, treating her other breast to the same as his hands stroked the rest of her clothes away.

Jane wasn't a passive partner. She caught his straining erection, rubbing up and down, causing him to pause and groan as she relished his response. When he moved to plant nibbling kisses up her throat, she sidled on the bed to bring her in more direct contact with his cock. She wanted that cock. So badly.

When he would have continued his gentle kisses, she turned the tables on him, swiveling to take him in her mouth, eliciting a string of curses that were music to her ears.

"Dammit, Jane! That feels so good!" His hand guided her head, tangling in her hair as his eyes followed her every movement.

It was a fantasy come true. Jane. Going down on him. In his bed. He was afraid to blink, lest she disappear in a puff of smoke.

She moaned around him, sending quivers of passion into him as he used his fingers to stimulate her clit and sink deep within her honeyed passage. She moved in time with him now, shuttling up and down on his cock, sucking deep, then teasing the head as he gasped. He was close now.

"Suck me hard, honey. I'm going to come!"

And with a harsh groan and a tightening of his entire body, he erupted into her mouth. For the third time. He cradled her head as she swallowed him down, taking every last drop he had to give and seeking more. She was a miracle to him.

After long moments, Mick flopped back against the bed, drained completely and eager for more, all at the same time.

"Give me a minute, honey, and I'm going to make you come so hard, you'll scream."

"Uh, you're going to have to give her a raincheck on that, Mick." Justin's voice sounded from just beyond his apparently all-too-thin bedroom door. "The bull we were watching is down. He looks pretty bad."

"Shit!" Mick cursed, clasping one hand over his eyes. He rubbed his face and turned to look at Jane. "I've got to go, honey. That bull is important and he's been really sick."

Jane sighed. "I know how important he is. Go tend to him, but hurry back."

She stroked his chest and smiled, making him feel luckier than any man alive in that moment, to have this woman's love and understanding.

"You're more important than the damned bull, but we need him to keep this ranch running, which means keeping you safe. If not for that, I'd let him die before I left you hanging like this." He kissed her, his lips practically begging for understanding.

She stroked his chest. "I know, Mick. And I understand. Really."

೫)೦೩೦೩

But Mick didn't get back to her that night—or even the next. He ended up babysitting the very sick bull most of the night, then collapsed onto the cot he kept in his office so as not to rouse the whole house when he came in. Caleb woke him with a late breakfast he'd brought over from the house and an update on the bull he'd taken over watching when Mick started to fall asleep on his feet.

Mick spent the next week between his office and the barn, with little time even to shower and eat. The animal was struggling, and he was key to their herd. Eventually, the stubborn bull took a turn for the better and it looked like he would survive given proper treatment, which Mick spent most of his time providing for the next few days.

Jane showed up at Mick's office in the middle of the following week, to provide the samples he needed to determine if she were pregnant. He'd barely seen any of the family except when they came to take over in the barn while he grabbed a few hours sleep. Jane was a sight for sore eyes and she brought the sun with her when she entered his little make-shift medical office. He took the samples he needed and she left him with a soft kiss. He ran the tests quickly, eager to share good news if he had it for them.

A short while later, Mick walked into the kitchen, grinning from ear to ear. He was glad the whole family was present for his big announcement. They would all be both happy and relieved when they heard the news.

"Jane is pregnant," he announced with a big grin.

He saw Jane's eyes widen, then fill with tears of joy, just as Caleb reached for one of her hands, squeezing tight as he smiled. Justin smiled too, putting an arm around her shoulders and tugging her close for a quick hug as she began to laugh and cry in earnest. She stood and hugged Justin back, then Caleb, then made her way on dancing feet to Mick, grabbing him around the waist and resting her head so trustingly on his chest it made him ache.

"Thank you, Mick. Thank you so much!"

He picked her up and spun her around. "I can't wait to meet my niece or nephew."

Mick released her and Caleb was there, his broad hand settling over her still-flat stomach, pressing gently. "This baby is going to know so much love," he said, making Jane's eyes fill again with happy tears.

The tears spilled over as she rested her head on Caleb's chest, accepting his love and his warm embrace. Caleb's eyes met Justin's over her shoulder.

"Thank you for this, Justin." Caleb grew serious and almost mystical. "Your children are going to reshape the world."

Justin laughed, uncomfortable with the weight of responsibility Caleb had just placed on him, but nodded. He was choked up in a way that he hadn't been when he thought about Mara carrying his son. Oh, he wanted his son, there was no doubt about that, but this child would be special too, because this child would be a part of Jane.

His heart nearly burst when he thought of sharing the coming months of her pregnancy with Jane. She was so damned special to him, so damned perfect. She was the finest woman he had ever known. And she was having his baby. Hot damn! Would wonders never cease?

Caleb released her and turned her toward Justin. She flowed into his arms and hugged him tight.

"I'm so happy!"

"No happier than I am," Justin said. "No happier than we all are. Think of it. In nine months, we'll all have a little rugrat to spoil rotten."

She swatted his shoulder. "You will not call our baby a rugrat!"

They all laughed as she pulled from his arms with a broad grin and shooed him to the table, where lunch was waiting. What had started out as an everyday meal turned into a celebration and the men toasted the happy event with a glass each of their hoarded liquor. Jane had learned to brew beer but they had a careful stockpile of vintage wine, whiskey and other liquors they used for only the most special occasions. Of course, Jane settled for fresh milk, but she toasted right along with them and the little house in the hidden valley rang with laughter and hope for the first time in years.

Chapter Nine

After lunch Caleb stayed inside with his wife, making plans and reveling in the joy of the occasion. It could have been bittersweet, but Caleb had long ago come to terms with what must be. His gift was both a blessing and a curse and he was sometimes at a loss as to know which it would be and when. But for now, he was glad of the coming child and at peace with the knowledge Justin's second child had almost as vital a role to play in the future of mankind as the first half-alien boy he had seen in his visions of the future.

He'd also seen recently—like a gift from a gentle and benevolent higher power—the faces of his own children with Jane. He knew for certain now that somehow Mick would find a way for him to have a few of his own children to raise and shower with love. The thought of them, as well as the thought of the nieces and nephews who would soon populate their home, was enough to hold him against the future. It was enough to know the happiness each of those children would bring to his sweet wife, whom he now shared with the only people in the universe he loved as much as he loved her.

Caleb spoiled Jane that afternoon. They sat on the couch after he did the cleaning up from lunch, not allowing her to lift a finger. He twirled her pretty hair around his finger as they talked about the future—the things he'd seen as well as the things they planned. She was excited about the baby, as was he, and he reassured her again that he was okay with the fact that the baby was Justin's biologically. The ring of truth in his emotions seemed to satisfy her that he truly was happy. He made her understand that as far as he was concerned, any child would be all of theirs, no matter which brother was the biological father.

She liked the idea and he told her just a bit of what he'd seen of their future brood. Jane had so much love to give, she was thrilled with the idea of a big family and raising them under the umbrella of her love and the guidance of the three strong O'Hara men.

Shortly before dinner, Caleb went out to join Mick, checking on the slowly recovering bull. He'd helped Jane get everything ready for dinner. All they'd have to do is put it on the table when they came in and he made Jane promise to let the men handle it, at least for this one celebratory day.

Mick was staring at the quiet bull when Caleb found him in the barn.

"How's he doing?"

Mick started. "He's recovering. I'd say he'll be fine with a bit more rest. The worst of it is over."

"That's good news." Caleb walked over to the stall and settled one arm over the top rail, looking in on the huge beast. "Jane is over the moon with happiness."

"That doesn't surprise me. I'm pretty excited myself. And a little scared."

"Scared?"

Mick turned toward him. "I've delivered my share of animals, but never a human baby. What if something goes wrong? We don't exactly have a hospital here. And I'm not an M.D."

"Brother," Caleb put his big hand on Mick's shoulder, "you're much better than any M.D. You love her. You won't let anything bad happen. Trust me."

Mick sighed. "Sometimes I wish I could see the future like you do."

"Don't say that, Mick. It's a burden I wouldn't wish on anyone." Caleb's thoughts darkened. "Oh, it's easy enough when things are going well and I'm seeing happy times, but knowing bad things are about to happen and being unable to do anything about them…"

It was Mick's turn to offer comfort. "I didn't think. I'm sorry, Caleb."

Caleb shrugged. "Don't worry. Right now I only see good things where our children are concerned. You'll do when the time comes. Don't worry about it."

ℰ𝒪𝒞𝒮𝒬

After a joyful dinner, the brothers cleaned up while Jane joked about the way they were treating her, but they could tell she loved the attention. Mick knew she wouldn't show for months yet, but he also knew he and his brothers would be watching her body for changes, enjoying each of the signs of her pregnancy as they experienced it with her. But for Mick, the pregnancy was a challenge to his somewhat spotty medical training.

After all, he'd planned to be a vet, not an obstetrician. He'd purchased all the medical texts he could after Caleb had moved them here and told them to prepare for the end of the world as they knew it. Before that, he'd never practiced medicine with anything other than animals as patients. Even then, he'd always been under supervision because he hadn't quite finished his schooling before the cataclysm.

He never imagined he'd be the only medical help available for both animals and humans. Not until Caleb told him what was coming. Then he'd spent the precious months of warning preparing himself to treat human beings and amassing a research library he could count on when he encountered something with which he had no real experience.

Childbirth was daunting, to say the least, but he knew he had to be strong for the family...and for Jane. He would stand by her, see her through all the changes she was sure to undergo in the next nine months, and not let on by the slightest hint that he was unsure of anything. She needed his confidence. She needed his strength. As she needed the strength of all the O'Hara brothers—each in different ways.

Caleb was her rock. He was her security in a world gone crazy, and Mick knew she loved him deeply. Justin seemed to appeal to her wild side. That tattoo of his and the Harley spoke volumes about what his life had been like before the cataclysm, even if he himself was tight-lipped about his adventures.

Mick didn't quite know what Jane saw in him. Sure, he'd been popular with the girls before the cataclysm and knew he wasn't hard to look at, but when compared with Caleb's steadfast bravery and Justin's devil-may-care toughness, he didn't think he had all that much to offer a beauty like Jane.

He'd admit she depended on him to a certain extent. The whole family did. He was the next best thing to a doctor and he tended to all the O'Haras—those on two feet and those on four. But that was no reason for her to give him the kind of love she'd shown since that fateful day they'd taken the irrevocable step into intimacy.

He tried not to focus on it too much, but every once in a while, Mick had to stop to think what in the world she saw in him. What would motivate a woman like her—with everything to give—to share herself with him? Other than the sheer goodness of her heart. He cursed inwardly as he thought again the damnable idea that he was some sort of pity fuck for her. She knew, as they all did, thanks to Caleb's visions, that there was no woman for him. Could she really be so giving she would take him into her body out of sympathy?

Mick hated the thought, but he knew his Jane had a heart as big as the world. If anyone would do such a thing, it was her.

He retired soon after supper, assuming Jane and Caleb would want some time alone. After all, Jane had been spending every night with Justin since he'd come back from town, making damned sure she got pregnant. It only made sense she'd sleep with Caleb again, now the deed was done.

He, for one, was glad. He didn't know if he could take another night of staring up at the ceiling while he listened to the faint sounds of pleasure coming from the room next to his. Even muted through the heavy walls, the sounds emanating from Justin's room were enough to drive Mick crazy, lying alone in the dark, hard and wanting something he rightly shouldn't be able to have. Neither should Justin, but that was almost excusable due to the need for Jane to get pregnant and Caleb's difficulty with that particular job.

Mick could almost justify the odd sort of assistance Justin was giving Caleb and Jane. And he couldn't help but wish circumstances had allowed him to be the brother called upon to render such assistance. But it was Justin's destiny this time, Caleb had said. That last part made him wonder... Would there really be a time when Mick was called upon to put a baby in Jane's womb? Would Mick get to deliver his own child of Jane's body someday? The thought made his heart catch, so he put it

136

away for later consideration. Right now, he had a hard enough time thinking about the blessed relief she'd given him with her mouth and hands.

Mick rolled over and let his mind wander to safer areas. He thought about the sick bull and the other various chores waiting for him in the morning. With thoughts of the vaccines he had to administer, he drifted off to sleep.

Only moments later, it seemed, he was roused by a light, feminine touch on his bare shoulder. A weight settled next to him on his wide bed, making the mattress dip just the slightest bit. Mick thought hazily that perhaps he was dreaming, but then his apparition spoke softly in his ear, her breath puffing past his sensitive skin and making him harden almost instantly.

"I'm all yours tonight, Mick. I want you to come in my pussy."

As he rolled over, his eyes opened wide and he realized that Jane was wearing only a thin nightie that she was in the process of removing. He sat up and stayed her hands with his own, holding her gently at bay.

"Jane, you don't have to do this."

She smiled at him. "But I want to. I've wanted to make love to you for a long time, Mick. Now is our time. Finally."

She pushed forward gently then, and he allowed her to push him back down on the bed, moving over him. She settled on his chest, her lips tracing over his chin and up to his mouth.

"I dreamed of you—of this—since I was a teenager."

"You're kidding right?" He couldn't quite keep the disbelief from his voice. "You don't have to lie to me to make this easier."

She sat up, staring down at him, then leaned over to turn on the bedside light. Her eyes were troubled.

"I'm not lying to you, Mick."

"Yeah, right. You always dreamed of fucking all three of us."

She flinched at his crude phrasing, but he wouldn't let himself feel even guiltier.

"When I hit puberty and started to think about what it would be like to be kissed by a boy, it was you I wanted to kiss me. Not Caleb. Not even Justin. It was you, Mick. But you never treated me as anything more than a friend, so I tried to stop thinking of you that way. The pattern repeated itself with your brothers, one by one. I'd just about given up hope of any of the O'Hara boys seeing me as anything other than a pesky little sister when Daddy passed on and Caleb started courting me." She hugged herself as she remembered the hard time in her young life. "My point is that I've wanted all of you at one time or another. Under normal circumstances, I would've been happy to live with Caleb for the rest of our lives, but things have changed, Mick."

"For the worse, if you ask me." Mick crossed his arms over his chest and ground his teeth. The delicate scent of her skin wafted over him, making him even hungrier for the release he now knew he could have in her arms. It was torture of the worst kind.

She moved closer to him, touching his arm and resting her cheek on his shoulder.

"Actually, I think I got the better end of the deal."

That startled a laugh out of Mick. "How do you figure?"

She turned mischievous eyes up to him. "You each only get one-third of me and I get all three of you. I don't have to choose between you anymore. I get all of you, just the way I've always wanted." His eyes widened as he looked at her and her hands grew bolder, moving down to cup his hardening body. "Don't

138

feel bad for me, Mick. Don't bother feeling guilty. I've wanted each one of you and now I get to have everything I always wanted. In fact, I'm feeling kind of guilty about it all, so you needn't bother. If anyone's getting away with anything here, it's definitely me."

She reached up and kissed him, stroking more boldly with one hand over his hardness and using the other to sneak up and unwind his arms, resting eventually on his pectoral muscle. Her fingers played with one nipple as he kissed her back for all he was worth.

She deftly freed him and started stroking. Kissing him deeply, she captured his groan in her mouth, answering with a moan of her own when his hands came up to push aside her nightie and gain access to her breasts.

"Mmm, more..." She sighed as his hand swept slowly up the inside of her leg. He pressed gently on her bud, already tight and wet for him. She kissed his throat as he bent his neck to lave the smooth skin above her breasts, working his way down slowly but surely.

He didn't speak as he moved with quiet urgency, reversing their positions so he was on top. He moved gently, but with a definite goal in mind as he removed his boxers, crowding her bare body with his and touching her from head to toe. He rubbed his chest over her nipples, back and forth, making her gasp as he found his place at the juncture of her thighs.

"Jane!" he whispered, his strangled voice raising her temperature even higher.

She spread her legs at his urging, knowing without being told that he needed to come inside her quickly, before he lost it completely. She was more than ready.

"I've wanted you for so long," she said at his ear, making him shiver as he positioned himself at the mouth of her womb. "Come to me now, Mick. Make me yours forever."

He pushed forward, sheathing himself in her with one strong glide as she gasped. His invasion was total and complete and she marveled at the feeling of having him inside her at last. He felt so right. Just as his brothers felt, each in their own special way. Mick felt thick and full, and the small curve of him touched an incredibly sensitive place inside her the other men didn't hit with such intensity. As he began to move, she felt the bundle of nerves inside her become more and more inflamed. She'd never had it like this before!

"I love you so much, Jane!" Mick gasped as he moved.

She felt his muscles clench as he fought off the orgasm that was so very close, but it didn't matter. She was panting, writhing beneath him now with every stroke as he hit her G-spot just right. She'd never felt such stimulation there before. It was almost too intense.

"Mick! I'm coming!" Her voice was nearly unrecognizable to her own ears. Who was that sobbing woman, so close to the pinnacle, her voice ragged with passion?

"I can't hold on much longer, love. Come now!"

She obeyed him with a cry as she came apart in his arms. It was the most mindless orgasm of her life and it went on as he continued to push inside her, hitting that magical spot with every long stroke. He rammed into her once, twice, then a third time before he tensed and the hot jets of sperm shot into her core. Her orgasm was fueled anew by the heat of his release beating against the tight bundle of nerves inside her.

Tears ran down her face at the intensity of their joining, but they were tears of incredible joy. Mick's body bowed above her, still caught in the throes of his own passion as he finally collapsed on top of her, utterly worn out. She stroked down the length of his legs with her own, holding him tight within her depths as he breathed raggedly, his heart pounding in unison against hers.

"I love you, Mick." She kissed his shoulder as he rested above her, totally drained.

Mick rose just a bit to look deeply into her eyes.

"I guess you do at that." His quiet wonder communicated through her empathic senses.

She felt he was coming to terms with this in his own way. It would probably take time, but this first complete joining had gone a long way toward making him more comfortable with the new arrangement. Inwardly, she was relieved. She loved him and she would do anything to keep him and their family safe from harm. And heck, if it meant more of these mind-blowing orgasms, she wouldn't mind a bit!

She smiled as he kissed her lips gently, almost like a benediction. Below, his body stiffened again, getting ready for another round. She clenched her inner muscles around him and was rewarded with a groan and a quick tickle as he moved his heavy weight off her. She was reassured by the smile in his gorgeous blue eyes as he caressed every inch of her.

"You are a miracle, Jane."

They made love long into the night. Mick hadn't had a woman since before the cataclysm and finally having Jane—a woman he loved dearly—made him extra potent. He let her sleep after the third time they made love, doggy-style this time, then woke her a few hours later to start all over again. She met him with an eager abandon that did more to convince him this was the right thing than all the words up to this point. He decided somewhere along the line to leave thinking for later. This night was for enjoying. And he enjoyed Jane's body in every way he could imagine.

Early the next morning, Jane slipped out of bed before Mick woke to start breakfast for the family. They took turns doing most of the chores but she claimed to enjoy cooking for the men who were always appreciative of the dishes she came up with for their various meals. Mick was a little stiff with his brothers, especially Caleb, when he first entered the big kitchen, but Caleb and Jane soon put him at ease. Still, he was looking at Jane with new eyes as she bustled around setting breakfast on the table with a glow he knew he'd put in her cheeks.

ഗ്രരഗ്ദരൂ

As the weeks wore on, Jane spent many nights in Mick's bed, as well as Justin's, sharing herself freely with the brothers and basking in their tender care of her. She slept with Caleb most often, but when the wanting got too hard to bear, she went to each of the brothers, who treated her like gold. She never had any complaints about any of her lovers and if they had problems with the arrangement, she didn't sense it from any of them. She was always linked to them, alert to any slight change in their moods.

They were careful of her, almost reverent in the way they worshiped her changing body and when the morning sickness came, all three helped her through it. Though Mick, of course, doctored her, putting all his hard-won medical knowledge to use as he held her through the bouts of nausea and vomiting, and made her eat plain foods until her stomach settled.

They all enjoyed her rounding tummy, and they made a special effort to make her day-to-day life easier. They carried everything for her and wouldn't let her strain herself in the kitchen garden or cleaning the house. They were also extraordinarily careful when they made love to her. She might have complained if she wasn't enjoying the exquisite treatment. The way they saw to her every need—sexually and otherwise— was marvelous, and she wouldn't change a thing.

Chapter Ten

"I have to go into town."

Caleb's words at the otherwise quiet breakfast table a few months later were met with worried silence.

"Isn't going to town getting a bit dangerous? I mean, the aliens could be coming any time now, right? I thought you told us to be wary of being caught out alone." Jane voiced what most of them were thinking.

Caleb sighed and pushed back from the table. "I know. It is dangerous. But it has to be done. There's someone I have to warn."

"I thought the visions had started to ease?" Mick asked quietly, his breakfast forgotten in the face of his older brother's quiet determination to put himself at risk.

"They have, but I need to do this."

"Can't one of us do it for you? I'll go, Caleb," Mick's eyes were almost pleading.

Caleb looked at his youngest brother hard. "Come with me, Mick, but I have to see this through myself. Otherwise the message may not get to her."

"Her?" Jane asked in surprise.

"Do you remember Una Johnson? The storekeeper's wife?" Caleb reached over and took her hand between both of his.

"Damn, Caleb," Justin spoke up for the first time. "Old man Johnson keeps her and their daughter under lock and key. How are you going to get a message to her?"

"I know. He's managed to keep them safe this long, but he won't be able to hold out against the aliens. Johnson knows us. I think he'll listen to me."

"All right then," Justin said, standing and throwing his denim jacket around his broad shoulders. "I'll cover you, Caleb. Let Mick stay here with Jane."

Caleb met Justin's eyes for a long moment. "No. You stay and guard Jane. Just in case my timing's off. You have the best chance of keeping her safe if you come under attack. Mick and I can handle the trip into town."

"Are you sure?" Justin's eyes were steely and as serious as Jane had ever seen. Caleb nodded toward Mick, who also stood.

"Let's go. The sooner we do this, the better chance we have."

With a lingering kiss for Jane, Caleb joined Mick outside. The brothers made their way to the small town just down the mountain from their secluded valley on horseback. They made good time and didn't talk much as they went, both fearing the arrival of aliens at every turn.

When they finally arrived in town, Bill Johnson was belligerent at first, but Caleb talked him around with a dire warning that seemed to take hold.

"My wife and daughter are none of your concern, O'Hara."

"You're right," Caleb agreed with a rueful twist of his lips. "But they are yours to protect. I know you have some telekinesis, as does your wife. Do you know what my gift is?" Caleb waited a beat to see if the other man had heard the

145

rumors about him. Precognition wasn't a common gift and those who did have it usually weren't as strong as Caleb. No, Caleb's foresight was an incredibly powerful manifestation, rarest of the rare.

"I see the future, Bill. And I've come with a warning for you and your family." Caleb took a folded piece of paper from his pocket and held it up before the other man. "There's very little any of us can do about what's coming, but for the sake of your wife and daughter, read this and make them read it too. I'm begging you, Bill. It could save their lives."

Johnson stared hard at Caleb, but eventually took the paper and pocketed it quietly. "Precog, huh? No wonder you knew when to come up here and bring your family. I've often wondered about what made you come north."

Caleb straightened and nodded. "My vision of the cataclysm was the strongest I've ever had in my life. Until now. Read what I've written about what I saw for your womenfolk, Bill. And know that running now will only kill you all outright. You have to tough out what's coming, but if you're prepared, your wife may be the key to your salvation."

Caleb knew Mick was listening to their conversation from over near the entrance and he sensed more than saw his brother perk up at his words to the other man. He knew he'd have questions to answer on the way home, but Bill surprised him by opening the stockroom door behind him and motioning his wife to come out of hiding.

"You heard, Una?" he asked his wife of twenty years with a tenderness that was shocking to the brothers who watched.

The older lady nodded, her eyes wide with fear. She turned to Caleb and grabbed his hand.

"Thank you for coming, Mr. O'Hara. Back when you first moved here, I knew your wife. She told me about your gift when the attacks started and I know she had complete faith in your visions. Thank you for coming here and sharing what you've seen with us, though I'm terrified of what may be coming."

Caleb nodded solemnly. "Remember your roots, Una O'Mara. Be sure to tell the woman who's coming your maiden name as soon as you can. Claim the protection of it for yourself and your family. It may stop her."

"How did you know my maiden name?" Una whispered in scared wonder.

Caleb smiled as gently as he could, trying to put her at ease. "The woman will be pregnant. That's how you'll know her. There's more in the note I wrote you. Details you should attend to as soon as you can. Time is short."

The older woman clutched her husband's arm. Her lips trembled, her eyes were wide and filled with tears as she faced Caleb.

"Bless you, Mr. O'Hara. Bless you for coming and for sharing your gift."

Caleb nodded silently to the couple and strode for the door. Mick followed him out waiting until they were well out of town before breaking the silence.

"So Bill Johnson's wife was born an O'Mara? And the alien scientist that's coming, who just happens to be pregnant with Justin's baby is named Mara. Isn't that a bit of a coincidence?"

Caleb shook his head slowly from side to side. "I don't believe in coincidence."

ഇ൦ൽ൙

Word came down a few days later that the aliens had come to the Waste. Mick intercepted wild cries for help from the few strong telepaths in the village and was able to learn the aliens had the area surrounded. No one was getting out. At least not alive.

They were taking prisoners and shipping them off to the alien city. At least that's where the few who could communicate with Mick thought the prisoners were being taken. Surprisingly, the aliens were being careful not to kill anyone unless provoked, which was quite a switch from their behavior since coming to Earth. Still, they had little compassion and no understanding of what it meant to tear families apart.

They took women away from their mates and put them in with other males, countenancing rape and even encouraging it, or so it seemed. Mick was aghast at the scenes described to him and his emotions boiled each time one of the village telepaths saw fit to update him.

They reached out for news and comfort. Mick hadn't known them well, but had a nodding acquaintance with most of the villagers from his infrequent trips into town. Still, it seemed like the O'Hara ranch was the only place free of the alien presence. At least in that, Mara had kept her pledge.

But the things Mick learned from the villagers made him sick.

Jane found him in his office one afternoon, tears in his eyes as he was told about the repeated, public rape of a woman who had been married to the town's barber. Daniel had kept her hidden, but the aliens found her and separated the long-married couple. They put her in a holding pen with twelve single men who hadn't seen a female since before the cataclysm and carefully noted the results like some sort of freakish scientific study.

"Mick?" Jane came up beside him, slipping her arms around his waist and leaning her head on his broad shoulders. "Is it bad?"

Mick turned and swept her into his arms, pulling her close, burying his hot face in her neck. "It's bad, darling. So bad."

"Tell me what I can do." She stroked his golden hair, seeking to comfort the ache in his heart.

"Just having you near helps, Janie. You are so precious to me."

She reached between them and unfastened the buttons to his shirt, knowing he needed more distraction, more distance from the thoughts that were plaguing him.

"I need you, Mick." She dropped to her knees in front of him, undressing him as she went. She was awkward with her big tummy, and though Mick tried to stop her, she would not be denied. With gentle hands she stroked him. Mick was already semi-hard from holding her and now he came fully erect, his cock hardening in her hands as she leaned forward to kiss him and suck him inside her warm mouth. She took him deep, swirling her tongue along the veins and curves, smiling as he gasped.

"Just like that, Jane." He closed his eyes in pleasure as she worked her magic on him.

Neither heard the door open, but both pairs of eyes shot open when Caleb started laughing.

"And here I thought you'd be suffering at the news from town. I should've known our Janie would comfort you." Caleb took off his work gloves and jacket as he moved behind her, supporting her body against his while she continued to suck on Mick's cock.

Justin was there too, clearing off the examining table in Mick's laboratory, spreading a blanket over the cool surface while he stripped off his shirt.

"Bring her over here, Mick. The tile floor is too rough on her knees." Justin watched with heat in his eyes as Caleb lifted her away from Mick and brought her to the table in his arms.

He wasted no time removing her stretchy pants while Mick moved up by her head to take off her top. She turned her head to the side and reached out with one hand to recapture Mick's cock, pulling him back to her. She hummed in pleasure as he gave in and pushed his length back into the warm cave of her mouth, looking helplessly at his brothers.

He sent a mental burst to them to help him out. At this rate he'd come way before Jane could be pleasured and he'd learned to be very careful of her. As empathic as she was, especially with her pregnancy adding all kinds of hormones to the mix of her volatile gift, he didn't want to hurt her—physically, mentally or emotionally.

Justin sat in Mick's office chair and rolled over to position himself between Jane's spread legs. He ran his hands under her butt cheeks, pulling her down on the table until she was at the edge. Mick groaned as he followed the clasp of her moving mouth with his cock and Caleb smiled at his predicament.

"I've always wanted to play doctor," Justin said from his seat, right at pussy level. He eyed her dripping folds with pure appreciation as he used his fingers to spread her wider. Caleb helped out by taking one of her legs and looping the knee over his arm as he stood by her side. Mick followed suit and held her other leg, spreading her wide for Justin's perusal.

"My, my. What do we have here?" Justin said with a false leer as he examined her folds. "I think I'll have to use the probe."

He thrust slowly inside her passage with one long finger, leaning down at the same time to lick her clit. He licked her and stroked inside as Mick fucked her mouth and Caleb bent to her breasts, pinching one nipple with his free hand while sucking the other.

Jane was nearly in orbit with the attentions of all three men. They'd been so careful of her since she'd begun to show her pregnancy, but she loved every minute of their sex play, as gentle as it was now or as raw as it had been in the short time before she was visibly pregnant.

Caleb's warm mouth teased her nipples, sucking and pulling with just the right pressure and making her pussy even wetter, while Justin licked her clit. His fingers were doing something wild inside her, curving and corkscrewing, making her squirm while Mick's cock pulsed against her tongue, almost ready to explode.

She wanted him to explode too. She would have sucked him off without any pleasure for herself, so concerned was she about his emotional state. She knew he wasn't thinking about anything but her lips on his cock right now, and how that made him feel. She was content her distraction had worked and even happier that all three brothers joined in putting their collective troubles away for just a little while.

Mick neared the point of no return and he tried to pull away, but she refused to let him. Her hand settled on his ass, pulling him closer even as he made the token gesture of pulling away. She knew from past experience that he loved it when she swallowed his cum and she wanted every last salty-sweet drop.

She hollowed her cheeks, sucking harder, gazing up at him. A second later, she felt him explode like a rocket deep in her mouth. She swallowed hard as he pulsed, streams of his cum soaking her and making her heart sing.

"Jeez, Jane!" Mick bent over, climaxing hard, his muscles trembling, his heart exploding with love that flooded her empathic senses. "Fuck!"

Caleb stood, watching over them, his own cock expanding behind his jeans as he teased Jane's pink nipples. It made him hotter than hell to watch his brothers being pleasured by his wife and vice versa.

She was so loving and so giving. It amazed him every time he saw her with one of his brothers that she was so willing to please them all. He'd asked her to do it as a way to keep them all safe from the alien threat, but damn if it didn't turn him on as well. He'd never been very kinky before the cataclysm, except maybe for a small dominant streak he tried to temper with Jane. Hell, he'd never had time away from the demands of raising his brothers and running the ranch to ever really explore the bounds of his sexuality, but he was learning fast that he liked to watch. Even more, he liked to watch Jane as she found fulfillment and know it was his brothers who gave it to her.

As Mick's cock slid from Jane's hot mouth, Caleb watched with avarice. He wanted to feel the heat and swirl of her tongue, and envied Mick the release she'd just given him. He knew the same would be waiting for him, if he just asked. They'd been careful of her since she started showing her pregnancy and the brothers had quietly agreed among themselves to ease off the vaginal sex a bit. Each of the brothers was good to go at least three or four times a night, but Caleb worried Jane's ripening body probably wasn't made to handle the kind of loving three able-bodied O'Hara brothers could dish out.

Caleb watched Mick ease back, enjoying the last caresses of Jane's hands as he sat for a moment to recover. Justin still had his head between her legs and she was squirming nicely, while Caleb's hand toyed with her nipples. Caleb was watching Justin's mouth close around her clit and suck hard when he felt her hand on the fly of his jeans. His gaze flashed to hers and he was enchanted by her smile.

"Are you sure you're up to this, Jane?" Her comfort was always his first priority.

She leaned up on one elbow and he moved quickly to help support her back. She put her hand around his neck and brought his face down for a kiss and Caleb felt his heart stutter and speed up. He loved the taste of her and the idea of what she had been doing to his brother just a moment ago. What's more, Jane knew he liked it and she bedeviled him every time. She smiled as she pulled back.

"I want you, Caleb. Come in my mouth, at least for a bit, okay?"

Caleb eased her back on the table, his hands caressing every inch of skin they touched with love. "How can I resist an invitation like that?"

He lowered his zipper the rest of the way and slid his cock and balls out as he eased the worn denim and white cotton briefs down just enough to give her full access. He sucked in a breath as her hands found him and caressed him before she brought him to her mouth.

He took over then, sliding in and out, holding her head the way he liked as she let him control the penetration. It was an act of trust that she'd learned when they first married and it never ceased to please him.

"You ready for a little double penetration, Jane?" Justin asked from between her legs, his words sending puffs of hot air

153

over her clit as she moaned around Caleb's cock. Caleb liked it and pushed deeper, watching as Justin stood and positioned himself at Jane's opening. Justin held both of her thighs in his hands, pushing her knees up and out enough to admit him, spreading her wide as he watched the progress of their joining.

Mick moved to stand at his shoulder, watching while he pumped himself. He'd quickly recovered from his first release and looked ready for more.

Justin turned his head to the side when he was seated fully within Jane and jerked his chin at Mick.

"Go suck her titties. Maybe she'll give you some hand action if you're nice." Justin laughed teasingly as he began thrusting, slow and easy, in and out of Jane's tight core. Caleb too was thrusting in the hot cavern of her mouth, getting off on the sight of the brothers pleasuring her.

Mick closed his perfect white teeth over the tight tip of her breast, startling Caleb. He never used his teeth on Jane, but she seemed to like it, so he filed his objection away for later discussion. He was learning a lot about what she liked and what she didn't like as his brothers expanded both of their realms of sexual knowledge and experience. And he was learning there wasn't a whole lot she didn't like. His Janie was a wild woman, and damn if he didn't love it.

Caleb saw her reach out to Mick. She fisted her hand around him and squeezed, rubbing up and down as Mick groaned and pulled away for a moment. When he returned, he had a bottle in his hand and he opened Jane's palm and squeezed a dollop of lubricant in her palm, spreading it around with his fingers. Together, they massaged his dick, making it shine with lubricant.

After a few strokes, Mick's hand fell away and Jane was free to increase the tempo and length of her motions. She never moved her head from Caleb's hold and he marveled at how she was able to take on all three men without losing track of herself in pleasure. Caleb stroked just a little deeper, pleased when she moaned around his cock.

"I'm coming, love," he warned. "I'm coming now."

She purred when he filled her mouth with cum, swallowing it down as she orgasmed around Justin's invading cock and her hand tightened on Mick. Caleb pulled away moments later, after she'd swallowed every drop.

Jane floated as Justin pumped into her and Mick's slippery cock slid through her fist. She'd had a lovely climax, but she knew from experience there was more to come from the O'Hara boys. Justin could ride her for hours and make her climax over and over again, and she intended to have all three of them between her legs if she could manage it.

They'd been limiting her, treating her as if she were made of fragile glass that would shatter if treated too roughly. Well, they'd gone overboard and she wanted to demonstrate graphically that she could handle their passion. She was only a few months pregnant and they were treating her as if she were about to give birth. Sure, she knew she'd have to ease off a bit as her time grew closer, but she also knew she would wait until the last possible moment to do so. She loved having sex with the O'Hara men almost as much as she loved them. And she wouldn't deny herself or them before she absolutely had to. It was time they learned that.

"I want to fuck your tits." Mick eased her hand away from his cock.

He looked down the table at Justin and the older brother nodded, taking a breather while Mick repositioned, climbing onto the examining table that was plenty wide enough for him to brace his knees on either side of her petite torso. Mick slid his lubed cock between the enlarged globes of her breasts while Justin renewed his efforts between her legs. With each stroke of Mick's cock, she bathed him with her tongue, her gaze meeting his with deviltry as he trembled.

She loved making this man lose his cool. Mick was so controlled, so deep, she loved making him lose that iron control, and she reveled in his passion. Of the three brothers, he was the deepest thinker. He would study her responses for hours if she let him, giving his all to her enjoyment and only rarely letting her push him beyond his own limits. She relished those times and basked in the ability to make her cool thinking man turn hot and wild.

She felt him drawing near his climax, felt his trembling as he in turn felt the jolts her body was taking from Justin's steady pounding in her pussy. Justin was increasing his pace, using his fingers to excite her clit and stroke her legs. Mick's strong hands pushed her breasts together while he tunneled through the softness, the lube making him slick, but she wanted to be slicker still.

"Come on me, Mick. I want to feel it now."

"Fuck, Jane!" Justin pumped faster, sliding into her with great care. "Suck his knob and get him off your chest."

Caleb moved closer, stroking Jane's hair. "Justin's right. This isn't safe. I don't want to chance any of us hurting you." He met Mick's eyes. "Finish and get off her, Mick."

Mick groaned, already in agony. "Nothing like a little added pressure. Thanks, guys."

Jane smiled as Mick tightened his grip on her slippery breasts. "Don't listen to them. I like you where you are." And to show him how much, she swiped her tongue over the tip of his cock again, sending him into orbit.

He came with a blistering groan, splashing his cum over her breasts and neck, even getting some of it onto her tongue as she reached out to lick him.

"Mmm," she hummed around his still-throbbing knob. "You taste good, Mick. So good."

Mick accepted Caleb's help to climb off the table after she'd finished licking him clean. She rubbed his cum all over her breasts. He helped her, letting her take his large hand and rub it all over her nipples.

"I like that." She sensed all three bothers' emotions as they watched her. The love bathed her senses in a warm glow that spiked toward Justin as he neared release.

"Come with me, Jane." Justin pushed deep, his orgasm crowding up from the soles of his feet. "Come for me now, honey."

He pinched her clit and with a scream, she came hard, his warm spurts of cum increasing her pleasure. He stroked through his climax and hers, drawing them out and making her hot again before he ever left her body.

Jane grasped Caleb's hand and met his eyes. "I need you, Caleb. I need you in me."

Caleb sucked in a breath. "I don't want to hurt you or the baby, Jane."

"You won't. I need you, Caleb. Mick, tell him!"

She pleaded with the family doctor to confirm the truth of her words. Mick moved between her legs and felt her pussy, apparently unable to resist stroking her clit and making her jump slightly as he gave her a cursory examination.

"As long as you have no pains that you're not telling us about, it should be fine," he confirmed with one last long caress of her clit.

"You heard him, Caleb." She lay back with a siren's smile. "Do me."

Chapter Eleven

Caleb wasn't quite used to his shy bride's new forthrightness and it never failed to excite him. Jane had been a virgin when they married, but she was quickly discovering her power over the three O'Hara men and learning how to tell them exactly what she wanted.

He moved between her thighs, savoring the feel of her legs around him. He, like his brothers, had been holding back a bit since she'd gotten pregnant, but he always wanted Jane. He'd take her twenty times a day if his body could manage it. As it was, he had to hold back so as not to hurt her and leave a little for his brothers. It was a noble sacrifice, he thought with a silly twist of his lips, but he loved them all and he would do anything for them.

Caleb let just the tip of his cock slide along her slit, teasing her before finally finding a respite inside her. He pushed in a short way, standing back and swiveling his hips, making her sensitive walls recognize their new inhabitant. Justin had pounded her and while Caleb liked that too once in a while, he had something different in mind this time.

Seeking Mick's assistance with a glance, he pulled out and turned her to her side, putting her legs together and pushing up her knees so her bottom was exposed to him and she was still comfortable.

"How's this?" he asked sliding inside. It was even tighter in this position and nearly made his eyes water with the pleasure bearing down on him.

"It's good, Caleb. So good." Her answer sighed through him, making him throb in the tight confines of her compressed channel.

He moved slowly, gratified when she came after only a few short strokes. He let her quiet down, then started once more, controlling her movement with Mick's help. Mick stood at her side, holding her knees so she was comfortable, taking pressure off her straining muscles. Of course, this put Mick's semi-erect cock in line with Jane's mouth again and she didn't waste any time sucking him in.

"Hurry it up, Caleb," Mick groaned as he hardened fully in her hot mouth, "before she cripples me."

Justin laughed with Mick as he came up beside them, recovered enough to stroke Jane's back as he'd been doing since her pregnancy started to give her backaches at night. He rubbed, offering comfort that became erotic given the situation, and lengthened his strokes down over the curves of her ass, squeezing and gripping, changing the amount of access Caleb had, just slightly, but enough to make her tremble with increasing need.

"Let it come, Jane," Justin whispered, bending down to slide his tongue into her ear. "Ride the wave."

She groaned deep in her throat as Caleb came hard, triggering her own deep climax. Caleb pistoned in and held, spurting into her.

"Sweet Lord, Jane!" Caleb whispered, caught up in climax. "Sweet, sweet, Jane." He stepped back when he finally could move again and helped turn her to her back and lower her legs to a more comfortable position. Jane pulled away from Mick and smiled up at him. The mischief in her gaze should have warned him, but he was beyond thinking.

"Now you, Mick. I want all three of you in me today."

"Jeez!" His cock twitched as she drew one finger from balls to tip. "Are you sure you can handle this?"

She smiled like a fallen angel. "Definitely. I want all three of my men inside me. Now."

So saying, she spread her legs wide once more, grasping Mick's cock and guiding him around the end of the table. She didn't let go even then, but positioned him, rotating her hips, making him stroke her with the head before moving him down to stroke inside. He slid in with a deep groan of pleasure.

"You're so hot, Jane."

He loved this. He loved her. And he loved sharing her with the only men on earth he would even consider as her mates other than himself. If it had to be this way, heaven knew he would enjoy fucking Jane with his brothers. It had been hard to accept at first, but now, after months of loving and sharing, it felt almost right. Almost. He still had pangs of conscience now and again, but the hottest orgasms of his life had a way of making any lingering doubts float away on a puff of air.

He stroked into her lightly at first, using his curved tip to hit the secret spot inside her that craved attention only he could give. He watched her eyes light up as he found the magic spot and felt her tremble from deep within. He sped his own rush toward ecstasy, rubbing more firmly inside while Justin's fingers moved down to stroke her clit, surprising him at first. He looked to the side, meeting Justin's devilish grin.

"Just lending a helping hand. I can't resist Jane's little clitty any more than I can resist her hot pussy." He smacked his lips as he turned to grin at Jane. "Let me play, sweetheart. I promise you'll like it."

"Like it?" she asked breathlessly. "I love it!"

Justin took the little nubbin of flesh between his fingers and squeezed, nearly rocketing her off the table. Her contractions sent Mick over the edge and he came hard and fast within her, his cum spilling out as her channel filled to overflowing.

"Son of a bitch!" Mick swore as Justin held on through the hard climaxes. He'd shared a lot with his brothers, but he'd never had one of their hands so close to his dick when he came. It seemed weird at first, but when Mick saw the glow on Jane's face, he realized she liked it a lot. He could get used to just about anything to put that dazed look of satisfaction on Jane's beloved face.

Mick knew Justin was kinkier than all of them, just as he knew Justin was in no way interested in men. But he had no shame when it came to bringing Jane pleasure, and that was a goal Mick could get behind. This kind of closeness when they shared her would just take a little getting used to. But he would get used to it, seeing as how she liked it so much. He'd do anything for Jane, including sucking her clit while one of his brothers stuffed her pussy. They hadn't done that yet, and suddenly it was something he wanted to try. It would make her come like a rocket, he'd bet.

But it would have to wait for another time. Their very own sex goddess was already asleep, replete with her many orgasms and plain tuckered out. Mick watched fondly as Caleb gathered her in his arms and carried her to the ranch house.

"We fucked her unconscious," Justin said with some pride as he dressed. "Not a bad afternoon's work, if I do say so myself."

෩෮෪

A few days later, Justin came up behind Jane as she watched a new foal gallop alongside its mother in the morning breeze. One of his large hands settled around her shoulders, drawing her back against his chest and the other palmed the swollen belly that held his child. He rubbed gently, bringing all three of them ease as he held her, watching the young foal's antics and enjoying the dewy morning.

"I wonder about my other child sometimes, Jane," he said, confessing his fears to the one person who might understand and sympathize. Or at least the one person he felt comfortable exposing his own weaknesses to. Jane had a heart as big as the world and he knew he held a place in it that was his alone. She also felt something for the child that would be born to Mara—a part of him and yet forever out of his reach. Jane had told him how she felt for the child and for him, and the half-brother or sister nestling under his palm. She felt for them all, and would nurture them all.

Jane put her hand over his. "I think about him too. He's going to be so alone with Mara—so emotionally isolated—judging by what you've told us about her. There's got to be some way we can get him away from her. Some way we can have an influence over how he's raised, to let him know he's part human and loved." Her gentle words stole his breath. "All children need to feel love. I want him to know it too, and for him to know you. He needs you, Justin, as you need him."

If his mind hadn't been focused before, Jane's words did the trick. He knew he had to somehow, someway, get his son to live with them. The O'Haras could teach him the way humans lived, loved and felt about the world and the people in it. He'd made it his goal—an impossible one, it seemed—to have some say, some influence over the child that would be born to Mara. He felt the need deep inside, and made a vow to himself. He would raise his son to understand his emotions, embrace them and be happy in his own skin. He owed the child that much and more, and he would see it done. Though he had no idea yet, just how.

⋙⋘

When a small silver craft circled the ranch, none of the O'Haras had any idea if it was a good or bad thing. Even Caleb hadn't foreseen this alien visit and he sent Jane indoors with just a look.

She went into the kitchen, but watched worriedly from behind the curtains. If the aliens wanted them, there was nothing they could do against their superior technology. She knew her men would put up a fight, but had little hope of success.

The craft hovered, then landed in the pasture, luckily away from the livestock, but still uncomfortably close to the house. A hatchway on the side of the ship opened and lowered silently. Shortly thereafter, several aliens appeared in the opening, cautiously stepping forward and down the small ramp onto O'Hara land.

Caleb strode forward as head of the family to meet them. He stopped several feet from the closest alien, a man who stood almost a foot taller than Caleb's own six feet two inches, with long flaxen hair pulled back in a neat, masculine braid, allowing his slightly pointed ears to show. The alien man had striking features, though his face held faint scars that made it more than obvious he was a warrior with many years of experience. He held his arms loosely at his sides but Caleb figured he had to have several weapons within easy reach, should they prove necessary.

Caleb didn't want to find out the hard way if his supposition was correct. He held up his palms and spoke without inflection.

"I'm Caleb O'Hara. I lead the family that lives here. We have no disagreement with you or your people. Why have you come?"

The alien soldier looked down at Caleb with indifference, yet his gaze measured and decided. He didn't answer, but made a small hand motion to those behind him and more activity ensued, though Caleb didn't dare take his eyes off the huge warrior facing him.

"Our mission is to find one called Justin O Hara. Do you know where he is?" The tall man spoke in a deep, almost rusty voice that had a hint of the musical lilt Caleb had heard the aliens possessed. The sound was pleasant and made Caleb want to hear more of the aliens' lyrical speech.

"I'm right here." Justin strode forward from the direction of the barn. Caleb knew Justin and Mick would have returned to the homestead as soon as they saw the alien craft descending. Apparently they'd ridden hard because Justin and Mick were both covered in dust and sweat as they got closer.

The alien warrior shifted his gaze to the two men who approached and his eyes narrowed. "You are the one designated Justin?"

"He is," said a new, higher voice from behind the alien warrior. All eyes turned to the newcomer, a tall, blonde woman who was heavily pregnant. She strode right up to Justin and placed a kiss on his lips, shocking most of those present. She was surrounded by an entourage of aliens, mostly soldiers like the one who still faced Caleb, but for one. The one at her right hand was an elderly man, shriveled with age, though still quite spry, and he had a slighter build than those of the warriors. He looked more like an accountant or bookkeeper, Caleb thought.

"Hello, Mara." Justin looked at the round swell of her stomach. "I didn't really expect you to come."

She smiled politely. "You requested that I visit before I gave birth and the opportunity presented itself. Plus, I must admit to curiosity about your living conditions. I have brought another researcher with me," she turned to indicate the old man. "This is Helas Prime. You may refer to him as Prime, since he is the highest ranked Helas onplanet."

Justin nodded to the old man. "It's a pleasure to meet you, sir."

Prime quirked his head as if surprised by the courtesy, then nodded back, observing all. Justin turned to Mick and Caleb who'd come up on either side of him in a show of support and unity.

"These are my brothers, Caleb and Mick O'Hara. Caleb is the eldest and Mick is youngest."

The aliens nodded to each brother in turn, their eyes searching over them for only they knew what. Mara moved her hand to her stomach as a very visible kick distended the top of her belly. She laughed and the tinkling sound was enchanting.

"Your child is very active," she complained with a grin.

Justin felt a bit more at ease, though he had no idea what all these aliens could possibly want with them. He feared for Jane, but so far things were friendly, so perhaps this would work out.

"May I?" Justin held one hand over the mound of her stomach. She nodded her permission, taking his hand and holding it to the place where the baby kicked. They were rewarded with another strong kick as the child made his presence known.

"That's my boy," Justin said with a pleased smile, ignoring the wetness behind his eyes. He thought he felt a flash of awareness from the baby as he moved his hand away, but he couldn't be sure.

Prime quirked his head at Justin and spoke for the first time, his voice a pleasant mid-range rumble. "How do you know it is male?"

Justin looked at Caleb. The eldest O'Hara nodded, then stepped forward.

"That's my doing," Caleb said clearly. "I sometimes have precognitive visions and in them I've seen this baby. It's a boy." The aliens looked intrigued.

"I would like to speak with you more about this, Caleb O Hara. Since the early days of this pregnancy, I have had strange dreams in which I think the baby may be communicating with me. At first I thought it was just imagination, but it has happened too often and too accurately for me to dismiss it entirely."

"Is that why you came?" Justin asked.

"That is a primary reason. I do not know what to expect from a Breed child and thought you might have some of the answers, but I also remember our conversation and how you wanted to experience this pregnancy if at all possible. So here I am, seeking answers and fulfilling my obligation."

Justin nearly winced. This woman truly had no emotion in her body.

"My brother, Mick, can probably help you with your questions. He's our doctor and is familiar with pregnant women." Justin paused, not sure how much to tell her. "He's

167

also a very strong telepath. If our boy is trying to communicate, chances are it's some form of telepathy, since I have a bit of that ability myself."

"Indeed?" Mara looked intrigued, a seemingly permanent state for the scientist. Just once Justin would like to see some other emotion on her face, something to indicate his son wouldn't grow up with a woman who only saw him as some kind of interesting lab rat.

"You should also speak with Jane."

Caleb's voice surprised the brothers. Justin hadn't been sure whether or not to divulge Jane's presence or keep her hidden, but Caleb was their leader and he'd undoubtedly seen things they would never fully understand. The brothers followed his lead, always.

"Jane is your wife?" Mara asked, apparently remembering the description of the family Justin had given her.

Caleb nodded. "She's also pregnant with Justin's child, and about as far along as you are, I think."

Mara's head tilted and a frown of concentration creased her light eyes.

"Justin's child?"

Caleb nodded again, though Justin shifted his feet, uncomfortable.

"Yes. I had an illness as a child that resulted in low sperm count as an adult. Jane's always wanted a child and I wanted that for her, so my brother, Justin, did the honors. It's not conventional and it's not the way things would have been done in the old world, before your people came, but we've come to terms with our new world as much as we can."

"Very sensible." Mara accepted his statement, not recognizing the emotional depth of their words or actions.

"Would you like to come inside and meet Jane?" Caleb asked politely, indicating the house in the distance. Mara nodded and ordered most of the warriors to stay near the ship, taking only the one who'd spoken.

"The leader of our guard will come as well. He is Grady Prime," Mara introduced the warrior succinctly.

"Highest ranked Grady onplanet?" Caleb asked with a wink that was totally lost on the aliens, though Mara did seem impressed with his logic. The soldier bowed his head briefly in acknowledgement as they all began walking toward the house. "Are all Gradys soldiers?"

Grady nodded affirmative though he remained vigilant and protective of the two scientists. "The Grady bloodline is warrior stock. Most end up in traditional warrior occupations."

"And you're the best of them. Impressive." Caleb shot his brothers a look that spoke volumes. They'd tread lightly around the big man.

Grady made Justin's neck itch, but he recognized the huge man's duty to the two scientists. Once upon a time Justin had been a soldier, perhaps not too much unlike the giant following so silently in their steps as they neared the house. His eyes shifted constantly, taking in all the particulars of the ranch and its inhabitants, assessing possible threats and routes of escape, should that prove necessary.

Justin was secretly glad his days in the U.S. Army Special Ops units were over, though he would never regret the skills he'd learned and the vigilance that was ever with him. It had always helped him before, and he hoped his training and experience would help him keep his family safe for years to come. Justin nodded to the seven-foot-tall soldier as he passed him, a nod of respect among warriors the alien man returned with not a little surprise.

Jane was nervous but only the humans could tell as she greeted the other woman, acting the gracious hostess in her large kitchen. She invited them to sit and was discomfited when the alien scientists sat next to her. Mara took the chair on her right and Prime seated himself on Mara's left around the large kitchen table. Justin stood behind them, resting against the countertop, ever vigilant, near the alien warrior who had taken up his post by the door. Caleb sat on Jane's left and Mick took the seat next to Prime, ready to help answer their questions and learn what they could.

"You carry Justin's child?" Mara asked bluntly.

Jane nodded, her hand reaching out under the table to grasp Caleb's. He was her strength. She would face these aliens with courage.

"Mick did some tests." She firmed her voice as the aliens' attention diverted to Mick. "He found out why Caleb and I hadn't succeeded in having a baby before, though we've been trying for a long time. We all decided together that Justin should give me a baby."

The aliens asked Mick the particulars of the tests he'd run and the technical reasons Caleb had difficulty impregnating his wife. The aliens seemed impressed by Mick's medical knowledge and spent several minutes talking with him in technical terms Jane had trouble following.

"This is very good news," Mara said, finally coming back to Jane and her baby. "We can compare the progress of your pregnancy with my own. The data will be quite interesting since both embryos have the same father."

"I've been keeping records of her pregnancy," Mick said quietly. "I'd be glad to make copies for you."

The aliens seemed pleased by the offer and made arrangements to do their own examination before they left the ranch. Mick also managed to get them to agree to let him examine Mara at the same time. Jane knew this was a coup and Mick would be certain to use his powerful telepathic gift to learn what he could of the half-alien boy in Mara's womb.

Both babies started kicking, and Mara grimaced at the twinge while Jane laughed. She saw the pain on the other woman's face and reached out as she would to anyone, her empathic gift making it difficult to see anyone in pain.

"I find it helps if you rub in a circular motion." Jane moved as if to touch Mara's swollen belly, but she stopped short to meet the other woman's eyes. "May I show you?"

Mara nodded, her lips twisted in pain as her baby continued to batter away at her insides. Jane touched lightly, rubbing in circles as she tentatively sent her emotions to the baby, wondering if she could reach him, young as he was.

She was shocked by the awareness that met her gentle empathic touch and the strength of the child. She could tell he was self-aware and aware of his mother and the doctors who touched her from time to time, but he was also frightened. No one he sensed had given him the hope of love and comfort he needed, so Jane sent waves of love to the child, easing him. He kicked a bit more forcefully at first against Jane's hand as she continued to rub Mara's tummy. He subsided, though, as she fed him all the love and reassurance she could, telling him without words it would probably be a while before she could touch him again, but promising she would always be there for him. That she would always love him, and so would his father and uncles.

She tried to reassure him as best she could that, though he might be alone for a while, the O'Haras would always love him and be there for him. They would be working to be with him, to touch his thoughts and love him as one of their own. She felt his fear subside, to be replaced by wonder at the world of love she promised him. And a beautiful sense of hope. She fought hard against the tears that threatened, but Mara didn't have a clue what the look on Jane's face meant. Mara only smiled in thanks when the pain of her baby's kicks subsided.

"I will remember that trick," Mara said. "Thank you, Jane."

Jane was forced to remove her hand, but she sent one last wave of love to the child, rocked to her core by the startling level of awareness she sensed from him. She knew her own baby wasn't nearly as self-aware, though each day the child under her heart developed a little more. Mara's baby was special in a way Jane had never experienced. She squeezed Caleb's hand under the table, telling him without words that something profound had happened.

They talked a few minutes more, then the aliens decided to look over Mick's medical office. As they all shuffled out the door and down to the small building that housed his medical equipment, Jane managed to pull Mick aside and tell him about her startling discovery. She knew Mick could telepathically send her message to Justin and Caleb, though she herself had very little telepathic ability.

When they reached his office, Mick gave the aliens a quick tour, then settled Jane on his oversized examining table. He watched carefully as Prime and Mara used small devices to record her vital signs and take something like an ultrasound image of her womb. He asked questions at each step, seeking assurance their technology would do no harm to the fetus or to Jane.

When it came Mara's turn, Mick explained the methods human doctors had traditionally used to track the progress of a pregnancy. He explained each as he used his own tools—blood pressure cuff, stethoscope, heart rate monitor, etc.—to do a cursory examination of Mara's distended stomach. While he explained to them on one level, on another he was communicating with the baby. He was amazed by what he found when he sent out his first tentative thought to the child in Mara's womb.

"I've shown you the basic human medical tests I can do here," he said quietly. "But there's something further we can do that regular humans, in the old days, could not." Standing back, Mick motioned Justin forward. The aliens were intrigued enough to let him continue. "You already realize your child may have some of Justin's extrasensory abilities. Justin is strongly telekinetic, but also somewhat telepathic." He turned to Justin. "You should be the first to really communicate with him, Justin. He's your son."

"You mean to say the fetus can communicate already?" Prime asked.

Mick nodded as Justin moved forward to put his hand on Mara's belly. Mick kept the scientists occupied with an explanation of human gestation and growth, giving Justin a moment to commune with his child.

Justin sent out his first tentative thoughts to the baby, shocked to his core when the child sent back a barrage of thought images. The boy had no real understanding of the wider world around him, but he knew sensations and feelings and he could communicate them using his already strong telepathy.

Tears formed behind Justin's eyes as he realized just how special his boy was. He sent the thought to him, trying to let the baby know how much he was loved by his father and that he could always come to his father for help and understanding.

"Is he speaking to you?" Mara's lilting voice interrupted, her hand moving to cover Justin's on her tummy.

Justin nodded. "He's communicating, though not quite in words. It's amazing."

"I take it this is not the usual course of events. Can you communicate with Jane's baby as well?"

Mick stepped up to answer Mara while Justin concentrated on the stolen moments with his son. "Jane's baby isn't very self-aware just yet. I've tried once or twice to see if I could communicate, but never received the kind of response we're getting from your child. Of course, that might also just mean Jane's child will not be as strongly telepathic as yours. It could be that Jane's baby has different gifts."

"My baby communicates with me empathically," Jane said quietly, coming forward. "It gets stronger each day, but it only started a few weeks ago."

Mara tilted her head. "This baby has been sending me dream images for much longer. I think the first one I made note of was only three weeks into the pregnancy."

"So early?" Mick asked. "Have they gotten stronger over time?"

"Yes, and I believe my ability to interpret his images has gotten better as well."

"He's telling me about a cold place," Justin said, concentrating on the images in his mind. "He doesn't like the cold, damp feeling, and he wishes you wouldn't stay there so long."

Mara laughed and the room was filled with the tinkling alien notes. "There are caves below the city where I go to visit some of our test subjects. It is rather cold and damp. I will endeavor not to visit quite so long for the baby's comfort."

"I'll tell him." Justin smiled, sending the thought to the boy. "He's grateful," Justin said after a moment, "and he seems to want to spend more time in a place where there's a lot of rainbow light and a very comforting, vibrating hum."

"The resonance chamber," Prime said quickly, nodding. "That must be what he means."

Mara nodded. "I enjoy the sound of the place as well and will do as he asks. It's very soothing there."

"He agrees. He likes the vibrations. They make him feel warm." After that he spent a few more minutes communicating back and forth, but when Mara asked what some of the dreams the baby had been sending her meant, Justin asked Mick to step in to try to decipher them with his stronger telepathy.

Mick spent some time helping Mara learn what the baby had meant with the dreams he'd sent, then saw an opportunity to advance the family's plan. They'd all discussed ways they could get this child under their protection, to raise him within their family, show him love, and teach him about the legacy of his humanity.

One of the dreams the baby had sent made them all laugh. The baby wanted her to eat more of a certain kind of vegetable because the way it rumbled in her digestive tract made him happy. It was hard to figure that one out, but Mick's medical training and strong telepathy allowed him to come up with the right words to explain what the baby sent. The other dreams were of a similar nature, and Mick tried to send back to the child how his mother didn't really understand all his messages, though she was trying. The baby seemed reassured by the thoughts Mick sent him and rested content in his mother's womb. When the last dream was explained to Mara's satisfaction, Mick struck up the conversation he'd been rehearsing in one corner of his mind.

"You know, we could help you with this kind of thing as he grows." His gaze sought and held Mara's, but he knew his brothers and Jane were holding their breath, waiting to see how the alien woman would respond. "If you'd bring him back here every so often, or let him stay with us once in a while, we could teach him about his extrasensory gifts and help him learn to both control and use them responsibly."

Mara seemed to consider. "Your suggestion has some merit. I will think more about this."

Mick sighed. He didn't want to push the woman. He didn't want to seem too eager and make her suspicious. He'd planted the seed and would wait to argue the case, if needed, when he had her decision.

As the conversation drifted, Mara looked at each of the brothers in turn. "You, Caleb, have the leadership qualities of Hara, and Mick, the inquisitive mind. But what of you, Justin? What did you do before my people came?"

Justin sighed heavily. He knew he had to tell the truth, though as a rule, he liked to keep his past private.

"Before the cataclysm I was a soldier. I was selected and trained as a special operative. If Caleb hadn't called me home, I would have stayed in the military, probably for the next twenty years or so, but I came home when my family needed me."

"You were a warrior. As was your ancestor, Hara." Mara seemed pleased, though it was hard to tell when she had so little emotion. "Hara was a great leader, a warrior educated in science and possessed of a daring that few of my kind still have. I see parts of him in all three of you."

"I'd like to read about him, if you have any historical records that could be translated into English you're willing to share." Mick's request seemed to surprise the aliens, but Mara smiled with something that approached pleasure as she thought about it.

"It would be fitting that the descendants of Hara make a study of his life and accomplishments." She seemed to be almost thinking out loud. "I will take your request under consideration. It is a reasonable and respectful one."

"You seem surprised," Justin said, a little insulted by her tone of astonishment that heathen Breeds could be either reasonable or respectful.

Mara tilted her head, his emotional tone completely lost on her.

"You have continually surprised me since the moment we met, Justin O Hara. You are not at all what I expected of Breeds. Especially males of your species."

Caleb stepped forward. "We're not all savages driven half mad by loss, lack of female companionship and rough living. I know a lot of the men living in the Waste are a bit odd, even among humans, but you shouldn't expect they're representative of all of humanity. We were a civilized, technologically growing and caring people before the cataclysm. We've tried to stay as close to the old ways as we could given the circumstances of our new world." Caleb's tone was patient as he tried to educate the alien woman who just couldn't comprehend the emotional toll the cataclysm had taken on the few survivors of humanity.

"Forgive my assumptions. We had reports of a much more primitive indigenous species when my predecessors formulated our plans for colonization of this planet."

177

"Well, your reports were dead wrong," Justin said, his anger showing in his words.

She turned her attention to him, her flat, unemotional eyes giving him chills.

"I am beginning to revise my opinion on that matter as well, but I must gather further data to draw reasonable conclusions. Regardless, what's done is done and we all must live with it. My people have no choice but to proceed with colonization of this planet. There is nowhere else for us to go."

"Why not? Surely there are other planets like this one in the galaxy," Mick asked, ever the scientist.

Mara nodded. "Yes, we found several with untuned crystal deposits sufficient to sustain us and dispatched other colony ships to each likely candidate. Our homestar went supernova and we had to relocate the populations of several planets. We are the survivors of Alvia Prime, the first homeworld. The inhabitants of Secundus and Tierti and so on were sent to other worlds, spread far across this and other galaxies. We do not expect to hear from them for many centuries. We can only hope they found their worlds to be as acceptable as we have so far found this one."

"Alvia? So then your race would be called Alvian?" Mick asked.

Mara nodded. "Yes. Is that significant?"

The brothers looked at each other and grinned. It was Jane who took pity on the aliens to explain.

"We had legends of a race called elves who looked a lot like your people. Tall, blond, pointy ears, musical voices." The scientists nodded, that inquisitive look back on their faces. "They were also believed to have magical abilities. I imagine your technology would have looked like magic to the less advanced people of this planet centuries ago and if your people

178

bred with humans and psychic abilities were the result, well, you can see how the legends now seem to have some basis in fact. It's not a far leap in our language from Alvian to elven, is it?"

Mara nodded again. "Fascinating," she said, turning to Helas Prime. "I believe this observation merits further study." The old man nodded in agreement and they asked a few questions about Earth's legends which the O'Haras answered as best they could.

Mara and Prime headed for the silver ship not long after, the giant, silent warrior at their back. The O'Haras went to see them off, but Caleb and Mick hung back with Jane while Justin said goodbye to the alien woman who was having his child.

"Thank you for coming here, Mara. I appreciate the opportunity to see you this way and share in my child's development." He placed a hand on her tummy, sending his thoughts to the baby, saying goodbye for now and telling him to be strong and to remember that his father loved him, always. Mara placed her hand over his.

"I have learned much here today. I wish to reassure you that our bargain holds firm. Your ranch will remain unchanged by my people's presence in the Waste and your family will not be taken for study or removed from here."

"I thank you for that."

"The debt is mine and it is an honorable one. You have fulfilled your part, now I fulfill mine." She made a gesture with her hands that seemed ritualistic. "I will try to return after the child is born so that we may compare him with Jane's baby."

Justin noted she wasn't coming back so he could meet his son. No, it was for the sake of her damned experiment that she would return. Again it amazed him how little feeling this woman had and how little she understood human sentiments. Perhaps his boy would be the one to teach her. Perhaps their son would show her the damage she'd done to human lives with her experiments, and help stop them.

But he was getting ahead of himself. The boy had to be born first, and Justin was just glad Mara had a reason to return so Justin could meet his son.

"We'll look forward to your visit," he said formally, leaning forward to kiss her cheek in farewell. She seemed surprised by the gesture, but returned it.

As the scientists turned to go, Justin nodded to the huge warrior who had observed all, a shadow who'd followed them around all day. Grady nodded back as Justin stepped away from the craft and joined his family. They moved well back from the ship, unsure how much clearance it would need to take off, but watched carefully as it lifted almost soundlessly into the sky and flew quickly out of sight.

Mara and his precious baby boy were gone.

For now.

Chapter Twelve

When Jane's baby finally made her appearance, all three men gathered to help and watch the miracle. Mick's sure hands caught the baby and took care of the necessary medical steps, then handed her off to continue his work with Jane.

It was Caleb who Mick handed her to, concentrating more on his patient who still needed his care than the symbolism of what he'd done. Though Justin was the biological father of this baby girl, Caleb was the leader of their strange little family, Justin thought later, realizing it was only fitting Caleb be the first to hold the newest member of their family when Mick had finished tending her.

Regardless, Justin got to hold her soon enough, Caleb handing her off to him with his big, surprisingly gentle hands and a look that told Justin he'd done good. Caleb had been giving his younger brothers that look since they were kids for various reasons, and it always made Justin proud, but this by far was the best feeling he'd ever had. Jane and he had made a precious baby girl and she was spectacularly beautiful to him.

ᏕᎧᏘᏘᏆ

The silver craft reappeared and landed in the home pasture about eight weeks later. Justin was glad he was nearby when he spotted the silver bird. Mara must have delivered her child by now, so perhaps she was coming to show him his son. Or perhaps the aliens were coming to take them all away. He had no real way of knowing except to trust in Caleb's vision. Surely Caleb would have warned them if something really bad were about to happen, but then, their gifts weren't always one hundred percent reliable.

So it was a cautious Justin who approached the craft from a distance, signaling Mick with a quick telepathic burst as to what was going on. He knew Mick could contact Caleb and marshal the meager forces of the O'Haras, should it become necessary.

The hatch opened and the old man he knew as Prime stepped out, followed closely by Mara, holding a squirming baby. Justin felt the region around his heart clench as he realized he was about to meet his firstborn son. Mara smiled and he was pleased to see it was a genuine smile that lit her eyes in a way she hadn't been capable of when he'd first met her. His son had done that. His son had brought at least a smidgen of true emotion to the otherwise cold woman.

She walked right up to him, passing Prime, who observed in his curious way.

"This is your son." Mara handed the baby over to him.

Justin was surprised, but caught the baby boy gently to his chest. He had experience with newborns now that Callie had come into the world and stolen his heart, but he still did the usual inspection, counting fingers and toes and smiling down at his little man with tears in his eyes. He was absolutely perfect, but Justin noted the slightly pointed ears that betrayed his mixed parentage.

"He's so beautiful." Justin's voice caught. "What have you named him?"

"He is called Hara, though I have not yet determined how to designate him. He is only partly Hara, but your bloodline is the stronger of our two. Mara is a lesser line given to scientists and questioners. Hara is a more dominant, honored bloodline."

Justin was a bit put off by her answer. "You said Hara was an explorer, right?"

She nodded eagerly. "One of our most famous, and a savior to our people when the Homeworld was on the verge of destruction. He and a few others brought hope to our people and planned for our evacuation into the far reaches of the galaxy. It is a proud heritage we thought lost until I met you. We've done detailed analysis of your DNA and compared it with historical records. We determined the Hara influence is very strong in you, even with all the human fluctuations."

"Well, he's an O'Hara, so I guess the name works, but I'll call him Harry." Justin bent to kiss the boy's forehead. "It's a pleasure to meet you Harry O'Hara. I'm your daddy."

Justin walked off a short distance, wanting some private space with his son and his almost overwhelming emotions. He knew Mara watched and studied his reactions, but she kept back, which was good enough for the moment. He needed time with his boy before she took him away again. A pang ripped at his heart when he thought he might never see the boy again. He'd only just met him, but already he loved this small bundle squirming happily in his arms. The boy looked at him with clear, sparkling blue eyes that reminded him strongly of the sainted woman who'd raised the O'Hara brothers.

Jane felt the emotional storm and decided she needed to help. She went outside cautiously, leaving Callie sleeping in the wooden carrier Caleb had lovingly carved for her near the door so she could hear her if she cried. Jane took in the varying levels of emotion with interest, noting the slight increase in emotion coming from Mara.

Prime was still basically a blank slate to Jane's empathic senses, but Mara had indeed changed, at least a tiny bit. Jane was glad of it. Perhaps the changes would continue and Justin's boy wouldn't be raised without any kind of love at all. She knew babies could die without affection and she feared for the boy.

She guessed she should be jealous of the other woman, and probably would have been of any woman who bore Justin a child in the old days—even if they'd never become lovers. Jane loved him. She always had. It was just that simple.

But that was also the reason she couldn't wait to meet Justin's son. Mara didn't matter to Justin, except as a means to keep them all safe from the alien threat. She knew that with utter certainty. Jane was secure in the knowledge Justin loved her. She knew for certain he felt nothing for Mara personally, other than disdain at her utter lack of emotion.

Jane was ultra-sensitive now to the waves of love and longing coming off him as he cradled his son in his arms for the first time. He'd felt the same sense of wonder and boundless love as he'd held Callie, she recalled fondly, and his heart was as open as she'd ever known it. She was happy for him.

As she studied Justin, she felt the decided curiosity of another presence. The boy himself. His emotional strength was amazing for such a young child and she found herself moving toward him slowly, wanting to strengthen the empathic connection that was beginning to form.

Mara sidetracked her with a greeting and Jane stopped, realizing she could help give Justin this time alone with his boy. None of them knew what Mara's plans would be for the child.

For all they knew, Justin would never see him again. Jane vowed to give him whatever time she could.

She drew the other woman into conversation after exchanging polite greetings. "Can you stay for lunch?"

Mara smiled and closer now, Jane was amazed to feel the increase in emotion coming from the alien woman. It still wasn't much, but it was a lot more than the last time they'd met.

"We would like to see your baby, as well," Prime reminded them as he joined the women.

Jane suppressed the pang of fear. These aliens held power over all their lives. She didn't think they'd harm her child, but she was a new mother with all those protective instincts surfacing for the first time. She had no choice but to allow them to see Callie, of course, but still she worried.

"She's in the kitchen." Jane led the way toward the house.

The Alvians followed her inside, leaving Justin alone with his boy. By the time they had finished looking at Callie and asking questions about her delivery and habits, Jane was glad to sense the other two O'Hara men outside bonding with their nephew.

"He remembers us, Mick," Justin marveled, his shining gaze meeting his brother's. "From before he was born. He remembers us all."

Mick's surprise was clear. "He's amazing, Justin. Just amazing."

"He's all I foresaw and more, Justin. He'll do great things for humanity, if he is well nurtured." Caleb touched the baby's soft cheek, squinting as he received impressions from the child.

"If we have anything to say about it at all, he will be. But it all depends on Mara." Justin knew the amazingly sentient baby was picking up on all their emotions and thoughts, though he was still developing his mental capacity. The rate at which he was developing was faster than a normal child, and the strength of his gifts greater. "God, he's special." Justin pressed another kiss to the boy's forehead.

"We have to get Mara to leave him with us sometimes, or at least to visit," Caleb said with determination that was answered in his brothers' eyes.

As it turned out, they didn't have to try hard at all to get Mara to let the boy visit.

"Do you have adequate milk for your baby?" Mara asked Jane bluntly, making Justin nearly choke as he entered the big kitchen with his son still in his arms. The other men followed close behind.

Jane was surprised, especially now that everyone was looking at her swollen breasts. But she was game to answer any question Mara might ask if it would help in some small way.

"Actually, it feels like I may have too much." She squirmed under their scrutiny.

Mick stepped forward, trying to help with the medical turn of the conversation.

"From what I've read, Jane's unusually productive, but it should subside as her body becomes accustomed to Callie's needs."

"Could she feed two infants?" Mara asked, surprising them all. But Jane stepped forward, hoping the question meant what she thought it did.

"Yes, I could do so easily."

"Then I will leave Hara with you for the time being." The pulse of joy that rushed through Jane from all the males in the room was lost on the aliens. "We have studied him all we can for now and my breasts do not have enough to sustain him. It is beneficial to have mother's milk, to pass along immunities, so if you have no objection, I believe he would be healthier if he fed from you for the next few months."

"I have no objection." What an understatement! A pang of joy sang through her. She'd do anything for Justin to have his son near for even a few short months. She knew from Caleb's visions that the boy would need to learn about humanity before he could become their champion. This was a small start in teaching him what the Earth had been before the aliens came. "I would be pleased to help him grow and be strong."

"We'll return in six months then to check his progress," Mara said, as if she'd expected no other answer, and stood to leave.

The men saw her out and Jane noted sadly that she didn't even stop to say goodbye to her newborn son. She was gaining some emotion, but she was still a long way from being anything even close to human.

After Mara and the alien contingent took off in their ship, Justin returned. He looked solemnly at Jane, the love shining in his eyes.

"Thank you, sweetheart. I know this can't be easy for you, but thank you."

His voice caught on the last word, bringing tears to her eyes. She felt the waves of emotion from him as she stepped forward to cup his cheek.

"I love you, Justin, and he's a part of you. I could do no less for either of you. It hurt me to think of that cold woman not understanding his emotional needs. At least I know while he's here, he'll feel all the love we have to give him."

Justin bent and kissed her lips sweetly, the baby held between them.

"You have such a big and pure heart, it constantly amazes me, Jane."

She turned to look down at the baby who was waving his arms to get their attention.

"We haven't been properly introduced yet, have we, Mr. O'Hara?"

"His name is Harry." Justin smiled at them both, handing her the infant.

"Harry O'Hara?" She smiled at the boy, touching his cheek and his cute elfin ears as she began to feel his intense emotions. "Oh, Jus," she whispered in discovery, "he's so much more self-aware than Callie is. He's amazing."

And as if mentioning her name woke the sleeping girl, a whimper came from the wooden basinet on the table.

"That's right." Justin picked up the pink bundle. "He hasn't met his sister yet." He kissed the rosy cheek of the girl and held her up so the two infants could look at each other.

Callie wasn't quite so curious yet, but Harry's laser blue eyes studied the girl and his little arms flailed toward her. Jane read the emotions coming from the boy, a mix of curiosity, love and a touching protectiveness.

Callie started to cry in earnest and Justin took her to change her diaper. Afterward, he found Jane and Harry in the room they'd set up as a nursery, Jane balancing the baby on her lap, contemplating him.

"What?" Justin could see the wheels turning in her mind.

She smiled self-consciously. "It's just going to be weird is all. I've barely gotten used to Callie and now I've got this strange baby to get intimate with in a matter of moments."

Justin sat on a bench next to her rocker, shifting Callie to one arm while he cupped the nape of Jane's neck with his other hand. He drew her forward, into his kiss, and she melted as she always did when he touched her.

"This is a noble thing you're doing, Jane. And if there's any way I can make this easier for you, I'll do it."

"For now, just stay with me. I need you with me. We both need you." She turned back to the baby on her lap.

Justin had watched her nurse Callie, but aside from some initial self-consciousness as she learned how to handle their daughter, she'd been calm. Now she seemed self-conscious all over again as she opened her blouse, letting her incredibly ripe breasts spill free.

"He's hungry." She chuckled nervously. "I can feel his hunger. Callie is too, but she's not quite as desperate as Harry is." She frowned. "I wonder what they've been feeding him."

Horror at the thought of his deprivation written plainly on her face, Jane settled the baby in the crook of her arm as she'd learned to do with Callie. Harry was already bigger than his sister, but his mother was a giant compared to Jane, so Justin figured that was to be expected.

When Harry latched onto Jane's swollen, distended nipple and began to suck, Justin caught his breath. It was such a beautiful thing to witness. It humbled him. Jane giggled as the baby slurped happily.

"He takes after his father, wouldn't you say?"

"That's my boy. He knows a good thing when he sees it and appreciates the finer points of a woman's body." Justin caressed Jane's other nipple with one gentle finger, enchanted by the dampness that signified sustenance to his children.

"You're beautiful, Jane. Have I told you that today?"

She smiled, charmed easily by his tender side, he well knew, though he would have been more than uncomfortable with any other woman seeing and feeling his innermost thoughts.

"No, I don't think you have, but it's nice to hear, especially when I'm still feeling so fat and unattractive."

"Unattractive?" He dropped to his knees, facing her. "Now where would you get a silly idea like that? I know you can feel how much we all love you."

She shrugged one shoulder, her breasts rising and falling as Harry sucked like a starving man. Jane's voice was a mere whisper when she answered.

"None of you seem to want me anymore."

"God, Jane! You've got to be kidding, right?" He cupped her cheek. She was reluctant to meet his eyes and embarrassed, judging by the flush on her cheeks. "We've been staying away from you because you just had a baby!" He saw tears in her eyes and leaned in to kiss her cheek. "We don't want to hurt you, Janie."

"Really?" She looked so unsure of herself, so hopeful, he was shocked. This woman had always been able to read the O'Hara men like a book. Why now was she suddenly so unsure of them?

He nodded, kissing her with a bit more passion this time.

"Really. But, Jane, you should know this. Why couldn't you feel it?"

"Her hormones are all out of whack." Mick spoke from the door, leaning against the frame, watching them. Justin had been so caught up in Jane's turmoil and his son, he hadn't heard his brother come to the door. He was glad to have Mick's medical insight into Jane's odd behavior. "Could be the normal upheavals in a woman's emotions and body after giving birth are interfering with her natural empathic ability."

"Aw, Janie, I've been taking for granted you knew how much I—" He found it hard to say how much he wanted her, loved her and missed her sweet body while she watched him with such hopeful eyes.

Mick walked further into the room, cupping Jane's cheek in one calloused hand.

"I think we've all been taking it for granted. I'm sorry, sweetheart. You're the most beautiful woman on the planet to me, in all your seasons."

Damn, Justin swore, he'd never known his studious brother was such a poet, but even he could see the love and desire in Mick's eyes when he looked at Jane. Maybe Caleb hadn't been so wrong in assuming Mick would've married Jane in the old days, given half a chance.

Callie started fussing, so Justin picked her up, soothing her as he watched Mick stare at Jane and his son. Harry's slurping was growing lighter as he became sated, and Callie was getting antsy to have her meal. Justin traded babies with Jane, rubbing Harry's back with gentle motions to bring up any air he might've swallowed.

Mick watched, his eyes deep and mysterious, though Jane didn't seem to mind. Still, Justin worried about the intense look on Mick's normally affable face.

"What's up, Mick?" He tried to sound causal.

"I just came to see if Jane and Harry were getting on okay."

Mick was more or less the family doctor, so Justin was thankful for his concern.

"I'm proud to report, your nephew is most definitely a breast man."

"Takes after his old man, eh?" Mick smirked.

Both men looked at Jane's swollen breasts with appreciation.

"A veritable chip off the old block," Justin agreed.

"Hmm, I can definitely see the appeal," Mick acted as if he were contemplating the question seriously, "but I'd have to say I like Jane's pretty ass best. I love watching her walk and seeing that little jiggle and bounce."

"Great!" she said with blushing laughter. "Did you have to remind me how fat my butt is?"

Mick's eyes narrowed. "I've told you before, Jane, you're not fat. You never were. Sure, you gained weight for the baby. That's only natural. And it looks great on you. You have nothing to be worried about."

"Except that none of you will touch me." She paled as the words left her mouth and her shocked expression made Justin laugh. He'd bet anything that she hadn't wanted to say those words out loud.

"Sounds like frustration talking to me, wouldn't you say, Mick?" Justin finished with Harry and placed him in the crib they'd made for Callie. It was big enough to hold both infants for now, though they might have to make some additional furniture as the babies grew.

Mick nodded conspiratorially at Justin. "I told you her hormones were out of whack. And I'm also pleased to report she should be just about ready to resume all normal activities."

"Are you sure?" Hope lit her pretty eyes.

"Well, it's been enough time, but you'll have to decide for certain what you want, Jane. I'd like to examine you again, but everything was healing nicely last time I looked."

Mick loved everything about Jane's body. He'd loved watching over her through the pregnancy and calming her fears as each new change came over her body. He'd loved rubbing her aching back and marveling over the formation of the baby as it started to move around and kick. And he'd absolutely loved helping her through labor and delivery, receiving that squirming bundle of energy that was his niece into his hands. It had been one of the high points of his life so far, and he knew it could only possibly be exceeded when he caught his own biological son or daughter from Jane's sweet body, in just the same way.

Mick's blood heated as he looked at her hopeful face. Callie finished nursing and Justin took the baby, rubbing her tiny back in the way he'd learned. Mick was glad Justin was dealing with the infant for now. His mind was full of scandalous thoughts about her mother. He held out his hand to Jane.

"Want me to take a look?"

Jane nodded, rising from the rocker with his help. She spared a glance for Justin, who was efficiently dealing with both babies, though his gaze followed them as they left the nursery. Mick led her to his room, wanting to see her reclining on his bed for the first time in quite a few weeks.

He helped her off with her jeans and panties, then assisted her onto the bed, settling between her legs. He had a few things he might need already laid out on his bedside table.

"I see you're prepared, as usual," Jane said with a smile that sent shockwaves through his eager body. "My very own boy scout." She stroked his golden hair as he moved within reach to kiss her gently, with reassurance.

"It's all I can think about, Jane. I want you so much." His whisper was desperate, and he felt her answering quiver. Mick backed off, giving her room in case she wasn't ready just yet. He'd die rather than force her into anything she wasn't ready for. "But I can wait. I enjoy watching you, Jane. I mean that. I can watch you and know at some point, maybe not today or tomorrow, but maybe in a week or so, I'll be able to show you how much I love you and bring you pleasure."

He loosened the hold he usually kept on his emotions and let her feel the pureness of his love. He knew she needed that from him, and he knew he'd done right when a joyous smile broke over her lips and her eyes filled with happiness and love. It nearly killed him when she looked at him that way, and he drank it in like a man dying of thirst.

"I want you so much, Mick. Take a look and tell me if it's okay. I've missed you."

Prodding him toward her feminine core, she spread her legs eagerly. Mick couldn't help but enjoy the sight. He was sure a stupid grin lit his face as he watched her pussy cream, waiting for his examination. Mick took what he needed from the table and forced himself to be as clinical and deliberate about this as he could. He'd never do anything to hurt her and he'd be damn well sure she was healed and ready for them before he gave his medical stamp of approval, such as it was, to letting her have sex again.

For the next few minutes, he noted the improvement in her condition since the last time he'd examined her. She was almost fully back to normal now, though she would never be exactly as she had been before the birth. She was even more beautiful to him now, in an odd way, having given life to such a precious child. She glowed, not just with the pregnancy, but with the power of a life giver.

"If you feel comfortable, I'd say you're ready. You healed up beautifully. You're a natural mother, Jane, and I couldn't be more in love with you." He kissed her again, longer this time, while one of his hands couldn't refrain from brushing lightly over her feminine curls. She began to writhe in the beginnings of pleasure as he pulled back.

"Are you sure you're ready, Jane?"

She nodded, but still he held back. "Caleb should be first," he bit out, knowing she was still Caleb's wife, no matter the concessions they'd made to the new world they lived in.

Jane shook her head. "He and I discussed this. Mick, you need me. We both want to give this to you. I want you to be the first since Callie came. The others can catch up the next time." She laughed with a shrug. "If such things matter. I can't believe how you men like to keep score! Caleb knew you'd be this way." She giggled and pulled him down for a deep kiss.

For his part, Mick was floored they'd discussed this. But he should have known. Caleb knew him better than anyone on Earth, including Jane, and that was saying something. Enough years separated them that Caleb had sometimes taken on an almost paternal role with him, rather than that of an older brother, and Mick loved him for it, though it could be annoying at times. This wasn't one of those times, however. This was one of the times when Mick could have kissed him for his generosity.

"If you're sure, then." Mick lost himself in her kiss, bringing his body completely over hers, reveling in the feel of her beneath him once again. He felt as if she belonged there, under him, for the rest of their lives. He removed the rest of her clothes and hastily did away with his own.

"It may be fast, this first time," he said near her ear, apologetically. "I want you so bad, Jane."

She ran her hands down his muscled back, comforting him.

"I feel how you need me. You have no idea what that does for me, Mick. Take what I can give you. Let me do this for you."

He moved between her legs, holding her gaze.

"My little Earth Mother. Always so giving, so understanding. I love you more than life, Jane." His whispered words were punctuated by kisses that grew increasingly heated as he positioned himself and pushed inside.

Chapter Thirteen

Mick came minutes later with a hoarse shout of completion as Justin watched, scandalized from the doorway. The little fucker had gotten off and left Jane hanging.

"You little bastard!"

Justin swept into the room and stopped near the bed. Reaching down, he lifted Mick's head from Jane's neck by the hair. Mick yelped and jumped off her, spinning to face the threat Justin presented. But Justin was on the attack.

"How dare you treat her that way?"

Jane sat up too, watching them with unfulfilled desire and worry mixed in her wide eyes.

"Justin, I told him it was okay."

Justin's gaze shot to her, incredulous.

"Okay?" He pushed Mick away and dropped to his knees beside the bed, cupping Jane's cheek. "Janie, it's never okay to be selfish. Especially with you." He turned cold eyes on his younger brother who sat dejected, confused and hurt on the other side of the bed. "We taught him better than that."

"I was going to make it up to her, if you hadn't interrupted."

"Damn right you'll make it up to her," he ground out.

"What's going on here? I can hear Justin growling from out in the kitchen." Caleb appeared in the doorway and Jane groaned. Caleb's anger was palpable. "Dammit! Did either of you shitheads hurt her?" Caleb rushed over to take her hand as Justin stood, his worry and anger showing clearly in the tight set of his jaw.

"I'm not hurt. Just mortified," she said weakly, trying to cover herself with the bedspread. But Mick was sitting on a part of it and she couldn't get more than a corner free until Caleb barked at Mick and pulled, wrapping her up tightly in his strong arms. He then turned to his brothers.

"I expect some answers from both of you," he said in that low, dangerous voice they'd all learned to be wary of as teenagers.

"Don't look at me," Justin said loudly. "I didn't jump her bones and leave her wanting."

Caleb's angry gaze swept to Mick, who was struggling to put on his jeans.

"Did you do that, Mick? To our Janie? Dammit, boy, I expected better of you."

"Now just wait a minute." Jane interrupted the brewing battle, trying to stop the recriminations all around. "I wanted him to do it. I told him to let go. I knew what I was doing."

"Damn, sweetheart, don't you think we know you would let us do whatever we wanted with you, regardless of your own feelings?" Caleb tried to soothe her. "You're too empathically attuned to us, and we have a responsibility to take care of you as you take care of us. Jerkoff there knows that. We all discussed it. He knows better than to let you make such sacrifices for our pleasure."

"But it wasn't a sacrifice!" She was more than frustrated now. "I wanted to feel what he felt at that moment. I never feel everything he feels, Caleb, except when he lets go."

Justin actually grinned for the first time since entering the room.

"So, what you're saying is that in your own empathic way...you wanted to watch?"

"Jeez!" Mick exclaimed from across the bed, and Jane's smile told them she knew Mick liked the idea.

Caleb seemed stymied for a moment while he thought through the turn of events.

"That leaves us with a few things to resolve," he said finally, in his methodical way. "First, Mick, you've got to stop shutting Jane out. She needs the emotional connection to all three of us—especially during sex—and if you cut her off, she's liable to do something like this, just to satisfy her empathic need." Mick looked properly shocked and chagrined, but Caleb wasn't done as he turned Jane in his arms, comforter and all. He shook a finger in her face, but not threateningly. "No more of this self-sacrificing bullshit from you. You tell him what you need and when you need it. Hell, Jane, I taught you that the first week we were married. All of us need honesty if we're going to keep this relationship working, agreed?"

Jane nodded soberly. "Agreed."

"And now, finally," Caleb sighed dramatically, "someone here needs to come." All eyes focused on Jane, now blushing fiercely under the comforter. "I take it Dr. Sensitivity over there has cleared you? You're healed enough?"

Jane nodded, and Caleb and Justin's eyes turned to Mick.

"She won't be fertile again for a bit, but we should start thinking about precautions until she wants to get pregnant again. Otherwise, she's good to go."

"Well then." Caleb grinned, turning Jane in his arms until he plopped her down in the middle of the bed once more. He unwrapped the comforter like she was a Christmas present, letting them all savor the sight of her creamy skin as it was unveiled. When she was bare, Caleb looked at Mick.

"You get to sit and watch how it's supposed to be done, bro." He then turned to look at Justin, a few steps to his right. "Shall we show him?"

Justin grinned, already palming the hard-on in his pants. It had been too long since he'd been inside Jane's sweet body. Too long since he'd been able to show her his love and appreciation for all her sacrifices for the O'Hara brothers. Jane was the center of it all. Without Jane there would be no reason to continue, but with her, the possibilities for the future were endless.

Caleb moved around to the other side of the bed, making Mick scoot to the foot of the wide mattress as he knelt at Jane's side and removed his clothes, kissing her. She was still excited, Justin could see, from her squirming. He stripped as he watched Caleb bringing her back to that receptive place where Mick had left her wanting. He shot a glance at Mick, letting him know with a short mental push that while they were disappointed in him, they still loved him and expected him to participate in Jane's pleasure as soon as she'd come at least once.

The agenda for the evening suddenly changed to pleasure. Jane's pleasure. And the brothers' pleasure as well, but she came first for all of them. She had to. Without her, there was no O'Hara family, just a small collection of lonely men. And now the babies. Jane had done that. She had brought new life both figuratively and literally to the O'Hara clan. She'd given so much of herself to them, it was only fair they spend the rest of their lives giving back to her. Starting here and now.

Justin stepped closer to the bed, naked now and straining to be near the woman he loved more than life. He knew his brothers loved her just as much, needed her just as much, and that was the only reason he was able to share in this odd arrangement. He knew she deserved all the love they had inside them and more, and he was more than willing to show her and let her feel every last emotion hidden deep in his soul if that would nurture her.

Jane's empathy was so deeply a part of her, it wasn't surprising she'd forgone her own pleasure in order to feel Mick's. That wasn't something Justin was happy thinking about. Jane needed to be protected. She always had. And the O'Hara men had the joyful duty of doing so. If that meant protecting her from herself or from them, then so be it.

He touched her hand as Caleb moved to kiss her neck, whispering of his own love for his young wife near her ear. Her gaze shot to Justin as he purposely sent her the emotions clogging his heart, making it hard to breathe. He would expose his last weakness to her if it would bring her pleasure. He could see from the dilation of her eyes how deeply she needed the connection. She shuddered as he sat on the side of the bed, bringing her hand to his thigh, smoothing gently and letting her feel everything that was in him in that moment. The next move was up to her and he wasn't disappointed when she turned her hand and wrapped it around his cock.

Justin sucked in a breath and let her know how deeply her touch affected him.

Caleb turned to Mick, who watched them all with growing arousal.

"Don't just sit there," he hiked his chin toward the adjoining bathroom, "make yourself useful. Jane needs our care now."

Mick saw Caleb's gaze go from the rather obvious trail of his semen leaking out from between Jane's plump thighs to his face and Mick felt even worse. Bad enough he'd let Jane's pleasure override his common sense, but now that his brothers knew what he'd allowed to happen, they'd never let him live it down. He felt like crap, but he also felt like a king that Jane would care so much—to want to know him so deeply—she would sacrifice her own pleasure in order to feel his.

He could only love her more for it—if that were even possible—but had problems letting her feel it. He always had. Ever since he'd come home from school to watch her marry Caleb. In those years, he'd learned to hide his emotions from her, for her own protection. He hadn't wanted to hurt Caleb or Jane with his deep, almost uncontrollable love for her. He couldn't love her just as a sister, not when he'd wanted her as a man since he was old enough to know what that kind of love was.

True, he'd never acted on it aside from one lingering kiss before he'd left for school, but he hadn't been in a position to offer her anything back then. Now, however, he would offer his very soul to keep her safe and protected within the shelter of their family. If that meant sharing her love with his brothers, well, he'd become used to it. Truthfully, seeing her with them turned him on, though he'd never had the wild sex life either of his older brothers had before the cataclysm. Still, he was learning the decadent pleasures of sharing, and by all indications, Jane loved it. Whatever made her happy, made him doubly so.

The thoughts rushed through his mind as he prepared a warm washcloth in the adjoining bathroom. He went back to find Justin licking one of her nipples as Caleb teased the other.

Her legs squirmed in a delicious way and Mick stopped to admire the scene for a moment, his cock getting even harder as he heard her moan of pleasure. Caleb looked at him and he moved again, placing himself between her thighs, using gentle touches to part her legs.

With tender strokes, he cleaned her, inflaming her at the same time. He played with her tight nubbin, squeezing gently, inserting his fingers and spreading the lubrication of her warm and willing body. He threw the washcloth aside, his mind on a new goal. He had to taste her. He wanted to lick her cream and bring her pleasure.

Caleb eased away from her and met Mick's eyes.

"Let her feel what you feel, Mick. She needs it." Caleb sat at her side, stroking her, quieter now as he watched over the loving of their woman.

Mick tried hard to let go of the control that had become so second nature to him, cracking open the wall around his emotions the little he could. Justin moved away as Caleb reached across Jane's body and touched his shoulder, and then Mick was looking into Jane's pretty eyes.

Slowly, he eased down, his tongue reaching out for her, his eyes never leaving hers. He knew his brothers watched. He could see their hands stroking her and holding her hands. He could hear their thoughts, though they didn't realize just how powerful his telepathy had grown over the years. Justin was as hot as Mick had ever seen him, watching him go down on Jane. But then, Justin was the most sexually adventurous of the three brothers. Mick could learn a lot from eavesdropping on Justin's memories, never mind his fantasies!

Caleb, as usual, put everyone's needs before his own. He had that in common with Jane. She cared only that all three of her men were as happy as she could make them. She wanted peace in their souls and would sacrifice her own, for them, any day of the week. Mick watched her eyes, knowing her chaotic thoughts, filled with a desperate yearning, not only to achieve fulfillment herself, but to bring it to all three of her chosen mates.

Mick frightened himself with his own desperate need as he nuzzled her, swirling his tongue through her slippery folds. He didn't want to scare her with the power of his emotions, but knew he had to give her something. He let her feel the love first, in small doses, watching her eyes go soft with pleasure as he released his emotions in time with the tugging of his lips on her distended clit. This was a pleasure only he could bring her.

The others could pleasure her physically, bombard her emotionally, but he could control both sides, tease her sensitive empathic senses with small doses of revelation. She was nearing her peak as he orchestrated her release. He sent out tendrils of thought to his brothers, reassuring them, asking their compliance with his wishes, though they'd never taken orders from him before in such a situation.

But all that was going to change, here and now. Mick needed to control this, and he knew he could make it more than good for Jane, and for his brothers. He watched as they returned to her breasts, and then he closed his eyes, concentrating completely on Jane's pleasure. It was the one thing in the world for which he would release the tight leash on his emotions. He flooded her with his love and desire as he thrust his tongue into her, stroking in time with the pulses of emotion he sent. He reveled in her scream of fulfillment as she thrashed so hard in his arms he had to restrain her legs in order to ride out this first orgasm. He stroked her with his tongue, not letting her come all the way down, but building toward another, quicker, even more powerful crescendo.

Jane cried out in ecstasy once more as the pulses of her body told Mick how high she'd gone this time. Once more he rode her through the storm, raising her up again, but this time, he held her there at the peak, knowing his brothers' thoughts as well as he knew his own. Not sparing a glance, Mick spoke directly to Caleb's mind, telling him what Jane needed, seeking his cooperation and agreement. His thoughts shifted to Justin, whose own telepathy was strong enough to pick up on a lot of what Mick was doing and got his instant agreement, tinged with admiration.

Mick moved away, making room for Caleb as the two men switched places. Caleb mounted his wife quickly, not giving her any reprieve from the straining pleasure, just as Mick had asked. He was proud his brothers trusted him enough to plan this pleasure for them all and knew from their unguarded thoughts they understood, to varying degrees, how he needed to do this to redeem his earlier lapse.

Mick was sharing a part of himself and his abilities with them they'd never seen before, and though he valued his privacy, he knew this was right. If he couldn't share with his family, then he was in an even sadder place than he'd thought. He watched as Caleb joined easily with Jane, setting a slow pace at first, careful of her healing body.

"Harder!" Jane demanded, desperation clear in her strangled cries. "Oh, Caleb, I need you!"

Mick smiled, watching her. He bent and silenced her with a deep and lingering kiss, letting her feel the love and pride he felt at that moment. She came again, with battering intensity as Caleb fucked her. Mick moved aside, kissing her neck as he directed Justin with a quick burst of thought. Justin leaned in and kissed her as deeply, as profoundly, letting his emotions wash over her in a constant stream. Justin couldn't control them like Mick could. But Mick used every shred of his control now, letting the heat of his emotions grow as he watched Jane.

Mick caught Justin's eye as he moved closer to her mouth. Jane practically swallowed him whole, she was so eager. She tongued him as his eyes rolled back in pleasure. Mick watched as she fisted the base of Justin's cock, the other hand surprising him as she reached out for Mick.

It looked like Caleb was nearing his peak, so Mick let loose with pulses of his own emotional need, tickling her empathic senses to new heights. Her body spasmed and her gaze shot to his. He stroked her hair as Justin pulled out of her mouth. She let Justin go with one last, long lick, and held Mick's gaze as she came hard around Caleb, spurring him on to his own release.

Mick kissed her, knowing Caleb was enjoying his moment inside her, pulsing out his release in her depths. Mick basked in their glow for a moment, pulling back to regard Jane as Justin moved to the foot of the bed.

"You know how much I love you?" Mick asked in a low voice. Jane nodded, her eyes tearing with joy. "You know I didn't mean to hurt you, right?" Again she nodded. "And you know how sorry I am, right?"

"I know it now," she whispered. "Your emotions are teasing my senses, Mick. You're still holding them back somehow—" She seemed confused as to how he'd managed it.

"All for your pleasure, darling. You know that now, right?"

She bit her lower lip and nodded again.

Caleb sat next to Jane's hip, having recovered enough to remove himself from between her thighs. "You've been holding out on all of us, Mick. When did your telepathy kick into high gear?"

Mick shrugged and he knew it didn't take an empath to see he was uncomfortable. Jane reached up to stroke his stubbled cheek.

"It doesn't matter," she reassured him when Caleb would have pressed for an answer. "What matters is that you're sharing now. Don't think I don't appreciate it. And don't think I don't love it." Her smile turned devilish as she let them all know how she enjoyed the pleasure he was able to administer both to her body and to her empathic senses.

"You ready for another round?" Mick asked with a challenging tilt of his chin. "I have a bit more to make up for with you, I think."

"You can make up to me all you want." She smiled and rose up just enough to twine her arms around his neck and bring him back down with her.

Mick nodded at Justin before kissing her deeply. He knew Justin would move between her legs and he also knew, as the family doctor, that his brother was in for a little surprise when he did. He couldn't wait to hear his reaction, and it wasn't long in coming.

"Oh, God, baby! You've never taken all of me before. Shit!" Justin was almost incoherent as he settled into her well-lubricated pussy. She fit him like she was made just for him.

Mick smiled, his eyes holding secrets. "Her body has changed a bit since the baby."

"I didn't think it could get any better, but holy shit!" He swore as he stilled to take a moment and just feel. "Jane, you're so perfect. I've never been this deep inside you."

Her eyes teared again, feeling his genuine happiness and awe, he knew. It was a special moment.

"Dammit, Mick." He looked up into his brother's dancing eyes. "You knew!"

Mick grinned at both of them, stroking Jane's swollen breasts with obvious appreciation.

"I admit I had some idea. Women's bodies change after giving birth, Jus. And after all this time, I knew what you enjoyed about her. I guessed the rest. She'll be able to take all of you now and still give that extra ridge that gets you off. I figured you'd be happy."

"Shit!" Justin's eyes clenched against the waves of pleasure. Not only was she taking him fully for the first time, but the thought of what was to come tantalized. He also realized in a stark moment of clarity that Mick knew things Justin had never spoken out loud.

"You little fucker," Justin cursed his brother good-naturedly. "After we finish here, we're going to have a little talk about how your telepathy has grown."

Mick laughed and bent to Jane's ear, whispering loudly so they all heard. "Did you know he really gets off when the tip of his cock hits your cervix? That's why he likes to go so deep and hard."

"Jeez!" Justin shouted, his cock pulsing as Mick painted the picture and his body began to slam into her, wanting that friction as she tightened around him in returning passion.

Jane cried out as Justin sought deep within her, finding the friction he needed, letting them all know how perfect she was.

"Shit, baby! It's never felt this good before!"

Justin came in a rush as Jane squirmed her pleasure beneath him, crying out at the depth of his penetration and clearly loving every minute of it. Justin was breathless as he collapsed on her, his seed spurting within her well-loved body.

He kissed her neck, her cheeks, her lips, murmuring words of his love and appreciation of her beautiful body as they both came down from a very high peak. Mick was there, at the head of the bed, grinning at them as Justin came back to himself.

"Dammit, Mick. I thought she was the one who knew all my secrets, but it's been you all along. How the fuck did you know about what I like?"

Mick shrugged. "After watching you with Jane so many times? It's kind of hard not to hear your thoughts at such moments—monosyllabic as they often are." Mick chuckled as his brothers stared.

Jane sat up as Justin left her body and sat on the edge of the bed.

"Then tell me, Mick, what do I like about your body?" Her voice was low, her eyes teasing.

"You like how the curve of my cock rubs your G-spot on every stroke," he answered, surprising everyone in the room.

"My very own G-Man," she agreed, trailing her fingers over his hard cock, rubbing the curve and just under the knobby head as he started to breathe hard. "I need you inside me. Now."

"No place I'd rather be." Mick groaned and took his place between her thighs. She was already so primed, Mick didn't need to wait for anything. He slid home and felt better than he had in weeks. He loved this special woman with all his heart and counted himself lucky to be a part of her life and her love. It still hurt to think about the way things should have been, but he tried hard to focus on what was, not what could have been. If only that task were as easy as it sounded...

Chapter Fourteen

Jane was feeding the babies the next day when Mick and Justin walked into the nursery.

"I've been working on a way to store milk so Jane doesn't have to get up in the middle of the night anymore."

"You can do that?" Jane's gaze shot to his.

"Shouldn't be a problem. We just have to figure the best way to get the milk from you and into the bottle."

"She's not a cow, shithead." Justin sounded scandalized, but couldn't take his eyes off Jane's swollen breasts.

"I know that, stupid, but if we could take some of her milk and put it in the fridge, she'd get a lot more sleep. One of us could get up to feed them. Plus," his eyes danced with deviltry, "I'd love to give it a try. Playing with Jane's breasts is so much more interesting now, don't you think?"

Justin's eyes grew darker and more passionate. He'd always loved her breasts. They held an even greater allure now. He loved watching her breastfeed his children. It was special with Callie, but even more so with the boy. Harry was aware in ways Callie was only just learning. He knew Jane wasn't his mother, but she said she sensed Harry loved her as part of his extended family, as his father's mate. And he loved her for nourishing him and loving him as his own mother couldn't.

It was weird, she'd said, that the baby was so aware of himself and his position in the family, but it presented a rare opportunity to teach and nurture him while they had the chance. Because after the six months his alien mother had allotted, they weren't sure if they'd ever see him again.

Justin watched Harry gurgle and slurp at Jane's breast and grinned. "I think our boy agrees with you, Mick."

"I know he likes my breasts better than his mother's, but I think that's just because I have what he needs."

"Janie," Justin's voice caught her attention, "you have what all the O'Hara men need." His voice dropped low. "You're our salvation." Justin picked up his sated son and rubbed his back with care. "You hear me, son? You should understand this. Jane is your mother. She's your human mother. Mara may have given birth to you, and you should respect her for that gift of life, but Jane is the mother of your heart." He turned his eyes to his woman. "Isn't that true, sweetheart?"

Jane's eyes filled with tears at the feelings coming at her from the males—especially the baby.

"It's true. I love him because he's part of you, but also because he's mine now too. He nurses at my breast and I couldn't love him more if I'd carried him in my womb. Callie loves him too," she said, "and he loves her, his sister, and will protect her all the days of his life."

"You feel all this from them?" Mick asked quietly, somewhat in awe.

Jane nodded. "More from Harry than Callie, but her love for him is undeniable. She wants to be near him every waking moment. As he does with her. But his feelings are more protective, more mature somehow, as if he's aware that she'll need his protection and love in the future, as he needs her love and acceptance."

"Wow." Mick shook his head. "I never dreamed babies had so much awareness."

"It grows a little each day. It's amazing to feel." Jane finished feeding Callie and moved her to her shoulder as Justin settled Harry down for a nap. He then took Callie from her arms and rubbed circles on the baby girl's back before putting her in the crib with her brother.

Mick was beside Jane now, massaging her breasts. "Nipples hurt?" he asked gently, watching the reddened tips as she nodded. "We were too rough last night. We're not used to sharing with hungry babies."

"I'm sorry, baby." Justin swore and dropped to his knees in front of her. He cupped one nipple in his palm as if to ease it, intrigued when he felt the wetness of her milk leaking onto his skin.

"It's okay, I'm just a little sore."

"In the old days," Mick confirmed, an amused light in his own eyes as he palmed her breast, "we would have bought you a breast pump. I wish I'd thought to get one when I was laying in supplies. But I can probably rig something. If we can store some milk in the fridge, you won't have to do all the feedings in person, as it were. We can take turns in the middle of the night, for example, and let you get some uninterrupted sleep once in a while."

"Sleep sounds heavenly."

"Then it's agreed," Mick said quickly, as if that's all he'd been waiting for. "I've got the equipment we'll need ready to go. We'll try this as soon as possible. Get them used to it a little at a time so you can get more rest."

"What sort of equipment?" Jane wanted to know, concern on her pretty face.

"Sterile bottles, rubber nipples, that sort of thing. I'll set it all up so we're ready to go when you are, okay, Janie?"

She looked at the sleeping babies with sad eyes. "I'll miss feeding them."

Justin scooped her into his arms and sat them both in the rocker. He cupped her bare breasts gently, soothingly, as he set the rocker in motion. His protectiveness was in full swing and he knew she felt the cherishing love that flowed from his heart to hers.

"It won't be every feeding, just the late night ones. You need your sleep, sweetheart. And we need this too. We need to bond with our children and care for you, and them. Let us do this for you."

She laid her head back on his shoulder, sighing as she gave in.

"Okay." She relaxed against him. She was so tired, she was practically asleep in his arms as he carried her from the nursery into his room, laying her in the middle of his bed. Mick had followed behind with her shirt, placing it on the chair by Justin's desk.

"She's beat," Mick whispered as the two brothers watched her sleep.

"Well, it's not as if we gave her a chance to rest last night." Justin's smile was full of male satisfaction and tinged with guilt.

"No, we didn't, did we?" Mick wore a similar expression.

"And it was mostly your doing, Mick." He turned to pin Mick with a curious look. "Now tell me, when did your telepathic abilities evolve to the point that you could read my mind when I'm fucking my woman?"

Mick shrugged as if it didn't matter, but Justin could see it did matter, a great deal.

"Not just then, if you want the truth. I can read you, Caleb and Jane pretty much at will."

"Holy shit," Justin breathed. "Dammit, Mick! You know every thought in my head?"

Mick smiled. "Not every thought, but quite a few of them."

"Why didn't you ever tell us about this?" Justin's tone was slightly accusing as he faced his brother.

"Why didn't you tell us you'd joined the Army?" Mick countered, shocking Justin.

"Damn." Justin shook his head in wonder. "I guess we all have our secrets, hmm?"

Slowly, Mick nodded. "Some more than others."

"And what does that mean?" Justin rounded on him as he ushered him toward the door so they didn't disturb Jane's sleep.

"I know you're kinkier than the rest of us, Jus. I've seen some of your memories of other women and some of your fantasies of what you want to do to Jane."

Justin rubbed a hand over his face. "Jane isn't to know, Mick, you understand me?"

"Why?"

"I don't want to hurt her. You should know that."

"Then what if I told you that she's been thinking similar thoughts for more than a while now?"

Justin's heart nearly exploded. "What kind of thoughts?"

"Thoughts of how it would feel if one of us took her in the ass."

"Fuck!" Justin slammed one palm against the wall, bracing himself. His knees went weak with the idea. "She wants that?"

"She's curious. I think she's more than willing to try it. She's been searching her limited knowledge for some way to take all three of us at once."

"Fuck." Justin cursed again, hardening at the thought.

"You've done ménages before, Justin. You need to lead the way in this."

₨₧₨₧

That thought heavy in his mind, Justin tried to stay away from Jane for the next few days, but she noticed and sought him out a few nights later, waiting for him in his room. She didn't ask questions she knew he wouldn't answer, but instead, just went to him, kissed him and dragged him down to his wide bed.

They made love gently, Justin's thoughts invariably turning to what Mick had said, but he shied away from the idea Jane might want to explore the rougher side of sex with him. Still, he couldn't help but think about it, and in the afterglow of their passion, he kept her close, lying over him like a blanket, his sated cock still resting within her tight channel.

"You're very conflicted, Justin." Jane propped her head up on one fist to look into his eyes.

He knew she could feel his every emotion and for a moment he wished he'd mastered the art of hiding at least some of his feelings from her, as Mick had done. But he knew it was impossible. He wanted to give Jane everything, including the darker side of his personality, which he'd kept successfully separate from his family up to this point. Mick's words made him think though, and once started, the thoughts would not cease.

Justin stroked her back, savoring her soft skin as he fought with his own desires. The last thing he wanted to do was scare her or hurt her in any way, and he was truly afraid of doing both if he ever unleashed the dark need within him on her unsuspecting and accepting body.

"Mick said some things," he said hesitantly.

She smiled, encouraging him. "What things?"

"Things that are better left alone." His curt tone should have stopped her, but she wasn't to be deterred.

"Nice try, but you're not getting off that easy. What did Mick say that has you so upset?"

Justin sighed, seeing no way to protect her from this.

"He said you were thinking...about this." Instead of putting it into words, he dipped one finger between her cheeks, settling warmly against the tight, hidden bud and pressing gently. Her eyes widened and he stifled a groan. He thought he saw interest flare behind the shock in her eyes and his cock twitched within her tight channel, intrigued at the thought.

"Have you...um... Have you done that before?" she asked in a small voice, her curiosity growing along with his dick.

Justin growled and nodded. "Yeah, I've done it more than a few times."

"You enjoy it?"

He nodded again, holding her eyes. "I like it, Jane. And the women I did it with enjoyed it too." He pushed his finger inside her to the first knuckle, enjoying her gasp. "Mick said you'd been thinking about it, but we don't have to if you don't want it.

I don't have to have this, sweetheart. I would never want you to do anything you were uncomfortable with."

"I don't know if I can, but I'd like to try." She squirmed on him. Her gaze held both concern and eagerness.

His cock hardened to an almost painful level with her words and he pushed his finger deeper, watching her reaction.

"God, baby!" He tried to steady himself, but was fast losing control. "We can try it, but we'll have to prepare you first so you're ready for it. Do you want to?"

She nodded, moving on him, the fire in her eyes leaping as he pulsed his finger inside her.

"Yeah, I want to, Jus. I want to do anything you want."

He slowed then, removing his finger, bringing her complete attention to his serious eyes.

"I don't want you doing this just for me, sweetheart. It has to be for you too."

"It's for all of us. I want to try it at least. I remember in the old days, my girlfriends talking about...um...triple penetration. I was intrigued back then, but I didn't really get how it could work. I think after spending the past months with you three, I'm beginning to understand it better, but I haven't done it yet, have I?"

His heart nearly pumped out of his chest at her shyly voiced words, but he managed to control himself, though his cock pumped into her with increasing need.

"No, not quite yet, sweetheart. And maybe not ever, if you decide you don't like using the backdoor." Jeez! Could he get any harder? He could feel her excitement as her inner muscles contracted around him. "But we can explore anything you like. I'll do anything for you. And anything to you."

"You're the brother with the reputation for being kinky, but in the past months you've never really shown me any kink."

"Janie, you were pregnant most of that time. I wasn't about to—"

"Ssh." She placed a finger over his lips. "I know. But, Jus, I'm not pregnant anymore." Her breath caught when he opened his lips and sucked her finger deep inside his mouth. He urged her to move as he released her finger with a little pop.

"Ride me, honey." He gasped and pushed her into a sitting position, enjoying the sight of her swollen breasts bouncing over him. He massaged her nipples with gentle touches that made them harden into long, tight buds. She looked at him with love as she moved, picking up his urgency and riding him with an eagerness that never ceased to amaze him.

He cupped her ass cheek with one hand, squeezing in a way he already knew she liked. But then he did something he'd never done with her before. He slapped her ass, making her jump. He watched her eyes widen, feeling the grip of her body around him as she creamed with pleasure. Just to be certain, he slapped her again, watching her startled reaction to the slight, stinging pain as her pace increased again.

Two more swats to her ass and she came in a hard rush, gasping for air as she draped over him. Justin wasted no time, rolling her under and spreading her wide with his knees to claim her pussy with hard, deep thrusts. He never thought he'd be able to really let go and release his inner Dom, but she surprised him yet again, taking his domination with an inner grace that astounded him.

ഇ രു ക്ഷ

After they'd rested a bit, Justin brought up the subject again. He had some serious questions to ask his daring little lover before he could take her to this next level—if he took her there at all. He also had to get his brothers' consent and agreement. He didn't want any one of them thinking he might somehow hurt or humiliate Jane.

Justin stroked her hair as she rested sleepily next to him in the big bed. He knew she was well aware of his emotions and this time, like so often before, it helped to know she understood where he was coming from.

"Did you like it when I swatted your pretty ass?" His breath whispered across her sensitive skin raising gooseflesh. He felt her shiver and smiled.

"I've never done that before, Justin, but it was...exciting. I don't quite understand it."

"You know I'd never hurt you." He waited for her nod. "But there's something about seeing the outline of my hand on your pink butt that gets me hot. Maybe it has something to do with my need to possess you in every way, or maybe it's a control thing. Hell," he ran one hand through his hair in frustration, "I don't know where it comes from, but it helps satisfy my need to dominate." He sat on the edge of the bed, resting his elbows on his knees. "I've known for a long time that I enjoy being sexually dominant. It's not an all the time thing with me, but I definitely enjoyed it when I found a partner who was willing to submit to me."

Jane wrapped herself in the sheet to keep warm. "Do you want me to call you Master?"

He jerked his head around, shocked by her words, but she was laughing, the light in her eyes bedeviling him. He hauled her into his arms and hugged her close, tickling her through the sheet.

"Do you want to be my love slave?"

She giggled and nodded her head as she gazed up at him. "Yes, Master."

He chuckled, letting her go. "All you need is a blonde ponytail and a little harem outfit and you'd be a perfect genie."

She folded her arms like the character on that long ago television show and they both laughed. But then he pulled her back into his embrace, his chest to her back as he wrapped his arms around her, resting his chin on top of her head.

"Maybe we can try the harem girl fantasy sometime, but as for the dominant thing, Janie, I really need to know if you're all right with it. And there's more to it, you know."

"You mean...uh...coming from behind, right? That's part of your domination thing?" He nodded against her head and he knew she felt every bit of the uncertainty rolling through his core. "I already told you I'd like to try it, Justin. I know you'll be careful with me and as long as it doesn't hurt me, I think Mick and Caleb wouldn't mind either."

"Mind?" Justin had to chuckle. "Honey, going in the backdoor is something most dominant men think about, but seldom find a partner adventurous enough to try. It requires your total submission and that's not something most women are willing to give to just anyone."

She turned in his arms. "Well, I wouldn't submit to just anyone, as you well know. I don't know if I can take it—physically, I mean—but I'm willing to try. Mentally, I'm more than willing to try just about anything you and your brothers want. I trust you."

That simple statement meant more to him than anything anyone had ever said to him in his entire life. This one woman's trust meant everything. Her love was the world.

He bent to kiss her cheek, awed by her all over again.

"I don't deserve you, Jane, but I love you with all my heart."

She turned and kissed his lips sweetly, then smiled up into his dark eyes.

"Do you want to let your brothers in on this before or after we give it a try?"

"I think before, sweetheart, if you're agreeable. I'd like to have them with us to make certain you're doing okay. Plus, I don't want them beating me up after the fact for pushing you too far." He wasn't really worried about his brothers pounding on him, but he knew they'd have a thing or two to say if he didn't clue them in beforehand and were reassured of Jane's acceptance.

"So, when? Tomorrow?"

Justin thought about the logistics. He'd have to get the men together first to talk, then bring Jane in so she could assure them—particularly Caleb—she was agreeable.

"Tomorrow afternoon, if you think you're ready."

Justin's plan worked like a charm. He talked with Mick and Caleb that morning and Mick helped him convince Caleb to at least talk to Jane about it. Mick had been reading all their minds and knew better than anyone that all three men had been thinking about being in Jane's ass while one of the others was in her pussy. The idea she'd agree to try it was difficult for Caleb to take at first, but Justin reminded him how adventurous Jane was. Mick heard all their thoughts and realized Justin planned to put them all to the test that very afternoon.

Mick excused himself and made a quick detour to his office to gather some items he thought they might need, including a lubricant he'd made from native plants. They'd used it before, but he'd had this situation in mind when he cooked it up. He'd seen this coming, even if he wasn't the clairvoyant in the family.

He entered the house to find the other two men already hard at work undressing Jane as Caleb kissed her hungrily and Justin worked on her lower half. Mick had followed the sounds coming from the largest bedroom and found the door open.

"What took you so long?" Justin grinned at him, distracted only momentarily from his task of uncovering Jane's luscious bottom.

Mick held up the squeeze bottle he'd procured and smiled back.

"Just laying in some supplies."

Justin nodded in approval as he saw what Mick had in his hands. They finished undressing Jane and lay her on the bed. Caleb kissed her, keeping her off balance while Justin spread her pretty legs far apart and settled between them.

Mick just watched for a moment, enjoying the view, but when his cock could take no more, he placed the bottle of lube within easy reach on the nightstand and dropped to Jane's side. He played with her luscious breasts while his brothers worked on the rest of her.

The three men spent a long time kissing and caressing her, but they'd agreed beforehand to let Justin be their guide in this new kind of love play. After Justin brought her to a first, hard peak with his mouth, they eased back a bit. Justin directed Mick with a nod and the youngest brother wasted no time laying down and rolling Jane to her side, sliding almost simultaneously between her luscious thighs. Mick made love to her with a gently rocking motion while Justin worked on her from behind. He grabbed the tube of lubricant and applied it liberally.

Mick felt the intrusion of Justin's finger through the thin membrane separating the space he occupied in her pussy and the rear entrance Justin was preparing. He felt Jane jump and sought her eyes first before looking over her shoulder to meet Justin's gaze. Justin appeared to know damned good and well Mick could feel every move against his cock and the devilish light in Justin's eyes only confirmed his suspicions. Justin deepened the caress, adding another finger when Jane was ready, and then another, stroking them both higher.

"Dammit, this isn't funny." Despite his words, Mick chuckled as Justin slid in again, making both Jane and Mick shiver.

"You look pretty funny from where I'm sitting," Justin smirked back. "If you could see the look on your face! You didn't bargain on what this would feel like, did you? Now just imagine how good it would feel if we both had our dicks inside her at the same time."

"Holy shit!" Mick gasped as the image made Jane clench around him. He moved fast and hard in her as she cried out in ecstasy, finding his own completion only a moment later. He pulled out and just lay there, breathing hard, trying to get his feet back under him.

Caleb sat silent at the head of the bed, watching the proceedings carefully. He hadn't said much yet, but Justin kept an eye on him, making sure he was okay with what he'd orchestrated so far. Caleb, he saw, was watching Jane, an indescribable look in his eyes that Justin wasn't quite sure how to decipher.

But he figured if Caleb had any objections, they'd come out when he got to the next step in this seduction. Jane was almost ready. She'd taken his fingers with good grace and seemed to enjoy it. She was stretched and ready. Now he'd let her take him at her pace.

"Are you still with me, Janie?" Justin leaned over her. She was still on her side, facing Mick, stroking his chest as he caught his breath. She turned dreamy eyes to Justin as he caressed the pretty, pink cheeks of her ass, dipping two fingers inside the opening he'd prepared.

"I'm with you, Justin. That feels so good." She squealed when he added more lubricant and pressed deeper. "Odd, but good."

"Want to try more?"

"Mmm-hmm. I want to try it all."

Caleb growled but otherwise kept his vigil at the head of the bed, observing. From that small, unintentional sound Justin knew his older brother was excited by what he'd witnessed. His role as protector made him sit back rather than participate this first time, though. He would never let anyone or anything push Jane too far.

Justin wasn't insulted. Hell, if the roles were reversed, he'd do the same. He knew Mick would too. All three of them shared the need to keep Jane safe from all harm—even from themselves.

Justin turned her onto her stomach, lifting her hips so she could rest on her elbows. She loved the way all three of her men tossed her around as if she weighed nothing at all. She loved how they mastered her and put her needs above their own. She loved the care they gave her and she just plain loved them.

Presenting her bottom to Justin, she looked upward to meet Caleb's eyes. She could tell he was horny as hell watching this little experiment unfold and it touched her that he was holding back to make sure she was okay. With shimmying moves, she moved up the bed while Justin and Mick placed a pillow under her hips. She felt more of the lubricant being squeezed into her as she reached out to fondle Caleb's thick erection.

He tried to move back, but she wouldn't let him.

"You're not getting away so easily," she whispered, stroking him through his pants. "I want you right here, where I can get at you, Caleb."

"You can have all you want later, but right now—"

"No buts, Caleb." She giggled. "Well, except—" she nodded over her shoulder to where Justin was stretching her even more before attempting entry, "—my butt."

Even Mick laughed at her little joke and Caleb gave in with good grace.

"Okay, rest your head in my lap, honey. That's it. Just rest there for now." He stroked her hair as she nuzzled him lightly through his pants. He was hard as a rock, but he wouldn't let her even unbutton his pants.

Caleb nodded to Justin. "You better get this party started, son."

She felt Justin shift then, and his fingers were replaced by the tip of his cock. He pushed slowly, letting her get used to him by small increments. She was nearly overcome by the sensations flooding through her as he moved forward inch by slow inch.

"Are you okay, Jane?" Mick was at her side, watching for any signs of distress now that he'd caught his breath.

Jane moaned as Justin slid in deep. He stayed there for just a moment, letting her get used to the feel of him, then pulled back, slowly and steadily, his movements smooth as silk.

"You feel so good, sweetheart." He watched them come together as he nodded to his brothers.

Mick and Caleb used their hands and mouths to drive her higher as Justin set up a slow, building pace. Within moments, she shuddered around him, the new stimulation too much for her to bear. The new, forbidden feel of him stimulated something inside that sent a torrent of sensation straight down her spine. She tingled and burned in the most exotic way. It was like nothing she'd ever experienced before and she knew in that moment, it was something she'd want again. And again.

Chapter Fifteen

By the time Mara returned at the end of six months, Harry had made an indelible mark on the family, and on his stepmother's heart. Aside from being there to supervise as Callie was examined by Mara and her companion, Prime, Jane did her best to keep clear of the Alvians. She couldn't hide her feelings easily and her heart was breaking as Harry's confusion grew. She'd done her best to communicate her deep and unending love for him as she held him that morning, watching the silver craft land in the pasture, even as tears ran down her face.

When the Alvians had been greeted and brought to the house, Jane had her tears under control, though her emotions were in a state of utter turmoil. Only her fear for the rest of the family kept her silent as Mara took the child of her heart away. These unfeeling aliens held all the power. The silent, giant warrior who accompanied Mara and Helas Prime was a living, breathing reminder of their power. If they wanted, they could easily destroy the O'Hara family, probably without a second thought. Jane knew that to protect her daughter and her men, she'd have to let Harry go with his mother, even if Jane's heart broke at the lack of love his natural mother displayed for her son.

Jane took Callie to the barn and holed up in Justin's garage while the silver craft took off, the two O'Hara women crying for their lost little man.

Justin found her there and joined the two females in a circle of love and grief. The other brothers knew how much they were hurting and let them be for a while, putting together a small dinner they all could share, as they shared their sorrow.

The house was remarkably quiet for the next few days, only the sounds of sadness permeated the walls. Callie pined for her brother, small as she was, and the O'Hara men battled with their anger and helplessness in the face of the aliens' technical superiority. Justin knew there was no way to steal his son back from the Alvian city. Though he'd been a Special Ops warrior before the cataclysm, even his skills were no match for the aliens' technology.

Likewise, it didn't sit well with the other brothers that they were so damned helpless against the Alvians. Late one night, after Harry had been gone only six days, the brothers sat at dinner with their mate, still subdued by sadness though they tried their best to show her how much they loved her and their baby daughter. Nothing and no one could replace young Harry.

"Dammit all to hell and back!" Mick slammed his fist down on the table, shooting to his feet as he became fed up with their inability to do anything but suffer. "Haven't they taken enough from us already? They stole our planet, killed everyone and everything we ever knew. Made us change our way of life and hurt the ones we love the most in the process, and now they take the most defenseless of us and subject him to God knows what!"

Mick's normally calm voice broke on the last bit and it was Jane who moved to take him in her arms as she met Caleb and Justin's eyes over Mick's shoulder. She soothed him, allowing him to crush her tight against his chest in his grief. Mick was habitually quiet, more prone to analyzing a situation until he understood it than reacting in anger, but he was out of control now. His emotions stormed around her, compelling her to comfort him, to be there for him.

"You never hurt me, Mick. I just want you to know that."

He stilled and held her away from him, meeting her eyes. The sorrow in his gaze was too deep to bear.

"You can't tell me having three husbands at once isn't wrong, Jane. But I'll be damned if I can give you up." He crushed her close again, closing his eyes on his brothers' objections.

"I thought we'd settled all this months ago, Mick." Caleb's strong voice rang through the room.

Jane, for once, felt everything Mick had been concealing behind that icy reserve he'd somehow learned. Her Mick was seething with guilt and anger that had no outlet. He hated the Alvians with a depth that shocked her and hated what he'd become because of them.

She staggered back from him as he let her go, but she refused to let him leave in such a state. She tried to block his path but he went around her and she had no option but to appeal to his brothers.

"Justin! Stop him!"

When Jane sobbed at the way Mick tore out of her arms, Jane felt Justin's anger surge. He tackled his younger brother and held him captive while Jane and Caleb moved in front of him.

"Let me go!" Mick tried to kick back at Justin, but he was too skilled a warrior to give Mick any opening.

"Calm down and let's talk this out," Caleb said in his steady, calm, determined way.

Just like that, Mick deflated. Jane felt the dam burst inside him as his emotions came pouring through. She nodded to Justin who lowered his brother into a handy chair. Jane immediately perched on Mick's lap, holding him close.

Justin pretended not to notice the tears in Mick's eyes, though he stepped back to let Caleb and Jane handle the situation. He was dealing with the grief in his own way but he trusted in Caleb's vision. According to his big brother, there was still a small glimmer of hope that somehow Harry would be returned to them.

Justin prayed daily for that to happen. He'd finally come to terms with the idea there was no way he could get his son back unless the Alvians gave him back. He'd even scouted the perimeter of the alien city, but he knew it was impenetrable to the likes of him. His only hope was that somehow Mara, or one of her kind, would have a change of heart and bring the boy back.

He watched over his family, ready to help if called upon, as Caleb crouched down in front of their youngest brother. Caleb spoke in his steady, deep way and Mick seemed to calm. Justin watched Jane for the signs. He knew when Mick was vulnerable like this, she would be feeling everything Mick did, and Justin could get clues as to how Mick was feeling by watching Jane. His brother had become all too adept at hiding his feelings to be able to read anything directly from his body language.

They all missed Harry, each having bonded with him in their own way. As his doctor, Mick had cared for the little tyke and checked on him frequently, helping Jane with both babies and making sure they were healthy. Mick was also the strongest telepath of the family and Harry was already communicating in his own way. Mick had shared more than one humorous story with them about the way his son viewed the world, and his beloved half-sister, from such innocent eyes.

While Justin might be the biological father of both babies, neither Mick nor Caleb seemed to love them any different than if they'd been their own children. The thought pleased Justin, knowing his brothers would be there for the children should something happen to him, just as he knew the brothers would be there for Jane. In this damnably uncertain world, that reassurance went a long way.

Mick quieted as Caleb reasoned with him. Jane sat on his lap, soothing him with her presence and her soft, stroking hands.

"Mick," she said, "you have to let go of this guilt you carry. If not for all three of you, I'd have been dead in the cataclysm. Even before that, if not for the O'Hara brothers—all of you—I don't know where I'd have been. After Daddy passed on, and even before that, you three protected me. You know how hard my gift was to live with in the old world. You three made my life easier, you made me whole. And now..." Tears choked her voice. "Now you've given me the best life I could possibly hope for. I wouldn't change a thing. Except perhaps for this lingering guilt you've been hiding. It's not good, Mick. And it's not right. The old world is gone. Only together can we live in this new one. And if I have no problem with it, then neither should you."

"But I love you so much, Jane." His whispered words carried to the other brothers, even if he hadn't wanted them to. "I didn't ever want to hurt you."

"The only way you could hurt me is to stop loving me."

Mick's eyes lightened and Jane's shoulders lost most of the tension she'd been holding. Justin could tell from Jane's response that Mick's storm was subsiding.

"Stop loving you?" Mick smiled up into her eyes. "Never gonna happen, sweet pea. I've loved you since you were five years old and I'll love you 'til I die."

Tears of joy ran down Jane's face as she kissed Mick, wrapping him tightly in her arms and planting small kisses all over his face and neck. When he started to return the favor, it was Justin who pulled the couple to their feet and directed them toward the largest bed in the house.

When Justin turned to leave after opening the bedroom door and ushering them inside, it was Mick who stopped him. The hand on his arm and the serious look in Mick's eyes spoke volumes.

"You've lost a son," Mick said with difficulty. "As did we all. I'm sorry, Justin. If there'd been a way to prevent it..."

Justin nodded. "I know. I feel the same. And I thank you for the sentiment."

"Get Caleb," Jane said, turning Mick's attention to her. "I think we all need some together time."

"Are you sure?" Justin knew she felt all their reactions and could tell how Mick was taking the idea. For his own part, Justin was always up for a ménage with her and his brothers. Hell, he was already getting hard, just thinking about it.

Jane held Mick's eyes as she nodded. "We're sure."

Justin turned quick as a flash to get Caleb, who'd been cleaning things in the kitchen and checking on Callie, asleep in her crib, letting nature and Jane's loving empathy run its course. Caleb didn't seem too surprised by the summons. He just grinned and followed Justin back down the hall to the bedroom, satisfaction oozing from him now the family was together again.

"Get on the bed, Mick." Jane's order surprised them all. She didn't often take a dominant role when she made love with any of the brothers, but they were all amenable to her desires. If she wanted to call the shots, they'd let her. In fact, it was kind of exciting.

Already naked and hard, Mick complied. He scooted to the middle of the huge bed, watching and waiting while his brothers kissed and caressed their woman. Caleb stroked her breasts while he kissed her deeply, and Justin's hands petted between her legs, his lips nuzzling the sensitive spot on the nape of her neck as he stood behind her. It was an enticing sight and Mick lay back, one hand stroking himself while he pillowed his head on the other, enjoying the view.

After a few moments, Jane turned in their embrace and stared directly at Mick, holding his gaze as Justin and Caleb's mouths found her breasts, their teeth raking gently over her nipples as she shivered. Mick smiled at the siren's call of her body, undulating with need while his brothers stroked her to a level of excitement they would all enjoy.

She moved slightly, stepping out of their embrace and put one knee on the bed. She crawled toward Mick's erection as if she only had that one single goal on her mind. Reaching, she took him in her hand first, then brought her mouth down for a quick lick.

Releasing his cock, she moved her lips up his body, nipping and kissing his rock hard abdomen, his chest, his neck. When she reached his jaw, she played a minute before locking her lips to his for a long, hard, deep kiss. All the while, she crawled over him, positioning her wet opening over his long, thick cock. She pressed down onto him as she released his mouth, then pushed up to present her breasts for his enjoyment.

"You feel so good, Mick," she breathed, concentrating on the youngest brother while the other two watched. She heard Caleb move toward the bed while Justin opened a drawer somewhere behind her.

She settled on Mick's cock, making a few up and down motions as if to accustom herself to his size and shape. She spread her slick essence over them both, but then stopped. Turning her head, she winked at Justin.

"Well, what are you waiting for?"

Caleb chuckled and Justin's devilish smile said the rest as he stalked over to the bed. Mick reached around her, lifting and separating the soft cheeks of her ass for his brother while Justin prepared her for the dominating entrance he'd taught her and that she'd come to crave.

"Your wish is my command, milady." Justin growled into her ear as he moved over her, taking his time but entering her with a gentle force that would not be denied. "Never let it be said I kept you waiting."

She moaned when he was in her fully, both men feeling the pinch of the double penetration and the way it made her tighter and impossibly hotter. Justin bit her neck as she arched back, then subsided, knowing there was a third element not yet in play.

Justin swiveled his gaze to Caleb as he took his favored position. He wrapped one big palm around Jane's head to support her as she took him into the warm, wet recesses of her mouth the way he loved.

"That's my girl," Caleb crooned to her. "Take it all, sweetheart. Suck me down."

With an unspoken signal, the three men began to move, seeking the pleasure they'd come to know with this woman they loved as no one else on Earth. They didn't share her like this often, but every once in a while this triple penetration bonded them, making them all greater than the sum of their parts, pleasing her and themselves in a way that was unique and special.

They moved on her and in her, each touching a special place in her body, in her heart and in her soul. They couldn't hold back anything from her at times like this—even Mick's reticence was blown to smithereens when he came with such abandon during their triple play. She relished these times, though they were challenging and incredibly naughty. Just the thought of this ultimate act had her blushing and eager when she dared let herself remember the pleasure these lusty men had taught her.

"Harder, Mick!" she cried when Caleb let her up for a breath of air, to be certain she was all right. Even in the deepest passion, each of the brothers cared for her every need. Mick complied and thrust harder, giving her the passion he'd been holding in check and she went down on Caleb even more voraciously than before.

"Dammit, Jane, I'm going to come!" Caleb's deep voice acted as a catalyst for them all. Jane came hard around the two cocks invading her body, squeezing them and quaking around them while the brothers groaned and held on for the ride. Caleb managed to restrain himself until she'd settled down and begun her second climb toward fulfillment, but then she looked up at him with those wide eyes and caught him off guard.

Caleb shouted as he jetted into her mouth, her eyes holding his as she swallowed him down. She licked and sucked to be sure she got every last drop of his essence, loving him with her tongue, her lips and her eyes.

"Jane," he groaned, letting her minister to his cock until he was clean. Caleb stepped back before she could suck him to full hardness again. He wanted this night to last and he'd have his turn inside her. After so many years, he knew Jane's passions and appetites perhaps better than any of them, but his brothers were fast catching up and even teaching him a thing or two about how to pleasure her. He kissed her once, in thanks, then watched as Justin moved carefully, in and out of her gently undulating backside.

"I wish you could see yourself as I see you," Caleb whispered, bending down near her head as he watched them move together. "I wish you could see how you look when we love you." Her gaze locked with his, Mick's eyes following. Caleb had all their attention at the moment. "If you could see what I see, you'd know how much you are loved, how much you are needed, and you'd never doubt."

Jane blinked. "I don't need to see it, my love. I feel it." Her smile broadened, the light of passion burning bright in her eyes as she climbed higher.

Caleb looked up at Justin. "Make her come again, Jus. Show her."

Justin took his brother's words as an invitation to ramp up their love play into a realm only he could take them. He pulled back, settling on his knees between her outstretched legs, his dick still within her, but at a slightly different angle. Slowly, he moved, watching the in and out action as he plumbed the depths of her ass.

"You've got such pretty cheeks, Jane." He gasped as he moved within her. "But they need a little pinking, I think."

Jane moaned as Mick's arms came from underneath to wrap around her shoulders and hold her down while Justin slowed his pace and moved back just a bit more. He brought one hand down in a stinging slap on her ass cheek jolting her. She clenched deliciously around the cocks still invading her body. Mick caught her small cry of surprise in his mouth, thrusting his tongue deep as Justin brought his other hand down, spanking her again.

"She's soaking me, Justin." Mick groaned as she clenched around him with each slap to her buttocks.

Justin continued the spanking, making her clench each time, approaching that pinnacle of arousal to which he wanted to coax her.

"Come now, Jane!" Justin ordered, delivering one last slap before rising up and sliding deep, all at once, back into her ass.

Jane screamed with delight as the pleasure/pain drove her over the highest peak yet. She came hard as Justin released within her dark passage. He groaned and collapsed over her back, sandwiching her quaking body between them.

He levered his weight off her after a moment, using care as he pulled slowly from her body. He smoothed his palms over her cheeks, now glowing a lovely shade of pink that threatened to make him hard all over again. He noted Mick was still hard within her, so he moved off the bed to let little brother have his turn leading this dance. He figured Caleb would be up for action any time now, but he needed to get cleaned up before he came back for more.

Mick rolled over, pinning Jane beneath him and rose up to his elbows, seeking her gaze.

"You know how much I love you?"

She nodded.

"I'm sorry I got upset before."

"Let's not talk about that now. But I understand better than you think."

"You always do." Mick rocked within her, still hard and wanting. "You up for another go yet?"

Snuggling into him, she grinned. "I'm getting there."

"Good," he crooned in her ear as he eased down and started moving more vigorously. "Because I need you now, Jane."

Mick rode her hard, bringing her to a pulsing orgasm with much less effort than he thought he'd need. He used his special trick of pulsing his emotions to stroke her empathic senses as he drove inside rubbing against her G-spot. She came in his arms as he took his pleasure, coming deep within her.

The brothers took her again and again that night, loving her long into the morning, taking short breaks for sleep and to care for her beautiful body. They pampered her and pleasured her and together they forgot some of the sadness that shadowed their days since Harry had been taken away. At least for a little while.

ℰ)ℭℬℜ

Deep within the alien city, Mara was unsure what to do with her problem. The problem was the child, Hara. He was not typical of Alvian offspring and she had a hard time understanding his needs. But she thought she might have a solution, recalling a Breed family that claimed kinship with her line when they were taken as test subjects.

Pushing a button on her console, she ordered the guards to bring the Breed family to her office. It was rare she allowed

Breeds out of their pens, but this particular group might prove as special in their own way as the O Hara Breeds, so she made allowances. She'd been observing them for some time and noted no outward aggressive behavior.

The door opened and a contingent of guards brought in an older woman, an older male and a younger female. It was the older woman who had claimed to be Mara, so it was to her Mara 12 spoke.

"You are of the line of Mara?"

The woman squared her shoulders and stepped slightly forward, demonstrating boldness common to most Maras.

"My father was named Seamus O'Mara, if that's what you mean."

"Before my people came, what was your profession?"

"I was a researcher. My field was pharmaceuticals."

Mara raised an eyebrow. This was a good sign. The line of Mara was almost always involved in the sciences. They were scholars and researchers by nature. That this Breed woman had been such was a good indication the line bred true even mixed so long with human DNA. She would make an excellent test subject, but would be treated deferentially since she could claim at least some shared Alvian DNA. Mara turned to the younger female.

"You are her daughter, are you not?"

The younger girl came forward hesitantly, but nodded.

"I was in college studying biochemistry when my father packed us all up and moved us here. We opened a shop and waited out the cataclysm in the Waste."

Mara's shrewd eyes turned to the male. He was not claiming to be Mara, but she had learned from her interaction with the Breed O Haras. Perhaps this male was important to the O Mara females on an emotional level she didn't pretend to comprehend.

"And how did you know to go to the Waste?"

"My auntie was a precog. She lived in Asia, but she called to tell me what she'd seen and warned us to get clear. She was always accurate with her visions, so I took her words to heart."

"And what is your extrasensory ability?"

"I have a bit of telekinetic ability." The man shrugged.

"Please demonstrate. Can you lift this cup, for example?"

The man called Johnson concentrated on the cup and it lifted about a foot off Mara's desk. She nodded and he set it down. She then turned her attention to the women.

"What are your talents?"

The older female answered first. "I have a bit of empathy and some telepathic ability, but my daughter Julie is a much stronger telepath than I am."

"Do you know anything about caring for infants?"

"I raised Julie, of course, and she used to baby-sit to earn extra money."

Mara came to a quick decision then.

"Good. I have a small child I need assistance with. I've been told he has very strong telepathic ability and he is able to send images to my dreams which I have a hard time interpreting. I could use your help with that."

Una beamed, a calculating light entering her eyes. "I love babies and I'll be happy to help, but I would like your reassurance that my husband and daughter will not be either harmed or separated from me."

Mara waved a hand. "I would like your daughter to assist with the child as well, so she will stay with you, naturally. And as long as you serve me and the child faithfully, your husband may stay with you."

"Thank you!"

Una tried to hide her elation but began to realize the alien woman didn't understand her emotion. Not at all.

And so Una O'Mara-Johnson came to be the personal nanny of Mara 12's child. The O'Mara family was installed in a much larger room than the one they'd been in before, on an upper level of the city structure, adjacent to Mara's own spacious quarters.

Una met the baby boy she was to care for and liked him right away. He was human. At least, she sensed emotion from him, which she didn't from any of the aliens. Una could feel him trying to communicate with her, but she didn't quite understand what he was saying. Julie had better luck discerning what he wanted, but it took at least a week before they realized the child was terribly unhappy away from someone he thought of as his mama.

Una had a grudging sort of respect for the alien woman. Mara had a vast intellect and she handled her authority as well as one could without emotions to guide them, but Una didn't dare speak her mind. She wouldn't rock the boat, lest her family be endangered. Still, she wished there was something she could do for the little boy who was more human than alien, though he did have those funny, pointy ears.

Julie and Una took turns caring for the boy. Una spent the day with the baby and Julie typically stayed with him at night. Mara had given Bill a small job to do to keep himself busy during his days, at Una's suggestion. He'd been a mathematician before the cataclysm, and a storekeeper after, so Mara gave him a job in her office doing inventory.

He excelled at it and Una guessed the job was also a test of sorts to measure their intellect. Mara was systematically testing them all in various ways, posing logic puzzles and noting their responses. Una noticed it almost immediately, but said nothing.

The family was performing much better than Mara had expected and as such, she had already decided to keep them separate from the rest of the Breeds. They demonstrated some definite Alvian higher brain function—even the male, though she had not traced his lineage yet. She wanted to study the interaction of their Alvian DNA with their human sides.

But Mara was still having disturbing dreams. She knew Hara was sending them, using his telepathic abilities that grew stronger with each passing day. She didn't understand the images, and they were puzzling her and disrupting her sleep.

She woke in the middle of the night from the latest of the dreams to hear Hara fussing in the other room. Julie was in there with him, so Mara asked the telepathic young woman if she could figure out what Hara was trying to tell her.

Julie and Mara had a long conversation and were still talking through the images Hara sent when Una arrived early the next morning to take over from her daughter. At first Una was appalled at what they were discussing, but then everything began to click into place.

"Mara." Una was hesitant, but this needed to be said. "May I ask who Hara's father is? I mean, it's obvious to me that he's at least part human."

Mara shrugged. "A man called Justin O Hara is the father."

Una reached out and sat heavily in the chair next to her daughter.

"Then I finally understand the message his brother Caleb brought to us just before your people came."

Mara looked interested, sitting forward in her chair.

"I have met Caleb and the others. He had precognitive visions, is that not right?"

Una nodded. "Caleb came to town just before your people arrived to deliver a message to our family. He was the one who told me to mention I was an O'Mara. He knew it would mean something to you. And he also said that I and my daughter had an important task to perform here. We were to act as liaison for one who could not yet speak for himself." Her gaze went to the baby. "I think now he meant we were supposed to help you understand what little Hara wants."

₧ℛℜ

A few days later, the silver craft landed in the far pasture once more. Jane was afraid when she saw the ship. She didn't know what might happen and she feared for her daughter. Mara had taken one of her children already, perhaps she wanted the other as well.

"Stay here." Caleb stopped to reassure her before he went out to meet the ship. "Don't worry. I think this might be good news."

That offhand comment gave her strength to wait the precious few minutes, holding Callie close in her arms. She felt the emotions from her missing baby long before she saw him. Harry was back!

Carrying Callie with her, Jane rushed to the back door, waiting only for Caleb's discreet signal that everything was okay before she raced out the door. Mara walked toward the house with Harry in her arms. The brothers were with her, smiling broadly as she spoke and then handed the baby to Justin.

"Hello, Mara." Jane fought for calm as she met the group. Mara nodded a cool greeting. "What's going on?"

Caleb put his arm around her shoulders, smiling hugely. "Harry's going to be staying with us for a while."

"How long?" Jane whispered, not daring to get her hopes up too high.

"Until he is grown more, at least," Mara answered. "The boy demanded to be brought back to you."

"Demanded?" Jane didn't see how a ten-month-old could demand anything.

Mick smiled and stroked Harry's downy head as Justin held him close.

"Seems our little man is quite the telepath. He managed to get himself understood well enough to convince his mother to bring him back, though it was a bit of a strain, considering his age." Mick's eyes crinkled up as he thought through the implications of Harry's astounding telepathic abilities. "I'll want to examine him to make sure he's okay."

Mara nodded, eyes alight with interest as she followed Mick toward his office, her companion Helas Prime in tow as they discussed the possibilities associated with Harry's extraordinary talents. Justin held back, giving Jane a chance to see Harry. She moved up close to father and son, laughing when both Callie and Harry reached out for each other. Callie's tiny hands waved toward her brother, but Harry had a great deal more motor coordination and strength. He nearly launched himself out of his father's arms in his eagerness to touch his sister and stepmother. Callie cooed and Harry giggled, clearly happy to see his female family members again. Jane bent down to kiss his chubby cheek.

"I'm so happy you're back." Her voice broke. "I love you so much, Harry O'Hara!"

She stepped back, right into Caleb's arms as Justin took the boy to Mick's office for a quick examination.

Caleb took his women back to the house. He was quiet, thinking over the possibilities he'd seen with his gift. The flashes had been quieting down lately, but the few he'd received revolved around Harry. He hadn't quite known how it would work, but he'd hoped what he'd seen of Harry's childhood on their farm would now come to pass. In the future Caleb had seen, Harry was happy and strong as he grew. Caleb felt free to share some of these visions with Jane and his brothers now that Harry was back.

For the next half hour he told Jane what he'd seen, watching as her eyes lit with a happiness he hadn't seen since Mara had come and taken Harry away. Their family was complete now—at least for the time being. Caleb didn't share too much of what he'd seen about the passel of kids they all had with Jane. No sense scaring her off! He chuckled as he thought of the bright future ahead of them all.

When the brothers returned with Mara and Prime, Caleb helped Jane rustle up a small meal for them all. They discussed Harry's telepathy and the way he'd made his demands known.

"He was able to enter my dreams even more strongly than when he was in my womb," Mara explained as they ate, shocking them all except Mick, who looked on with narrowed eyes. "In the dreamstate, he was able to express his desire to return here by injecting images of your farm and your family into my mind directly. In addition to that, Una O Mara and her daughter were able to communicate on a more direct level with him, much like Mick can do. After several double blind tests it was confirmed he was actually communicating via telepathy and the message was made clearer."

Caleb nearly crowed as tears of relief crowded behind his eyes. His dicey trip into town all those weeks ago had been worth it after all.

"You have Una, Julie and Bill together, I hope?" Caleb had to put in a good word for the family if he could.

Mara nodded. "I have given them quarters near my own. The women were assisting with the care of the baby, but now I will give them tasks more suited to their scientific minds. It is interesting to see how the Mara genetics blend with human DNA. The male is good with numbers, though I am uncertain of his genetic make-up. Still it will be useful to study his DNA in relation to his daughter, and the women have petitioned me repeatedly to keep them all together."

"I hope you'll do so." Caleb spoke quietly, his voice low and rumbling in a way that the family recognized as his statement of will. Even Mara seemed to recognize the note in his voice as her head tilted, listening and thinking.

Slowly she nodded. "I have already given my word to Una O Mara. Like you and your family, she is known to carry DNA of my race. I could do no less than consider her wishes as they submit to our study."

"Thank you." Caleb's words were heartfelt and perhaps the tone communicated itself to Mara because she nodded with both respect and acknowledgement.

"I took Hara's wishes into consideration as well. It is quite obvious he is not like my people and judging by your reactions to his abilities, he is not like your people either. Still, I think his needs will more easily be understood by you, since you share extrasensory abilities. He has a depth of emotion my race has long put behind us and though it is in our distant past, our scientists duly documented the needs of children born to our more emotional ancestors. I've consulted the historical records in great detail and came to the conclusion his demands to be brought back here were better answered than denied."

"Human children need love and affection. They can die without it." Mick put in from the side of the table.

Mara nodded. "So too were our people, once upon a time. Even now, the incubator stations have attendants who come in each day to simply touch our newborns. Even without the same emotional makeup of our ancestors, the touch of another being is important to the youngest of us." She turned back to Jane. "Hara made it plain he needed you and your family to thrive and even though he was created to be the subject of study, he is still a member of my race, as well as yours. As such, he has certain rights. One of which is a decent environment in which to grow."

"So you'll let him grow up here, on our farm?" Jane seemed to want to be sure before she got her hopes set.

Mara nodded. "I will, of course, be monitoring his progress and will expect regular reports from you, Mick." She turned to the doctor of the family, then nodded to her alien companion. "Prime will give you a list of items we wish you to monitor in his development and equipment to record your observations and transmit them to me. I will also visit every six solar months to see him for myself, and compare his growth with Callie's."

Mick nodded and Jane smiled broadly. Caleb felt a vision coming over him and was helpless to stop it. He let it come, tuning out the conversation that continued around him.

When he came back to himself, Mara and her friend Prime were standing to leave. Caleb caught the speaking glances from his family and knew they'd picked up on his little vacation from the conversation but were covering for him. Caleb walked out with the group, escorting Mara and Prime back to their ship. Just before they boarded, Caleb stepped forward and took Mara by the hand, surprising her, he could tell.

"You've made a good decision here today, Mara. Future generations of both our peoples will benefit by your willingness to open your mind to other possibilities, and your conscientious study of your people's past."

Mara cocked her head to one side as she considered Caleb's words. He saw the light dawn in her eyes when she remembered his precognitive powers.

"You've seen this?" she asked in a whisper, as if she were truly astounded by the idea.

Caleb nodded solemnly. "By your actions here today, the possible futures have coalesced into more certainty than I've seen in a long while. I can tell you this—your son will be a great leader for both our peoples in his time. He will broaden your understanding of your own genetic code and bridge the gap between what's left of humanity and your culture. He will be an instrument of healing—for this planet and for our peoples."

Mara looked almost afraid, though it was doubtful she could feel fear. Intrigue showed more than anything else in her expression. Caleb almost feared he'd said too much, but the scientist in her won out as he breathed a sigh of relief.

"I will look forward to learning what he has to teach." She gave him a small nod, shaking Caleb's hand in the human gesture she'd apparently learned from watching the people she studied in her city. It was a sign of respect that wasn't lost on him and he returned the gesture with genuine warmth.

"You are a credit to your race, Mara. I thank you for trusting us with your son. He will know only love and happiness here with us, and will grow to be a strong man who will make you proud."

"Thank you for sharing your vision of the future with me. I will hold it as a hope in my heart." Mara touched her brow in a sign of respect he'd seen in his visions of the aliens and he followed suit, surprising her, he could tell.

The silver craft took off as soon as they'd boarded and the O'Hara family converged on the kitchen for a celebration. Harry was welcomed with kisses and hugs, the baby smiling happily to be back among his true family. He reached out with his chubby hands for his half-sister and Jane settled the babies next to each other so they could touch and coo, reestablishing their bond.

Caleb looked on, proud of the family they'd formed from the wreckage of their world. They were happy and healthy and God willing, they'd have a good future together. Jane came and cuddled under his shoulder as he watched his brothers play with the children.

"This is a happy day for the O'Hara clan, Caleb."

He hugged her close. "A happy day for humanity, my love."

She pulled back to look up at him. "Then all that saving the human race stuff is really going to happen?"

Caleb nodded as the brothers looked up, having heard her question.

"Let's just say, with the events of today, it's much more likely than not that our Harry will play a very important role in the continuing safety of our family, and humanity as a whole."

Justin picked up his sleepy son, worry in his eyes. "That's an awful tall order for such a little guy, Caleb."

The eldest O'Hara nodded solemnly.

"He's already done more than any child his age should be able to, Justin. Give our boy a little credit. He's up to the challenge. He'll make us all proud."

About the Author

To learn more about Bianca D'Arc, please visit www.biancadarc.com. Send an email to Bianca at Bianca@biancadarc.com or join her Yahoo! group to join in the fun with other readers as well as Bianca! http://groups.yahoo.com/group/BiancaDArc/

Look for these titles

Now Available:

Maiden Flight
Border Lair
Ladies of the Lair
The Ice Dragon
Prince of Spies
Lords of the Were
Forever Valentine
Sweeter Than Wine

Coming Soon:

Wings of Change
FireDrake

An ancient evil is stalking the twin alpha rulers of the werefolk and the half-were woman who is destined to be their mate…if she lives long enough.

Lords of the Were
© 2006 Bianca D'Arc

Fulfilling her mother's dying wish, Allie climbs a wooded hill just before midnight on Samhain—All Hallow's Eve. At the top, she finds an overgrown, magical stone circle, and her destiny. Waiting for her there are twin alpha *were*wolves who will be her sworn protectors, her mentors…and the loves of her life. If she lives long enough.

Overprotective is just one word to describe Rafe and Tim. Sexy is most definitely another. But their newfound love and all their skills—both mundane and magical—will be tested by an ancient evil. A hostile human mage and a misguided vampire hunt them, servants to secret plans of the ancient *Venifucus,* a society dedicated to destroying women like Allie.

They will earn unlikely allies, including a half-fey knight imprisoned Underhill for centuries. But will it be enough to battle the evil that stalks them? Will Allie's men be strong enough to let her aid them in her own defense? Only together can *were*, fey and vampire defeat this latest threat and learn that love does truly conquer all.

Available now in ebook from Samhain Publishing.

*How would you feel if you found out life, as you know it,
is all a lie?*

New Beginnings: Carpe Diem
© *2006 Tilly Greene*

After the third world war, Earth is drastically damaged. By the 23rd century generations have passed, the facts twisted, history revised so it is unrecognizable and below ground a utopian society is established. Or is it?

Major Cooper Sayer, an imposing intelligent member of the special security forces, and Maris Gower, a peaceful soul who works in the New American Central Library, are an officially partnered couple. Life is comfortable, full of love for each other, and yet it took them less than fifteen minutes to decide on making a risky change.

With the dangers of residing below ground growing daily and the low life expectancy rate continually dropping, chances of a long and happy life together are becoming remote. The complete trust Maris has in Cooper is never questioned, even when he tells her they are going above for a chance at a longer life. A place that she has always believed meant instant death.

The adventure starts now.

Available now in ebook from Samhain Publishing.

Discover the Talons Series

5 STEAMY NEW PARANORMAL ROMANCES
TO HOOK YOU IN

Kiss Me Deadly, by Shannon Stacey
King of Prey, by Mandy M. Roth
Firebird, by Jaycee Clark
Caged Desire, by Sydney Somers
Seize the Hunter, by Michelle M. Pillow

AVAILABLE IN EBOOK—COMING SOON IN PRINT!

WWW.SAMHAINPUBLISHING.COM

GET IT NOW

MyBookStoreAndMore.com

GREAT EBOOKS, GREAT DEALS . . . AND MORE!

Don't wait to run to the bookstore down the street, or
waste time shopping online at one of the "big boys." Now,
all your favorite Samhain authors are all in one place—at
MyBookStoreAndMore.com. Stop by today and discover
great deals on Samhain—and a whole lot more!

Samhain
Publishing, ltd

WWW.SAMHAINPUBLISHING.COM

GREAT
cheap
fun

Discover eBooks!

THE FASTEST WAY TO GET THE HOTTEST NAMES

Get your favorite authors on your favorite reader, long before they're
out in print! Ebooks from Samhain go wherever you go, and work with
whatever you carry—Palm, PDF, Mobi, and more.

samhain
publishing Ltd

WWW.SAMHAINPUBLISHING.COM